Jaroslav Kalfař

Jaroslav Kalfař was born and raised in Prague, Czech Republic, and immigrated to the United States at the age of fifteen. He earned his M.F.A. at NYU, where he was a Goldwater Fellow and was one of the three nominees for the new NYU E.L. Doctorow Fellowship Award upon graduating. He lives in Brooklyn. ⸱ ⸱ his first novel.

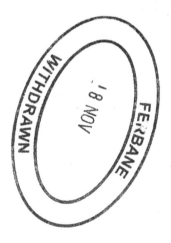

'A superb debut'
Literary Review

'Dizzyingly inventive, alternately lyrical, earthy, silly and sad.'
TLS

'Funny, humane and oddly down-to-earth ... Reading *Spaceman of Bohemia* reminded me of the thrill of unearthing *Everything is Illuminated* from the mound of entries to the *Guardian* First Book Prize ... Kalfař's writing has the same hyperactivity, the fidgety contempt for generic boundaries, as that of the young Jonathan Safran Foer.'
Guardian

'A frenetically imaginative first effort, booming with vitality and originality ... Kalfař's voice is distinct enough to leave tread marks. He has a great snout for the absurd. He has such a lively mind and so many ideas to explore ... he has an exhilarating flair for imagery'
New York Times

'[An] excellent debut ... could mark the launch of an astronomical career'
The Times

'The best, most enjoyably heartbreaking, most fun book you'll read this year'
Darin Strauss

'Outstanding ... simultaneously shocking, terrifying, wondrous, funny, and beguiling'
Los Angeles Review of Books

'Zany'
Hari Kunzru, *New York Times Book Review*

SPACEMAN
OF BOHEMIA

JAROSLAV KALFAŘ

SCEPTRE

First published in Great Britain in 2017 by Sceptre
An Imprint of Hodder & Stoughton
An Hachette UK company

This paperback edition published in 2018

4

Copyright © Jaroslav Kalfař 2017

The right of Jaroslav Kalfař to be identified as the Author of the Work has been asserted by him in accordance with the Copyright, Designs and Patents Act 1988.

'The Sun Clock' by Karel Toman translated from the Czech by the author

A CIP catalogue record for this title is available from the British Library

Paperback ISBN 978 1 473 63999 7

Printed and bound CPI Group (UK) Ltd, Croydon CR0 4YY

Hodder & Stoughton policy is to use papers that are natural, renewable and recyclable products and made from wood grown in sustainable forests. The logging and manufacturing processes are expected to conform to the environmental regulations of the country of origin.

Hodder & Stoughton Ltd
Carmelite House
50 Victoria Embankment
London EC4Y 0DZ

www.sceptrebooks.co.uk

For my grandfather
Emil Srb

A house in ruins. Through the cracked walls
spread gluttonous ferns,
and the parasitic bands of lichen.

On the ground sprouts delphinium,
a nettle forest. The poisoned well
a water trough for rats.

The frail apple tree, split by lightning,
forgets whether it once bloomed.

On clear days, singing goldfinches
fall into the ruins. On sunlit bright days
a clock's arc lives
on the facade, capricious and joyful
the shadow of time dances,
and recites solemnly to the skies:
Sine sole nihil sum.

For everything is a mask.

—Karel Toman,
'The Sun Clock'

PART ONE

ASCENT

The Losing Side

M Y NAME IS JAKUB PROCHÁZKA. This is a common name. My parents wanted a simple life for me, a life of good comradeship with my country and my neighbors, a life of service to a world united in socialism. Then the Iron Curtain tumbled with a dull thud and the bogeyman invaded my country with his consumer love and free markets.

Before I became an astronaut, the bogeyman and his new apostles asked if I'd like to change my name to something more exotic. More Western. Something befitting a hero.

I refused. I kept it as it was: common, simple.

SPRING OF 2018. On a warm April afternoon, the eyes of the Czech nation gazed from Petřín Hill as space shuttle *JanHus1* launched from a state-owned potato field. The Czech Philharmonic Orchestra wafted the national hymn between the city's Gothic towers, accompanying the countdown until, finally, the crowd gasped as the shuttle sucked and burned its cryogenic propellant and exploded upwards, all nine million kilograms of it, give or take the eighty kilograms of its single human inhabitant.

In a flash, *JanHus1* branded the hundred spires of the city with a dove-like stencil. Citizens and tourists alike followed the shuttle on its spherical climb until at last it vanished in the sunrays, reduced to a shadow captured by a few sharpshooting camera lenses. Leaving the vessel to its new fate in the heavens, the chattering citizens then descended Petřín Hill to quench their thirst for beer.

I witnessed my nation's triumph on a flickering, soundless monitor. It took about an hour to get used to the vibrations of the seat savagely bruising my buttocks. One of the chest constraints had cut through my suit and into my areola, and I could not ease its grip. The launch chamber in which I sat was the size of a broom closet, a collection of phosphorescent screens, anorexic panels, and the spaceman's throne. The machinery around me, unaware of its own existence, quietly carried me away from home, indifferent to my discomfort. My hands shook.

I had refused to drink water before the launch, despite the insistence of my handlers. My ascent was the fulfillment of an impossible dream, a spiritual experience that could not be matched. The purity of my mission would not be stained by such an undignified gesture of humanity as urine making its way into my Maximal Absorption Garment. On the screen before me, my people waved flags, clutched sweating bottles of Staropramen, traded koruna bills for plastic shuttles and spaceman figurines. I searched for the face of my wife, Lenka, hoping to catch one last glimpse of her sorrow, a reassurance that I was loved and feared for, and that our marriage could withstand my eight months of absence, or worse. Never mind that my throat was parched, that my tongue scraped along the rough flesh of my gums, that the muscles in my body tensed and cramped as every basic comfort of human existence disappeared mile by mile, sliced away by the layers of atmospheric divisions. I owned these moments of history. Schoolchildren would repeat my name for centuries to come, and a sculpture of my likeness would inevitably join the lineup at Prague's wax museum. Already the billboards littering the horizons of Bohemia displayed my face looking upwards with practical gusto. Gossip magazines had suggested that I kept four mistresses and struggled with a gambling problem. Or that the mission was fake and I was merely a computer-generated image voiced by an actor.

Dr. Kuřák, my state-appointed therapist, had insisted that my launch would be filled with pure terror—a lone human being traveling to the unknown, living at the mercy of technology, indifferent and silent. I did not like Dr. Kuřák. He stunk of pickles and was a pessimist disguising himself as a man with experience. He had been in charge of preparing my fragile psychology for the mission, but mostly he had taken notes on my fears (food poisoning; caterpillars; the existence of life after death, as in the possibility that life could not be escaped) with a ferocity that suggested he hoped to pen my official biography. He had recommended that during my ascent I consume my favorite childhood candies (Tatranky, layered wafers dipped in chocolate, which I'd stashed in the compartment to my left) and ponder my scientific duties to the world, the immense privilege I was honored with, to bring the Czechs their greatest discoveries since Jan Evangelista Purkyně had recognized the individuality of fingerprints, or perhaps since Otto Wichterle had invented the soft contact lens. My imagination embraced these ego arousals, and into the silence of the chamber I began to whisper my Nobel Prize acceptance speech, until my thirst became unbearable. I violated my resolve and pressed the H_2O switch, and the liquid flowed from the container underneath my seat to a straw attached to my shoulder. I was subject to my own physicality, a dwarf climbing a beanstalk to arm-wrestle the colossus, a cellular structure of banal needs for oxygen, for water, for the release of waste. *Banish the dark thoughts, drink your water,* I whispered as shots of adrenaline sharpened my senses and dulled the aches of my body.

Nearly a year and a half ago, a previously undiscovered comet had entered the Milky Way from the Canis Major galaxy and swept our solar system with a sandstorm of intergalactic cosmic dust. A cloud had formed between Venus and Earth, an unprecedented phenomenon named Chopra by its discoverers in New Delhi, and bathed Earth's nights in purple zodiacal light, altering the sky we had known since the birth of man. The color of the nighttime universe as observed from Earth was no longer black, and the cloud rested, perfectly static. It posed no immediate danger, but its stoic behavior tantalized our imaginations with dreadful possibilities. Nations scrambled to plan missions that would allow them to capture the particles of the mysterious Chopra and study these microscopic pieces of worlds beyond our own for chemistry and signs of life. Four unmanned shuttles had been sent to test Chopra's qualities and to carry samples back to Earth, but the probes had returned with empty bellies and no useful data, as if the cloud were a fata morgana, a collective dream of billions.

The next step was inevitable. We could not trust machines with the mission. A remote-controlled shuttle transporting German chimpanzee Gregor was dispatched to fly through the cloud and ensure that, with adequate protection, a human inhabitant could survive within Chopra long enough to observe and analyze samples manually.

Gregor had returned to his laboratory cage unharmed just as a new behavior was observed in the cloud: it began to consume itself, the mass of its outer layers dissipating and vanishing inside the thicker core. Some spoke of antimatter, others assigned the cloud organic properties. The media offered speculations—which of the world's governments would be brazen enough to send humans four months from Earth, toward a cosmic dust cloud of unknown and potentially lethal particles? Whispers, nothing but whispers from the Americans, the Russians, the Chinese, even the Germans, who had declared themselves the most serious about Chopra, given their offering of Gregor.

At last, an announcement came from a country of ten million, my country, the lands of Bohemia, Moravia, and Silesia. The Czechs would fly to Chopra and claim the mysteries it held. I would be their champion, the one to bring home the fanfare of scientific glory. In the words of a poet drunk on absinthe, reprinted in every major newspaper the next day: "With *JanHus1* lie our hopes of new sovereignty and prosperity, for we are now among the explorers of the universe. We look away from our past, in which we were claimed by others, in which our language was nearly eradicated, in which Europe covered its eyes and ears as its very heart was stolen and brutalized. It is not only our science and technology traveling through this vacuum; it is our humanity, in the form of Jakub Procházka, the first spaceman of Bohemia, who will carry the soul of the republic to the stars. Today, we finally and absolutely claim ourselves as our own."

As I prepared for the mission, my daily routines became public property. The street in front of the apartment building where Lenka and I lived was so littered with media vans, snacking journalists, photographers situating their elbows on cars like snipers, stray children looking for autographs, and general onlookers that the police had to put up barricades and redirect traffic. Gone were my lone walks around town, the quiet contemplation of which apple to choose at the market. I had been assigned a posse that trailed me everywhere, for safety (already unhinged letters from fans and would-be lovers had flooded in) and assistance—helpers for grocery shopping, for fixing stray hairs on my head, for speaking. It wasn't long until I couldn't wait to leave Earth and, again, enjoy the simple luxury of solitude. Silence.

Now the silence was another unwelcome noise. I opened the snack compartment and bit into the Tatranky wafer. Too dry, a bit stale, tasting nothing like the childhood peace it was supposed to evoke. I needed to be elsewhere, in the comfort of a time I could understand, the life that had brought me to *JanHus1*. Existence runs on energy, a fluid movement forward, yet we never stop seeking the point of origin, the Big Bang that set us upon our inevitable course. I turned off the monitor broadcasting my nation's festivities and closed my eyes. Somewhere in the deep circles of time colliding with memory, a clock ticked and tocked.

MY BIG BANG occurs in the winter of 1989 in a village called Středa. The leaves of the linden tree have fallen and rotted, and those uncollected have spread their brown mash across the fading grass stems. It is the morning of the Killing, and I sit in my grandparents' apple-scented living room, etching the image of Louda the pig in my sketchbook. My grandfather rubs the blade of his killing knife on the oval sharpener, taking a break here and there to bite into a thick slice of bread covered in lard. My grandmother waters her plants—the massive foliage of purple, red, and green surrounding every window—while whistling to the rhythm of a ticking clock. Below the clock hangs a black-and-white picture of my father as a schoolboy, smiling widely, the expression so earnest and unguarded, a smile I've never seen on his adult face. Šíma, our fat cocker spaniel, sleeps beside me, breathing hotly, reassuringly, onto the side of my calf.

This is the slow, silent world of a small village hours before the Velvet Revolution. A world in which my parents are still alive. In my near future awaits freshly cooked goulash, pigs' feet with home-made horseradish, and capitalism. My grandfather has banned us from turning on the radio. The Killing Day is his day. He has been lovingly feeding his swine, Louda, with a mixture of potatoes, water, and bulgur every morning and afternoon, scratching the animal behind the ear and grabbing fistfuls of his fatty sides, grinning. Louda is so fat he will burst if we don't kill him today, he says. Politics can wait.

This living room, this fireplace warmth, these rhythms of song, blade, dog, pencil, growling stomachs—perhaps somewhere around here a spontaneous release of energy occurred, sealing my fate as a spaceman.

My parents arrive from Prague at two o'clock. They are late because my father stopped by a field of daisies to pick a few for my mother. Even in an old blue parka and a pair of my father's sweatpants, my mother looks like one of the redheaded, milk-skinned actresses who play comrade damsels on TV, replete with the look of strong femininity and fierce dedication to the Party. Father's whiskers are grown out more than I'm used to because he no longer has to shave for work. He is skinny, his eyes are puffy from the slivovitz he has been drinking before bed. Over forty of the neighbors gather, along with the village butcher who will help Grandpa with the slaughter. My father avoids eye contact with the neighbors, who aren't familiar with his line of work. If they find out he is a collaborator, a member of the Party's secret police, they will abandon my grandfather, my grandmother, they will spit on our family name. Not publicly, but with the quiet hostility born from fear and distrust of the regime. This revolution speaks against everything my father stands for. The neighbors are nervous with their hunger for change, while my father blows smoke through his pale lips, knowing that the same change would put him on the wrong side of history.

The yard is long and narrow, lined on one side by my grandparents' house and on the other by a towering wall of the next-door cobbler shop. On any other day it is littered with cigarette butts and Grandma's gardening tools, but on the day of the Killing, the dirt and patches of grass are swept clean. The garden and sty are separated from the yard by a tall fence, creating an arena, a Colosseum for my grandfather's last dance with Louda. We form a circle around the yard with an opening for Louda's entry. At five o'clock, Grandpa releases Louda from his pen and slaps him on the ass. As the pig runs around the yard, excitedly sniffing our feet and chasing a stray cat, Grandpa loads his flintlock pistol with gunpowder and a lead ball. I say good-bye to Louda, who's growing tired and slow, by patting him on the nose before Grandpa drags him to the middle of the circle and knocks him on the side with his boot. He puts the gun behind Louda's ear and the ball cracks through the skin, the flesh, the cranium. The pig's legs are still twitching when Grandpa cuts the throat open and holds a bucket underneath to collect the blood for soup and sausage. A few feet away, the butcher and the village men build a scaffold with a hook, and pour boiling water into an industrial tub. My father frowns and lights a cigarette. He isn't fond of the animal-killing business. Barbaric, he would say, to harm animals just going about their existence on this earth. People are the real bastards. My mother would tell him to stop putting such things into my head, and besides, he isn't exactly a vegetarian, is he?

The bristly hairs fall off Louda's pink body inside the tub. We hang him from the hook by the legs and slice down the middle, groin to chin. We peel off skin, carve bacon, boil the head. My father checks his watch and walks inside the house. Through the window, I watch my mother watching him speak on the phone. No, not speak. Listen. He listens and he hangs up.

In Prague, five hundred thousand protesters flood the streets. Broken riot shields and bricks line their path. The ringing of keys and bells overshadows the radio announcements. The time for words has come and gone—what exists now is noise. The chaos of it, the release. Time for a new disorder. The Soviet occupation of the country, the puppet government backed by Moscow, all collapsing as the country's people call for freedoms of the West. To hell with these parasitic, ungrateful fucks, the Party leadership declares. Let the imperialists take them straight to hell.

We boil Louda's tongue. I pierce cubes of it with a knife and bring it to my mouth, hot, fatty, delicious. Grandpa cleans the pig's intestines with vinegar and water. This year, I am given the honor of the grinder—I stuff the sliced chin, liver, lungs, brisket, and bread into a hopper plate and push down while I turn the lever. Grandpa scoops the mash and stuffs it inside the cleaned intestines. He is the only man in the village who still makes *jitrnice* with his hands instead of using a machine. The neighbors wait patiently for these party favors to be done. As soon as Grandma divides them into packages, still steaming, the guests begin to leave, much earlier than usual, and half of them are not even close to drunk. They are eager to get back to their televisions and radios, to see about the events in Prague. Šíma begs for scraps and I allow him to lick lard off my finger. My mother and grandmother take the meat inside to bag it and freeze it, while my father sits on the couch, looks out the window, smokes cigarettes. I walk inside to enjoy the sharp scent of dinner goulash.

"Too soon to tell," my mother says.

"So many people, Markéta. The Party wanted to send the militia out to disperse them, but Moscow said no. You know what that means? It means we're not fighting. The Red Army isn't behind us anymore. We're done. We should stay in the village, safe from the mobs."

I go back outside to see Grandpa, who places a wheelbarrow in the middle of the yard. He loads it with dry logs and uses them to make a small fire. The dirt underneath our feet is soggy with organ blood. We slice bread and toast it to go with dinner as the sun sets.

"I wish Dad would talk to me," I say.

"The last time I saw this expression on his face was when he was a kid and a dog bit his hand."

"What's going to happen?"

"Don't tell your father, Jakub, but this is not bad."

"So the Party will lose?"

"It's time for the Party to leave. Time for something new."

"But then we will be imperialists?"

He laughs. "I suppose so."

Above the trees lining our gate, a clear horizon of stars blankets our view, so much clearer when not obscured by Prague's street lamps. Grandpa hands me a slice of bread with a burnt edge, and I accept it between my lips, feeling like a man on television. People on television eat slowly when faced with a new reality. Perhaps it is here that a pocket of new energy bursts through the firm walls of physics and singles out a life so unlikely. Perhaps here I lose the hope for an ordinary Earthling life. I finish the bread. It is time to go inside and hear my father's silence.

"Twenty years from now, you will call yourself a child of the revolution," Grandpa says as he turns his back to me and urinates into the fire.

As is usually the case, he is right. What he doesn't tell me then, perhaps out of love, perhaps out of a painful naïveté, is that I am a child of the losing side.

OR PERHAPS NOT. Despite the discomfort of my spaceman's throne, despite the fear, I was prepared. I served science, but I felt more like a daredevil on his dirt bike, overlooking the powerful gap of the world's greatest canyon, praying to all gods in all languages before making the leap for death, glory, or both. I served science, not the memory of a father whose idea of the world had crumbled over the Velvet Winter; not the memory of pig's blood upon my shoes. I would not fail.

I slapped the Tatranky crumbs from my lap. The Earth was black and golden, its lights spreading across the continents like never-ceasing pebbles of mitosis, pausing abruptly to give reign to the uncontested dominion of dark oceans. The world had dimmed and the crumbs began to float. I had ascended the phenomenon we call Earth.

The Spaceman's World

WAKING TO THE OCCASION of my thirteenth week in Space, I unstrapped myself from the Womb and stretched, wishing I had curtains to spread or bacon to fry. I floated through Corridor 2 and squeezed a pea of green paste onto my blue toothbrush, courtesy of SuperZub, a major distributor of dental supplies and mission sponsor. As I brushed, I ripped the plastic off yet another disposable towel, courtesy of Hodovna, a major chain of grocery megastores and mission sponsor. I spit into the towel and looked closely at my gums, pink as a freshly scrubbed toddler, and the bleached molars, a result of my country's top dental artistry and a meticulous oral hygiene routine aboard the ship. Though I had resolved that I would no longer do so, I felt with my tongue around one of the molars, and a familiar pain intensified. Despite the high marks I had received from my dentists before takeoff, this tingling of decay appeared during my first week in Space, and I had kept it secret ever since. I was not trained for tooth extraction, and where could I find a good Space dentist? Would he bring his own nitrous oxide, or would he gather it from Earth's polluted atmosphere? I grinned to myself but refused to laugh. Never laugh out loud at your own jokes, Dr. Kuřák had advised. It is a sure sign of a deteriorating mind.

Perhaps the most jarring part of the mission was how quickly I'd adjusted to the routines. My first week in Space had been an exercise in uninterrupted expectation, as if I were sitting in an empty movie theater, waiting for the hum of a projector to light up a screen and chase away all thought. The lightness of my bones, the functions of my machines, the creaks and thuds of the ship as if I had upstairs neighbors, they all seemed exciting, worthy of wonder. But during week two, the desire for something new was already setting in, and the act of spitting toothpaste into a disposable towel instead of an earthly sink lost its novelty. By week thirteen, I had forever abandoned the cliché of treasuring journey over destination, and in the daily tedium I found two methods of comfort: the thought of reaching the dust cloud to harvest its onerous fruits, and speaking to Lenka, her voice a reassurance that I still had an Earth to come back to.

I floated on through Corridor 3, unfastened the pantry door, and slathered a chunk of Nutella on a white pita. I flipped it up and watched it quiver through the air, like a pizza maestro spinning his dough. Food was my silent co-conspirator on this flight away from home, an acknowledgment of sustenance and thus the rejection of death. The ship burned its fuel and I burned mine, the chocolate-flavored protein blocks and the dehydrated chicken cubes and oranges, sweet and juicy inside the freezer. Times had changed since astronauts relied on a diet of powders as rich and enjoyable as expired packets of Tang.

As I ate, I knocked on the dead-eyed lens of the sleek surveillance camera provided by Cotol, major manufacturer of electronics and mission sponsor. One of the dozen broken cameras on the ship, failing one by one as the mission went along, causing the company embarrassment and heavy losses in the stock market. No one could figure out what had gone wrong with the devices—the company even put three of their best engineers on a conference call to guide me through a repair process, broadcasting the video feed online in hopes of reestablishing their brand. No luck. Of course, I did not disclose the presence of insistent scratching that resonated throughout the ship whenever one of the cameras went offline, skittering away quickly as I approached from beneath the corner. Such hallucinatory sounds were to be expected, Dr. Kuřák claimed before the mission, because sound is a presence of something earthly, a comfort. No need to chase ghosts. Besides, I did not mind that the cameras no longer observed my every step—I could enjoy violations of my strict nutritional guidelines with sweets and alcohol, I could skip workouts, I could move my bowels and enjoy onanism without worrying about my guard dogs watching. There was great pleasure in being unseen, and perhaps it was best that the world's collective imagination was teased by the denial of a 24/7 video feed of their Spaceman in sweatpants.

The day ahead was to be a pleasant one. After finishing a few usual menial tasks—testing Ferda, the cosmic dust collector and the tech star of my mission; engaging in a halfhearted cardio session; and running diagnostics on my oxygen water tank—I was to have a few hours of peace and reading before dressing myself for a video call with my wife. Afterward, I was to enjoy a glass of whiskey to celebrate being only four weeks away from my destination, cloud Chopra, the gassy giant that had altered Earth's night skies and escaped our attempts to study it. After penetrating the cloud, I was to gather samples with the help of Ferda, the most sophisticated piece of Space engineering to ever come from Central Europe, and study them inside my custom-designed lab on my way back to Earth. This was the reason the Space Program of the Czech Republic had recruited me, a tenured professor of astrophysics and accomplished researcher of space dust at Univerzita Karlova. They had trained me for spaceflight, basic aerospace engineering, and suppression of nausea in zero gravity. They asked if I would take the mission even if there was a chance of no return. I accepted.

Thoughts of death visited me only as I fell asleep. They came as a slight chill underneath the fingernails, and left when I lost consciousness. I did not dream.

I wasn't sure whether I was more anxious about reaching the

mysteries of Chopra or about the upcoming conversation with Lenka. Conducting an Earth/Space marriage through these weekly video feeds felt like watching an infection claim healthy flesh inch by inch while making plans for next summer. After these thirteen weeks, I noticed that there was a steady rhythm to human longing.

Monday, raw stage: God, babe, I miss you. I dream of your morning breath on my wrists.

Tuesday, reflective nostalgia: Remember when the Croatians stopped us at the border and tried to confiscate our schnitzel sandwiches? You unwrapped one and started eating it, shouted at me to eat too, shouted that we would eat them all before crossing and show those fascists what's what. I knew I'd marry you then.

Wednesday, denial: If only I wish it just right, I'll be back in our bedroom.

Thursday, sexual frustration and passive aggression: Why aren't you here? What is it you do with your days as I spit into a blue towel—courtesy of Hodovna, mission sponsor—and count the hours separating me from gravity?

Friday, slight insanity and composition of songs: *A scratch you can't itch. A scratch you can't itch. Love is that scratch you can't itch. Scratch you can't itch, oh oh.*

During the first few weeks of my deployment, Lenka and I would overstep the conversation limit of one hour and thirty minutes allotted by the space program. Lenka would close the dark blue privacy curtain and take her dress off. The first time, she wore brand-new lingerie she had just picked up that morning, black lace underwear and a black bra with pink edges. The second time, she wore nothing at all, her body clothed only in the gentle blue hue reflecting along her skin. Petr, the mission operator, allowed us to take as much time as we needed. There wasn't much logic to the limitations, anyway— I could chat with Lenka all day long and the automatic trajectory of the shuttle would go on uninterrupted. But the world needed this narrative, Mr. and Mrs. Spaceman's tragic separation. What kind of hero gets to chat on the phone?

During the past few calls, however, I had become thankful for the time limits. Lenka would grow desperately quiet before our first hour had expired. She would speak softly and call me by my first name, instead of the variety of pet names we had devised over the years. There was no discussion of nudity or physical longing. We did not whisper our wet dreams. Lenka scratched the edge of her right ear as if she was having an allergic reaction, and didn't laugh at any of my jokes. Always tell jokes to an audience, never to yourself, Dr. Kuřák had advised. Once you trap yourself into believing you can be your own company, you will cross the dangerous line between contentment and madness. Good advice, though difficult to practice in a vacuum. Lenka was the only audience I cared about. The emptiness of Space could not match the despair I felt when her laughter gave way to static silences.

Searching for the source of this decay, I'd been obsessing over my last night and morning on Earth with Lenka as I performed the menial tasks aboard *JanHus1*. I tested filtering systems, looking to squash any bacteria that might mutate unpredictably within the cosmic conditions and infect me with a vengeance unknown on Earth. I studied data to ensure the smooth recycling of oxygen (provided by a tank of water I often wished to dip myself into, like a careless vacationer plunging his body into the sea of a sunnier country), and I recorded the depletion of supplies. Around me, the shuttle hummed and cooed in its droning baritone, unaware, carrying me to our joint destination without asking for advice. I checked needlessly for deviations from the trajectory—the computer was a better explorer than I could ever be. If Christopher Columbus, that celebrated phony, had possessed a GPS as sophisticated as mine, he could have reached any continent he desired with wine in hand and feet elevated. Clearly, the thirteen weeks of the mission had offered much spare time to obsess over my marriage.

Three days before my deployment, Lenka and I had gone to Kuratsu, a favorite Japanese restaurant of ours in the Vinohrady district. She had worn a summer dress with yellow dandelions and a new kind of perfume, the scent of cinnamon and oranges soaked in red wine. I wanted to crawl under the table and nuzzle my face in her lap. She said that my sacrifice was noble and poetic, fitting these abstractions between powerful chews of her tuna tartare. Our lives were to become a symbol. I squeezed lime over my noodles and nodded at her words. Her voice spoiled the ecstasy of my cosmic exploration—I wasn't sure whether the entirety of the universe was worth leaving her behind, with her morning rituals and her perfumes and her violent outbursts of panic in the middle of the night. Who would wake her to say that she was okay, that the world was still whole? A camera flash blinded us. The spices burned along the edges of my tongue and for the first time, I did not know what to tell my wife. I dropped the fork. I apologized to her.

"Sorry," was how I put it. Just like that, a single word thrown in her general direction. It echoed through my mind afterward. Sorry, sorry, sorry. She stopped eating too. Her neck was slender and her lips so ambitiously red. This wasn't my sacrifice—it was ours. She was allowing me to go. She who had napped on my shoulder while I pored over astrophysics textbooks and tests from my students. She who had ecstatically dropped her cell phone into a fountain when I told her I had been selected for the mission. Mortality was not discussed, only the opportunity, the honor. She did not comment on the negative pregnancy tests filling our wastebasket while I spent my days getting used to the lack of gravity in the SPCR training pool, coming home with muscles cramped and speech reduced to "Hungry, sleep."

I never found out whether she accepted my apology. We picked up our forks again and finished our meal to the silent company of onlookers' cameras collecting our likenesses. We kissed and drank sake and spoke of traveling to Miami after my return. Finally, we took our own picture of this last dinner on Earth, and posted it on Facebook. Forty-seven thousand likes in the first hour.

As soon as we arrived home that night, I loosened my tie and retched. The antinausea medications had worn off with the alcohol at dinner, and my body had returned to its natural state of revolt against the strains of training for spaceflight, fighting lack of gravity with ceaseless vomiting. While I dry-heaved over the toilet, my gut hollowed out, Lenka ran her fingers through my hair. I told her we needed to give it another try, right then, if she could only wait for me to brush my rancid teeth. She said it was okay. I knew it wasn't. She waited in bed while I washed myself off, and with shaking arms I crawled on top of the bed and slid my tongue along her collarbone. She arched her back, grabbed at my hair, pushed herself toward me while I rubbed my palm along my flaccid cock. We caressed and twisted and sighed and in the end she gently pushed on my chest and said I needed sleep. I was sure the timing was perfect, maybe destined—husband and wife conceive; husband leaves for Space and discovers great things; husband returns to Earth with a month to spare to become a father. Lenka put lotion on her arms and said we'd get it right after I came back, without a doubt. See the doctor again. Solve the problem. I believed her.

The night's disappointment wasn't my main concern. It was the violation of a ritual I committed during my last morning with Lenka. When I was still an Earthman, I didn't have much use for morning rituals. Why should one spend time staring out the window, sipping lip-burning liquids and cooking feasts on hot surfaces when the world outside was so fresh and ripe for the taking? But my wife loved these mornings. She wore a robe (why not get dressed?), made eggs, bacon, rolls, and tea (why not buy a doughnut and a cup o' black before getting on the metro?), and talked about our hopes for the day (as long as we are not dead or bankrupt, three cheers) while I played along. But why shouldn't I have allowed myself to be tied to this slice of domestic sentiment, to relax my thigh muscles and help scramble the eggs, to take occasional glances at her slim ankles as she danced through our home in her daily festival? Lenka fried up thick slices of bacon, not prepackaged but obtained from the corner butcher, the slabs still stinking of living beast. She presented them to me as an offering, a coercion into her leisurely morning attitude, knowing my ache to move, my eagerness to wrestle the world. She knew this was her power, slowing the pace of our living to a soothing dance, regulating my heartbeat through her touch, her voice, her curves. Through pork grease spilling across porcelain. This was one of the many clauses in our contract, this bacon and grace exchanged for my compliance, and never once did I violate it. Until the last Earth breakfast with my wife.

I woke up that morning with the familiar nausea from the anti-gravity dive training, popped a few acetaminophens, and walked into the kitchen to find breakfast already waiting on the table. Lenka sipped from an oversized mug and cradled a laptop on her thighs, building a budget presentation. She closed it when I entered.

"It's getting cold," she said.

"Not today," I said.

"What?" She crossed her arms.

"I don't want it today. Not hungry."

She opened up her laptop again, wordlessly, going against another contract of ours, a ban on screens whenever we sat over food together.

I sat and I drank some tea, pushing the plate away. I pulled up email on my phone, feeling no need to defend myself. I did not want to ritualize the morning that day. The way our lives were about to change, the pretense did not fit in. Perhaps I was too ill, or scared nearly to death, maybe unstable, but I broke a clause of our contract unpredictably and absolutely, a violation that never fully disappears from the record of life. After a few minutes, Lenka dumped my breakfast into the trash.

"Last time, then," she said.

PERHAPS I ASSIGNED too much importance to this single moment. Perhaps not. But today, during our video chat, I was going to ask Lenka whether she felt the same way about our long silences and lack of humor. I would tell her how much I'd been thinking about the morning I rejected her ritual. I would ask whether she read the newspapers predicting the likelihood of my return. I would tell her that lately my nights (or periods of sleep, to be more precise, but Dr. Kuřák had recommended I hold on to the concept of day and night) had been filled with plates of bacon spitting grease, my tongue slithering in anticipation of carnivorous fulfillment. I wanted bacon on my Nutella sandwiches, my celery, my ice cream. I wanted crumbles of it sprinkled into my nose, my ears, between my thighs. I wanted to absorb it into my skin, revel in the busty pimples it would cause. During this call to Lenka, I needed to address my violation of the contract, beg for forgiveness. Never again would I refuse something she offered with her own two hands.

The call would reunite us. Kick-start a new wave of long-distance passion that would make the triumph of the mission that much more satisfying.

I entered habitat and nutrition data into the logs, leaving out my splurging on chocolate spreads and cider. I recalibrated Ferda the dust collector, ran internal diagnostics to ensure the filters were clean and ready for Chopra's offering. Having completed my preparations, I killed some time reading *Robinson Crusoe*, a favorite of mine from childhood that Dr. Kuřák had recommended I bring to create "an association of comfort." More obviously, Dr. Kuřák offered, I should take Crusoe as the perfect example of a man who embraces solitude and turns its crippling tendencies into opportunities for self-improvement.

Eventually, an alarm on the central computer announced it was five o'clock in Prague. I stripped into a black T-shirt, turned on my electric shaver, and ran it over my cheeks, chin, and neck as the machine collected and trapped the scruff. A stray hair follicle in zero gravity could be as dangerous as a bullet on Earth. The stress of the impending call with Lenka had pushed on my intestines all day, but I'd held out to make sure I wouldn't have to go twice. I entered the toilet through Corridor 3 and activated the air purifiers. The fans soaked up the stale air and replaced it with a vanilla-scented conditioned breeze. I strapped myself to the toilet and pushed as its vacuum pulled at my ass hairs and transported the waste out of sight. I read more about Crusoe—after all, the toilet was where my love for the book had originated. As a child, I'd suffered from yearly bouts of the intestinal flu, putting me out of commission for two or three weeks at a time. While I shat water, weakened from a diet of bananas and rice soaked in pickle juice, over and over again I read about Crusoe's solitude. *Thus we never see the true State of our Condition, till it is illustrated to us by its Contraries; nor know how to value what we enjoy, but by the want of it.* This was the very same copy I'd read as a child, yellowed and torn, abused by the coffee stains of my great-grandfather, who had stolen the book from the house of a Nazi captain whose floors he was forced to scrub. Even through the vanilla scent, I caught the stink of an intestinal system grown discontent with irregular eating, stress, a diet of processed foods and frozen vegetables, and water that tasted of chlorine. I studied the unkempt bush of pubic hair that sprawled to the sides of my skinny legs. There used to be muscle there, definition carved by years of running and cycling, now lost to pale flab that my halfhearted cardio session on the treadmill couldn't keep away. I wiped with wet disposable towels, pulled up my pants, and cleaned the sides of the toilet.

Afterward I dressed in a white button-up and a black tie, the same one I'd worn to my last romantic dinner on Earth. I removed the boxer briefs I'd been wearing for five days and exchanged them for a new pair. As an Earthman, I had always refused to go on a date without changing my underwear immediately before. I opened the compost chute and threw the underwear inside—another recent development in space travel, whereby a combination of bacteria and minor organic garbage was unleashed on the underwear, breaking them down until little remained. This ensured I did not have to sacrifice storage space or shoot my filthy knickers into the cosmos.

I looked myself over in the mirror. The formerly well-fitting button-up hung from my thin shoulders like a poncho. The tie saved it, kind of, but nothing could make my scarecrow arms and collapsed chest look particularly healthy. The thinness of my frame responded to the ache in my bones. The circles under my eyes spoke of the nightmares interrupting my sleep and fleeting visions of long, arachnid legs creeping within the darkened corridors, a secret I kept from my reports and therefore from Dr. Kuřák's thirst for madness. According to Central, I was doing fine. Good heartbeat, great results on psychological tests, despite the verbal dialogues I was having with myself before bed. Central knew best.

I floated into Corridor 4, an improvised lounge, and strapped myself to a seat facing the source of my connection and entertainment—the Flat, its large sleek screen responding flawlessly to touch, its Internet connection provided through satellite SuperCall (major provider of wireless services and mission sponsor). It boasted a database of ten thousand films, from *The Maltese Falcon* to *Ass Blasters 3*. I had limited access to social networking—all communication with the outside world had to go through Central, of course, then public relations, then the office of the president, then back to public relations—but I had the rest of the Web at my disposal, with its magnificent power to entertain any brain on any subject anywhere it could reach its omniscient fingers. I had to wonder: if we could only give a simple laptop to all the starving and the overworked, blanket the globe in the warmth of unlimited Wi-Fi, wouldn't the starving and the overworking be so much more pleasant, unlimited streaming for all? In my darkest hours on *JanHus1*, when my eyes hurt too much to read and I was certain something was stalking me whenever I turned my back, I watched dozens of videos of Norman the Sloth, a lazy, always-smiling creature whose owner had the ingenious idea to dress him up in boot-cut jeans and a cowboy hat. I grinned at Norman's sloth shenanigans and spoke to him under my breath. Norman.

Above the Lounge rested one of the last functioning surveillance cameras on the station, its blue dot of consciousness radiating proudly and watching me live.

Thirty minutes until connection time. I played solitaire, ran my hand over my cheeks to confirm I hadn't missed a spot. I imagined Lenka getting dressed for me, pulling the smooth tights over her coffee & cream–colored legs, stopping just below the half-moon dimple on her lower back. I practiced my greeting:

Ahoj lásko.

Or, *Čau beruško?*

Perhaps casual, *Ahoj Leni?*

I spoke the words in different intonations—higher, lower, gruff, sensitive, semiwhisper, imitation of my own morning voice, Darth Vaderesque, childlike. None of it sounded right. What could I say next?

I love bacon now. I want to feed it to you with my fingers while we sit on a beach in Turkey or Greece. Nothing tastes quite right in Space. I crave the taste of you.

I would remind her of our best days. Of the day we drove out to the lake, smoked pot underneath oak trees, spoke about the places we would travel. We made out in the car and returned home just in time to eat chocolate croissants and fall asleep on a bed filled with crumbs, our chins stained with wine and saliva. Bodies sun-drained and calves coated in rough sand.

Or the day we snuck into the astronomical clock tower and fucked so hard we defaced a national treasure.

Or the evening we married, in the middle of a Moravian vineyard, buzzed and barefoot. We didn't have to work for happiness then. It simply existed.

This was the one. A break to the streak of our distant, alien conversations. I just knew it. Maybe she'd even close the call booth privacy curtain again. Let me see the reflection of jazz club blue.

A shadow of hairy, arachnid legs peeked from beneath the Lounge counter.

"Not now," I said, my voice shaking.

The legs disappeared.

Two minutes until the call. I closed all other windows and glared. Would she call early? Even a few seconds would amount to an endless stretch of hope. One minute. She would have to call first. I couldn't seem desperate. Ten seconds late. I couldn't give in. Car trouble? One minute late. I breathed deeply, the heart rate statistics on my wristwatch hastened. Two minutes. Fuck. I pressed the dial button.

Someone answered. The expected face of my wife morphed into a gray, stained privacy curtain pulled all the way behind an empty chair.

"Well?" I said to no one.

A large hand, knuckles sprouting patches of red hair, gripped the curtain. It hesitated. No body yet, but I knew this was Petr.

"Hi, yes, I'm waiting," I said.

The hand pulled the curtain aside and finally I could see the entirety of Petr, mission leader, in his usual black T-shirt, the faded Iron Maiden tattoo on his forearm, a shaved head shiny with perspiration, a biker's beard extending well to his chest. He sat down and closed the privacy curtain behind him. My pointer finger twitched.

"Jakub, looking sharp. How's things?" he said.

"Fine. Lenka ready yet?"

"Have you eaten?" he asked.

"Yeah, it's in the report. Where is she? Today is Wednesday, right?"

"Yes, it's Wednesday. How's the nausea? Are the meds working?"

"It feels like you should be hearing me," I said, arms folded. Petr tapped on the desk with his knuckles. For a while, we were silent.

"Okay," Petr said, "all right. I'm an engineer. I'm not really trained for this. It's chaos around here. We're still trying to figure out what happened."

"Happened?"

"So, Lenka came in a few hours early today. She fidgeted a lot, wore sunglasses inside. We put her in the break room with some coffee. A few of us tried to talk to her and she just kind of nodded at everything. Kuřák spoke with her for a bit too. And then, twenty-five minutes before your call, she just got up and walked out, walked to the lobby, and our guy down there chased after her, asking what was going on, did she forget something, and she put a cigarette in her mouth and said she needed out."

"She doesn't smoke anymore," I said. "Never mind. When is she coming back?"

"I don't know. She jumped in her car. I went after her. She locked the doors and then the car wouldn't start. So I just stood there, she fidgeted with the key, the car coughed, stalled. So she rolls down the window and asks me if I could give her a jump. I told her I couldn't,

I took the bicycle to work today, but I could grab one of the guys from upstairs. And then she just cried, and she told me she couldn't handle any of this, that she didn't know why she thought she could, that she couldn't believe you left the life you had. She punched the steering wheel and turned the key again and the car started. Then she sped off, almost ran over my foot."

I looked into the blue eye of my webcam, the last working lens capturing my likeness on the ship. Should I name it? It studied me so loyally. I tapped on it in acknowledgment.

"I have absolutely no idea what you're talking about," I said.

"I don't either, Jakub. Maybe she's going through some things? I've got people calling her number on a loop. I've got a guy calling her mother. We'll call some friends. But she just ran off. I guess that's what I'm telling you. She just ran out of that lobby like Beelzebub was chasing her."

"She wouldn't do that," I said. "She knows how much I need to hear her."

"Look, we'll find her. We'll figure out what's going on."

"She didn't say anything else to you?"

"No."

"You promise? I fucking swear if you're lying, or if this is some kind of joke—"

"Jakub, your vitals are a mess. You need to try to focus on the mission right now, stuff you can control. We'll find her. She's just having a moment. It's going to be all right."

"Don't tell me what I need right now."

"Stay with the structure. What were you going to do after the call? Dinner?" Petr said.

"I was going to masturbate and read," I said.

"Okay, well, I didn't need to know all of that, but you should proceed with your day. Keep a clear mind."

"I don't want to do that."

"Have a protein bar. Do some cardio. That always helps m—"

I ended the call and unfastened myself from the chair. I slid the tie off my neck and let it flicker down Corridor 3, then unbuttoned my shirt and ripped it off my back. Petr's voice sounded through the intercom, the last resort of forced access into my world.

"You're on a mission, Jakub. Focus. It's not easy for Lenka. Let her do what she needs."

I pressed the intercom button to reply.

"I survive on these calls. I sleep thanks to them. Now she can't do it anymore? What does that mean?"

I craved Mozart, gummy bears, rum cake, the curve underneath Lenka's breast where I could slide my fingers for warmth. The closest comfort on the ship was the remaining three bottles of whiskey the SPCR had reluctantly allowed me to bring on board. I tilted one of the bottles and dipped a finger inside, then spread the flavor along my tongue.

"Through these months and through these miles, Petr, I can't shake the vulgar sense that somehow I got fucked on this."

He was silent.

The nausea came with the usual urgency, as if an invisible hand squeezed my medulla and clawed at my stomach lining. She had left. She needed out, she said. Where was my wife, the woman I hallucinated about as I attempted to sleep vertically, the woman for whom I was to return to Earth? Where were the decades of dinners and illnesses and lovemaking and images of our coalescent lives? She had walked into the Space Program of the Czech Republic headquarters in her sunglasses and couldn't stand to wait and talk to me. She had told a man she barely knew that she needed out. As if I no longer existed.

Lenka left me. The silences had led to this. I had read her exactly right.

She had left me once before, in those weeks around the anniversary of my parents' deaths, when I hid out in my office for days at a time and left her alone after the miscarriage. But back then, my legs were bound by gravity and I was able to run after her to the metro station, to beg her in front of all the people waiting for their train, to tell her I'd never leave her alone again (yes, I saw the lie now, as I floated inside my vessel), and by the time the train arrived, she allowed me to kiss her hand and to take the suitcase, and we walked home, where we could begin the negotiation of repairing our battered union. There was no such possibility here. Every hour, I was thirty thousand kilometers farther away from her.

By INSTINCT, I made my way to the lab chamber. Life made sense inside labs, it was measured and weighed and broken down to its most intimate essentials. I removed a plate of cosmic dust, an old sample, from its container, slid it underneath the microscope, and focused. It was the Space genome, the plankton of the cosmos, water turned to wine, and it whispered to me, revealed its content. Another sip of whiskey as I gazed at the milky crystal of silicates, the polycyclic aromatic hydrocarbons, and that omnipresent vermin, H_2O in solid form.

Yes, of course, this was why I had been put on Earth, to collect the pieces of universe and within them find something new, to throw myself into the unknown and bring humanity a piece of Chopra. What marriages I failed, what children I could not bring into being, what parents and grandparents I could not keep alive, it did not matter, for I was above all these earthly facts.

There was no consolation in it. I slid the dust plate back inside its container.

As I exited the lab, shirtless, again I spotted the shadow.

"Hey. You," I said.

I wondered, not for the first time, why I was addressing an illusion.

The legs quivered, hesitated, then skittered around the corner. I pushed on. I heard the legs scratching along the ceiling, as if tree branches were scraping the vessel's windshield. Behind Corridor 4, the shadow rested. There was nowhere else to escape. I was unafraid, which frightened me. I swam forward.

The smell was distinct—a combination of stale bread, old newspapers in a basement, a hint of sulfur. The eight hairy legs shot out of the thick barrel of its body like tent poles. Each had three joints the size of a medicine ball, at which the legs bent to the lack of gravity. Thin gray fur covered its torso and legs, sprouting chaotically, like alfalfa. It had many eyes, too many to count, red-veined, with irises as black as Space itself. Beneath the eyes rested a set of thick human lips, startlingly red, lipstick red, and as the lips parted, the creature revealed a set of yellowing teeth which resembled those of an average human smoker. As it fixed its eyes on me, I tried to count them.

"Good day," it said.

Then:

"Show me where you come from."

A Very Deep Fall

THE ALIEN CREATURE RAKES through the confines of my mind, gently but resolutely. It is seeing *me*. It is studying *me* to the very core of my genetic code. The tips of its legs strum on threads of memory, a rhythmic twitching within my brain matter. It shuffles through the history of my heredity, the origins of my nation, what brought both me and the name Jan Hus to the cosmos. The feeling is not entirely unpleasant. Together, we see Hus, a man of God whose name is engraved upon my ship. He preaches the words of John Wycliffe from a small cathedra in the public square of Univerzita Karlova. God's people, he says, are made up of his common children, all pre-elected to be saved—they are not the visibly identified members of the Catholic Church. God's favor can be neither bought into nor spoken from the lips of a golden-plated old man. The organization of religion is self-defeating, a trap for sin. Hus does not speak with hatred, but with the soothing composure of a prophet—a man who *knows*. And the people listen. Students gather with quills in hand and their hearts are moved. Bohemia must be freed from the tyranny of religious institutions.

The image changes. The creature has gotten hold of something else. It sees me falling.

I often try to forget the date, but the creature's cerebral strumming has brought it to the center of my consciousness—March 26, the spring following the Velvet Revolution. I am ten years old. That morning, my parents take the cable car from their Austrian hotel in the Alps to Mount Hoher Dachstein. This vacation is to provide them with much-needed alone time before my father's trial for the role he took on as a ranking member of the Party, namely the torture of suspects during interrogations. My parents risk adding to the charges by violating the court order to stay in the country, but my father says that marriage should not be subject to the whims of judicial systems. As my parents enjoy the view of the Alps and, I assume, pretend that the virginal mountaintops can distract them from the dread of punishment ahead, I spend time in Středa with my grandparents. Grandpa takes me to the garden and we pick a basketful of sour apples, and some strawberries. I eat four apples, wash them down with a sip of cola, and finish with creamed strawberries for dessert. I collect spiders from the space underneath the rabbit coop and throw them to the vicious chickens, watch as they peck the arachnids apart leg by leg. Nobody wants to speak with me about the future. No one wants to tell me what will be done to my father, why my mother does not sleep and why her forehead sweat reeks of wine, when we can stop watching every news segment on every station as if the anchor's hand could reach out at any moment and grab one of us by the throat. There is no space for my questions.

On the Monday my parents are to return, Grandpa takes the early train to Prague with me and walks me to school. All day I fantasize about the Austrian chocolates and fancy salamis my parents will bring back.

I wait in the school lobby, next to the doorman's booth, for my parents to pick me up. At four o'clock, Mrs. Škopková approaches me, hands folded behind her back, lips pale. In a quiet voice, she tells me that there has been an accident. My parents cannot, *presently*, pick me up. When will they come? I ask. Mrs. Škopková apologizes to me, and I ask why, and she asks whether I need something. My grandfather will send a taxi to recover me. I'd like some chocolate, I say.

She puts on her coat. Ten minutes later, she is back with a Milka bar in her hand. The label shows the picture of the purple Milka cow grazing in a pasture in front of the Alpine mountains. Mrs. Škopková apologizes again. The cable car collapsed, she says before she leaves. Your parents... The doorman glances at me over his crossword puzzle.

The driver picking me up is an old man who smells of pancakes. His hands shake as he drives. He makes the two-hour trip to Středa, turning the radio volume up when I ask what he knows about a cable car falling down a mountain in the Alps. My grandfather awaits us in front of the gate. He gives the old man money and takes my suitcase. In my hand, I hold an empty chocolate wrapper. Grandpa's gray whiskers reach to his lips. The skin sinks deeply into his cheeks, and his eyes are barely open. Inside the house, Grandma drinks slivovitz and smokes cigarettes at the table. I have never seen her smoke before. Šíma sleeps underneath her legs, wags his tail lightly when he sees me, but then again closes his eyes and exhales shallow breaths, like he knows this is no time for pleasure. Grandma kisses me on the lips. I go to the couch and lie down and their voices reach me through the rhythm of that damned clock, always nagging, asserting itself harshly over the tranquility of smoke.

My grandparents take turns explaining. Earlier that morning, my parents boarded the cable car to get to the top of Mount Hoher Dachstein. I stare at the ceiling and remember my father's enthusiastic lectures on the workings of cable cars. Aerial tramway ropes are made of dozens of individual steel strings with hemp running through the middle. I imagine my father's lips moving behind the tram glass, re-explaining this to my mother as she admires the albino behemoths ahead, nearly lost in the morning mist. Somewhere down the line, a string pops. And another. And another. The tram is suspended in midair as Earth's physics race to catch up. In my imagining of the event, influenced by watching Laurel and

Hardy every night before the evening news, the car falls very slowly, and the bodies slide back and forth as they grab on to each other, until they are forced into a dying waltz, ladies and gentlemen locked arm in arm, exclaiming vintage expressions like "Oh dear" and "I never." But this serenity of initial suspension—this antigravity waltz—is interrupted as the falling car gains speed. A gentleman accidentally touches a woman's midriff, and she slaps him across the cheek with a leather glove. The car wobbles and its occupants hold on to each other's ties and skirts, pulling off pants and wigs, the slapstick shenanigans of the silent film era. I'm not sure how these cast members die, whether their bones burst through their flesh, whether they die on impact, spines and skulls thrown over the sharp edges of black rock.

We occupy the living room, and Grandma sings a song I have not heard before about a young man leaving a hop farm to court a girl in the big city, winning her in the end by brewing miraculous beer made from hops his mother packed for the journey. Grandpa smokes, sucks from a warm bottle, coughs. Šíma whines for some food. I hold the Milka wrapper. Grandma speaks to me, but I cannot unseal my dry lips, cannot recall the sounds of our alphabet. I'm looking for my parents in all this snow. The ceiling cracks along the corners and a daddy longlegs crawls out.

Two days pass, and I move only to urinate in the chamber pot Grandma has left next to the couch. I hear Šíma lapping from it when nobody's looking. Grandma tries to feed me, but I can't open my mouth. She wets my lips with water. Grandpa rubs my feet and my hands with his callused fingers, stained yellow. I hold the Milka wrapper. When my grandparents go to sleep, they pull a blanket over me and Šíma snores at my feet, his whiskers wet with urine. This makes me love him more. Grandpa stays up late to watch football and all the American movies the privatized channels can now show. He knows I watch from the corner of my eye, a brief distraction from my search for the bodies, and I angle my head to get a better look at the man in a fedora who whispers to the beautiful blonde. The glow around her hair, her refusal to look the man in the eyes, gives it away—she has a secret. Their lip movements do not match the Czech words they speak. Neighbors come by every day to speak of condolences and God, but Grandma keeps them at the doorstep and thanks them quietly. He was such a good boy, they say of my father. They don't say he was a good man. I hold the Milka wrapper and I imagine standing among these Austrian mountains as frost causes phlegm to drip from my nose and sting my upper lip. My fingers are black and dead. The world is too vast and there are so many places where humans perish quietly. What good am I, a thin purse of brittle bones and spoiling meat? I can't find my parents. On the fourth day, I smell like the couch, a mix of dog, detergent, and spilled coffee. My calves cramp and my stomach feels disembow-eled. Grandma wears a black dress and blush on her cheeks. Her lips will not cease trembling to the rhythm of her shiny cross earrings. She does not like God but she loves the cross. Grandpa stands over me in a black suit jacket and slacks, a shocking variation on his usual wardrobe of muddy overalls and old army jackets. He holds a plate filled with rotisserie chicken, bread, and butter.

"You need to get up and eat," he says.

My eyes are with the ceiling cracks, and my fingers are out-stretched, wishing to peel back the layers of plaster. My right leg cramps. I grit my teeth and ignore it.

"You don't have to go to the funeral, but you have to eat," he says.

"They found the bodies?" I ask.

"We never lost them. It took a while to get them here from Aus-tria. I want you to think about whether you want to come with us. Nobody will be upset if you don't."

My search for the bodies was pointless, then. He grants me a few minutes of silence, then forces my mouth open and shoves a piece of chicken inside. He takes the Milka wrapper from my hand and throws it inside the cold chamber of the stove. I chew, and the salt and flesh feel so good they make my eyes water.

"You have to get up now," Grandpa says. "You have to be a person."

I resist, reject. The creature loses the thread of my life, and we return before Jan Hus. King Wenceslas no longer protects him — Hus has officially been declared a heretic by the church, a stigma as permanent as a birthmark. The Romans now consider Bohemia a nation of heretics. Hus wears a simple white robe and climbs atop a spotted, undernourished horse. Sigismund, king of the Romans and heir to the Bohemian crown, has promised Hus a safe passage and lodgings if he attends a council of church leaders to explain his betrayal. Does Hus sense treachery ahead? It is hard to tell, for his eyes are always set forward, as if he sees wonders beyond reality, as if he can penetrate dimensions and pick at concealed truths. Hus arrives at Konstanz and lives, unharmed, in the house of a widow. Her long, dark hair reaches to her knees and her shoulders sink from the disappointment of dead love. She never looks Hus in the eyes, yet speaks to him sternly, as if addressing a misbehaving little boy. She makes thin vegetable soup for him, and Jan soaks his bread crust in it, careful not to soil his beard. He tells the widow that no earthly group can provide true salvation. His faith will not be prescribed or dictated. The books he loves and hates will not be burned. His nation will not be blacklisted on account of greed. Against orders from his hosts, Hus preaches in Konstanz — his conviction is a compulsion not subject to self-preservation. The widow kisses him before he is imprisoned. The men condemning him set a sign on his head: *Heresiarch*. Leader of heretics.

Seventy-three days he spends in a castle dungeon, his arms and legs chained, eating bread gray with mold. When he is questioned, the councilmen spit and ask him to recant, but he will not. A man is free, he shoots back. Man is free under God.

The sentence is death.

The executioners have a hard time scaling up the fire—simply put, Hus's body hesitates to burn. In an attempt to help, an old woman from the audience throws a handful of brushwood on the pile, blows a little at the impotent flames. "Sancta simplicitas!" Hus cries out from the stake as his feet redden. *Holy Simplicity.* At forty-four degrees Celsius, the proteins within the series of cells known as Jan Hus begin to break down. As the temperature rises, the initial layers of skin peel back like those of a kielbasa. The thicker dermal layer shrinks and splits, and a yellow fatty paste leaks out and burns with a low squeal. Muscles become dry and contract. Bone burns stubbornly, though, as if the solid foundation of man were not the soul (nowhere to be seen), but this brittle framework. Here is Jan Hus, and he is dead. A space shuttle will someday carry his name.

The creature has ahold of me once again. I am on the couch; my grandparents are dressed for a funeral. I hold the plate my grandfather has given me, and I eat the chicken and dip bread in the grease, then wet my fingers and pick at the crumbs.

"I'll stay here," I say.

Grandpa takes the plate away and picks me up. He squeezes so hard I can feel the food moving through my body. He puts me down on my feet, and Grandma kisses me with lips tasting of lard and alcohol.

The silence in the living room changes during the hours of their absence. I am alone. Šíma is in the yard, sniffing out mice. The clock ticks obediently, mechanical and dead. The steel strings pop one by one and the tram halts suspended in the air for one long second before it begins to fall. I turn the TV on, six o'clock news. Small

37

business grows, the communists are long gone, and we are free to live as we like. Free to travel, free to kiss, free to remain silent as the tram falls down and down until we are free to die. Free to be as we like. My grandparents come home at seven and I sit in the same chair, and I don't remember how I got here, and I don't know what I plan to do next—until suddenly I am no longer the sole inhabitant of *JanHus1*, and I am left sweating and looking upon my visitor.

"Sancta simplicitas!" the creature says. "You are what I'm looking for."

The Secrets of Humanry

S KINNY HUMAN," THE CREATURE said. I ignored it and stared at the empty whiskey bottle.

The words didn't travel through my ear canal or vibrate through my eardrum, didn't fill my skull as a human voice would. The sound was a dull ache, a mild brain freeze.

I turned my back and pushed forward. Pressure around my temples forced green and blue stains into my vision. Had I been using my legs, I surely would've stumbled from wall to wall, feeling my way around like a drunkard or a blind man. But the lack of gravity allowed for flawless transportation, and without looking back, without acknowledging the scratching and breathing behind me, I made my way back to the Lounge and strapped myself down into the Flat chair. I watched, transfixed, as whiskey slithered up and down my cosmic glass, a shape engineered to resemble spaceship fuel tanks: sharp edge around the bottom, round on top, almost, just almost resembling the human heart. The liquid traveled inside the container in undisciplined blotches until I sucked it out and released it into my bloodstream.

The liquor burn fueled my anger, a spinal tap—I was a slave unshackled, bent to seize the reins of *JanHus1*, this magnificent steel beast, and plunge it into the planet that had spawned me. The labor, the isolation, the physical deterioration, all endured so that my wife could simply disappear. I plotted an apocalypse: somehow I would turn *JanHus1* into a sentient meteorite, turn it around, and drive it directly into the Earth. Somehow I would cut off the influence of physics over the shuttle, crash it through the atmosphere, and set the planet ablaze. My charred body would come back to life just so I could seek out Lenka. I would sit her down for a cup of coffee amid the end of civilization and ask her what it had felt like when she woke up one morning knowing she wanted *out*, whatever that meant.

Love could turn us all into war criminals. The Flat came to life and showed three email notifications, one of which was a reminder that my live blogging Q&A session with selected Earthlings was to begin in an hour. The feeds of my conversations with everyday citizens: children wearing T-shirts with my likeness silk-screened on them, women who couldn't stop referring to my wife as "so lucky," people who asked the simple questions, as in, was I allowed to have a beer, and how did I cope without a shower? Video technicians smoothed out my space-worn facial features, so painfully emphasized by the crisp image of high definition, by applying airbrushes and filters, making me look fresh and tight-skinned, because what is a hero who loses his looks really worth?

Not doing it, I replied to Petr's reminder.

"Skinny human, you have already acknowledged my existence," the creature said. "It is unreasonable for you to ignore it once again."

I let the whiskey bottle hover, a gesture much less satisfying than smashing it against the wall.

"I am sorry about your female partner. For what it is worth, the sociocultural rituals of your society seem to be in conflict with biological reality."

I looked up at it. The voice was high-pitched, childlike, yet a deep growl accompanied every word, like a malfunctioning radio. Its teeth were frozen in a cramped grin, and all of its eyes blinked at the same time.

"What was that?"

"Pardon me?"

"What were you doing to me? I felt it."

"I am a traveler," it said.

"Dr. Kuřák is going to love this," I said. "This plays exactly into his expectation. Reliving traumas, personification of fears, that son of a bitch."

"How would you respond?" it said.

"I wouldn't."

"Yes. Your mind is riddled with nonanswers. River dams that trap the wild joy of water for the sake of practicality. A poet human said that."

"I'm gassy. Exhausted."

"It is of utmost importance that we speak to each other."

"I need to sleep you off. Like a stomachache."

I floated off the chair, down Corridors 3, 2, and 1, back into my personal chamber, where the Womb spacebag awaited. Many Czech children on Earth had their own replica in their rooms, only horizontal, resting safely atop their beds. I glanced behind me a few times to see the creature follow, all eight of its legs smoothly rowing back and forth, back and forth, like the paddles of an ancient ship on its way to war. It seemed to be able to adjust its position and altitude regardless of the vacuum, as if it weren't subject to physics. For a moment, I observed its anatomy in detail, pondered the size of the joints set along the legs, the roundness of the belly, the dark irises of the eyes all focused in the same direction—could they do otherwise, did the nervous system provide individual control over each? The eyes were directed toward me, always toward me, and I shook my head and pleaded with myself to cease this study of an imaginary being.

Dr. Kuřák was an expert on hallucinations—in fact, he had admitted that the concept made him *giddy*. He was very careful to explain the distinction between hallucinations—a perception in the absence of stimuli that nevertheless holds the qualities of real perception—and delusional perceptions in which a correctly sensed stimulus, or, one could say, a real thing, is given some additional, twisted significance. For delusional perceptions, Dr. Kuřák chuckled, see Kafka. While Freudian theories proposed that hallucinations were the manifestation of subconscious wishes, perversions, even self-flagellation, newer waves of less ego-obsessed psychologists suggested that hallucinations had to do with metacognitive abilities, or "knowing about knowing." Dr. Kuřák was a bona fide Freudian, thus insisting that should a crisis occur during my time on *JanHus1*, the entire mythos of my childhood would come pouring out, filling the darkened halls of the ship with visions of horror, fear, pleasure, the naked body of my mother and erect phallus of my father, dreams of misdirected violence, and yes, perhaps even a "friend." Whatever the theory, my predicament was the same. Kuřák's predictions of madness seemed to be coming true.

The thing to do, of course, was to touch the creature. Hallucinations cannot be touched without dissipating. But what if I took the thin hairs on its legs between my fingertips and felt them, rough and long, or perhaps smooth and warm, felt them and thus had to declare them real? Was I, Jakub Procházka, ready to acknowledge an extraterrestrial without losing the last bits of control over my psyche? The consequences of this finding—existential, cosmic, unprecedented in the history of man—were too large for my one person. I slipped inside the sleeping bag and fastened the straps around my legs and shoulders. I turned down the light dial and the yellow hue of the room changed to a deep dark blue. Even the little bit of light that remained irritated my eyes and I pulled the zipper over my face, sighing at the darkness.

"Skinny human, at this moment I am in great need of your attention," the creature said.

"Vanish."

"I am a scholar, or rather, an explorer, like the great Columbus of your people."

"Columbus wasn't so great."

Speaking to the creature felt more appropriate while my face was concealed. I was only a man mumbling to himself under the blanket, a thing no less common than singing in the shower. So what if something spoke back?

"What is it you're exploring?" I asked.

"I have been circling your orbit. Learning the secrets of humanry. For example, the commitment of dead flesh to the underground. I would like to bring such tales for the amusement and education of my tribe."

"I've really gone past the breaking point."

"The cardiovascular organ managing your biological functioning is setting off irregular vibrations—a bad sign, I think. I will leave you to rest, skinny human, but tell me, does the ship's pantry have ova of the avian kind? I have heard great things, and I would delight in consuming them."

I shut my eyes aggressively. In the videos I had watched in training, a retired Chinese cosmonaut said that falling asleep on Earth was never the same after he returned. In Space, sleep is the natural state of being. Because the environment is unresponsive to human action—the vacuum has little patience for attempts at conquest—life becomes a specific trajectory of very basic tasks, aimed at bare survival. In Space, we submit reports, repair machinery, struggle with dirty underwear. There are no sexual interests, no work presentations to dread the next morning, no car accidents. The closer we are to the stars, the more controlled and boring our routines become. The old astronaut said that being in Space meant sleeping like a toddler once again. So unburdened, one was tempted to suck one's thumb.

But sleep would not come. I reached into an inside pocket of the Womb and removed a bottle of Sladké Sny, powerful sleeping drops developed by Laturma, major pharma manufacturer and mission sponsor. Their use was restricted to bouts of insomnia threatening to interrupt the astronaut's lifestyle cycle—frequent use would lead to dizziness, confusion, and addiction. Since I was already suffering from the first two symptoms and couldn't care less about the third, I took a triple dosage, spreading the bitter liquid along my tongue and swallowing with a brief choke. Within seconds, the tips of my fingers felt numb and my thoughts lost focus. As I hibernated, I could still sense it out there, a tension around my temples keeping tabs even when the creature could not see me. Though I blamed the awareness on the chemistry affecting my brain, it couldn't be denied—for a moment just before my loss of consciousness, I was glad. Glad that the creature was with me, real or not, searching the kitchen for eggs.

I AWOKE TO the darkness of the Womb, but I could not move a single limb. I was acutely aware of my spine, the snake of vertebrae holding me together, and I imagined what it would be like if someone peeled it off like a layer of string cheese, whether my bones would burst out of my flesh and the idea of self would collapse into a pile of perfectly unraveled parts. Did people with actual paralysis perceive their spines in the same way? I felt horror for them. The creature was strumming again, bringing about thoughts without my consent, but there was nothing I could do but take it, take it until the paralysis subsided and I would be, once again, protected by slumber.

The creature found it. The moment that had propelled me upwards.

Seven years into my marriage, I published my findings on particles within the rings of Saturn, the first tangible payoff for my lifelong obsession with cosmic dust. I toured Europe to lecture, and I was offered tenure at Univerzita Karlova for an assistant professorship in astrophysics. Four years into my somewhat satisfying tenure, Senator Tůma summoned me to his office to "make an offer." I arrived in a black tie and a new sweater-vest, certain that the government intended to recognize my achievements with a grant or an award.

Tůma was from the new generation of senators. While the old boys wore ill-fitting suits to disguise beer guts, combatted balding by wearing bigger eyeglasses, and blamed their public alcoholism on stress-related illness, Tůma was a dedicated vegetarian, a weight lifter, and a skilled rhetorician. The day the senator spoke to me was also the day he had first caught the attention of the media. Earlier that morning, the minister of the interior had been arrested for corruption and the coalition government had been attacked by the opposition for attempting to bury the scandal by buying off witnesses. Being a member of one of the coalition parties, Tůma made a statement on the stairs of Prague's district court while pouring coal ashes over his own head. This was a vintage gesture, appealing to those Czechs who favored conventional wisdom over the uncertainty of progress, symbols over factual integrity. With the gray specks covering his shoulders, hair, and cheeks, Tůma declared that Czech politics had become those of individual interest, catering to whoremongers, greedy swine, and common thieves. Hand over heart, Tůma pledged to shake up the coalition from within. I did not much care for politics.

Tůma entered the office and brushed the ashes off his suit with a handkerchief. His assistant brought him a wet towel and a can of diet cola. With his eyebrows still wet and his suit pale, he looked me over. I laughed at him when he told me that the country was building a space program. He laughed too, and poured me a bit of cola, asking whether I'd like rum or *fernet* in it. I declined.

Tůma walked to a table by the office window, and tugged at a curtain covering something tall and slim. The cloth fell to the ground and there it was: three thick cylinders connected by flat panels, a dozen solar wings extending to the sides, a beautiful dark blue finish. The entire model resembled an insect one might expect to find in the era of the dinosaurs, when nature was at once more creative and more pragmatic. Emblazoned on the middle cylinder was the country's flag—a blue triangle for truth, and two horizontal lines: red for strength and valor, white for peace—and next to it rested those words: *JanHus1*. I asked if I could touch it. Tůma nodded with a smile.

"Surely we can't afford this," I said.

But we could. Tůma named the long line of corporate partners willing to burn capital on mission sponsorship. He was to present the mission to the Parliament the following day. The Swiss were prepared to sell an unfinished spacecraft they no longer needed.

"You want us to try to reach the Chopra cloud," I said.

"Of course I do."

"You want us to go first. Even if we might not come back."

"But Gregor made it back, and look how well he's doing!"

Tůma traced the edges of the cylinders with his finger, studying me as I took the spacecraft in. A child's voice inside me encouraged me to pick it up, run outside the office, and find a quiet room in which I could admire it alone.

Tůma sat back behind his desk and cleared his throat.

"We pushed against the Austro-Hungarians when they tried to burn our books and ban our language. We were an industrial superpower before Hitler took us for serfs. We survived Hitler only to welcome the economic and intellectual devastation by the Soviets. And here we are, breathing, sovereign, rich. What next, Jakub? What is the vision for us, what will define us in the future?"

"I heard that milk prices will be through the roof next year," I said.

"Ha, a skeptic! I love skeptics. They keep a democracy honest, but they don't always think big. Think bigger. What makes a country great? Wealth, army, healthcare for all?"

"I leave that to the professionals."

"The greatness of a nation is not defined by abstracts, Jakub. It's defined by pictures. Stories that carry by mouth, by television, immortalized by the Internet, stories about a new park being built and the homeless being fed and bad men being arrested for stealing from good men. The greatness of a nation is in its symbols, its gestures, in doing things that are unprecedented. It's why the Americans are falling behind—they built a nation on the idea of doing new things, and now they'd rather sit and pray that the world won't make them adapt too much. We won't be following the Americans to that place. We won't be following anyone. We're going to take this spacecraft and send it to Venus. A nation of kings and discoverers, yet the child across the ocean still confuses us with Chechnya, or reduces us to our great affinity for beer and pornography. In a few months, the child will know that we are the only ones with the stones to study the most incredible scientific phenomenon of this century."

I remained expressionless. I did not want him to know he had me, not yet.

"You think the public will agree?" I said.

"What do our people want the most right now? They want to know we aren't the puppets of the EU, or the Americans, or the Russians. They want to know that politicians are making decisions on their behalf, not on the behalf of businessmen and foreign governments. This is the growth they crave. We defeated the communists decades ago, Jakub. We can't ride that wave forever. The republic will never have the agriculture of Latin America or the natural resources of Ukraine. We don't have America's megamilitary or the fish monopoly of the Scandinavians. How do we get ahead in this world? Ideas. Science. This country needs a future, and I will not lie comfortably in any deathbed until I get it."

I sipped on the cola and looked around the office. Not a single item was out of place, as if no one ever walked around and picked up the hockey trophies, the pictures of his wife, no one ever napped on the leather sofa underneath the window overlooking downtown Prague. The office was arranged as neatly as the man's life.

"And what do you need from me? Counsel?"

"From what I understand, in front of me sits perhaps the most qualified cosmic dust researcher in Europe. You discovered a brand-new particle of life! That must feel extraordinary."

His assistant entered the room with a bowl of garlic soup and a plate of blood sausage, fried potato croquettes, and aromatic horse-radish. The senator cut into the sausage and some grease landed on his ashy tie.

"Sure, sure, counsel is good, Jakub, but we are looking for more." He set his utensils down and took his time chewing, swallowing all of his food and smirking at the impatient hand tapping my knee. "We want you to be the first Czech to see the universe," he said.

I felt light-headed. I drank some of the cola, regretting I hadn't asked for alcohol.

"You're a vegetarian," I said.

"In my office, I'm a man. I trust you'll keep the secret. I trust we'll trust each other. What do you think of my proposition?"

"It's hard to believe a single word."

"Extraordinary, Jakub, is not only your discovery on Saturn. I know who you are. You and I, we need to do this together. Your father was a collaborator, a criminal, a symbol of what haunts the nation to this day. As his son, you are the movement forward, away from the history of our shame. Jakub Procházka, the son of a loyal communist, the glowing example of a reformed communist (you're not still a communist, are you? Good, good). A man who grieved through the death of his parents, who grew up in a humble village on the humble retirement pay of his grandparents, and despite all odds unleashed his brilliance upon the world, becoming a heavy-weight best in his field. The embodiment of democracy and capital-ism, while also a humble servant to the people, a seeker of truths. A man of science. I want to put a Czech in Space, Jakub, and that Czech will be you. Europe will scoff at us, burdened taxpayers will cry out in skepticism. But there is a future here, meaning for the country, and we can sell it as such with you on the packaging. The spaceman of Prague. The transformed nation embodied, carrying our flag into the cosmos. Can you see it?"

I saw it. I saw it and I bent over as something groaned deep within my gut.

The senator's canines once again sank into the pork as horse-radish sweat broke out on his forehead. He was so different from his television appearances, animated, loud, uncontrolled, ruddy-cheeked, and I thought, here is a man who devises a different identity every time he enters a room, and I shouldn't trust such a man. But I did anyway.

I straightened my shoulders and cleared my throat, steadying a shaky hand on my knee, heavy with the destiny this stranger had just offered. Deepening my voice to match the seriousness of the moment, I said, "Well, shit."

The government had approved the mission almost unanimously within the next three days. Within the week, I was seeing the skel-eton of *JanHus1*, its side still marked by the Swiss white cross in its sea of red. I shook the hand of the man with an Iron Maiden tat-too. Within two months, the world knew who I was and where I was headed. The shuttle had been completed. Lenka wore a black dress to the unveiling party and shook hands with the president. She gracefully carried on the conversation when I ran to a bathroom stall to retch. And within six months, I was waking up aboard *JanHus1*.

I UNZIPPED THE WOMB and made my way to Corridor 2, where the dreaded treadmill awaited. I didn't hear the creature moving around in any of the corridors, and thought that perhaps I had really slept it off. Central required that I exercise two hours a day to slow down bone loss, but lately I had been devoting less and less time to the hamster wheel, preferring to spend it in the lab. I pulled at the harness attached to the wall and slid the straps around my shoulders, grounding myself on the small gray pad underneath my feet. That was the sole benefit of the machine—it made me feel as though I was walking on Earth's sidewalks again. I started with a warm-up walk, then adjusted the speed. Strain cut into my weakened calves, and I breathed out loudly so that I would no longer ponder the creature, the disappeared hallucination. I sprinted to the point of nausea so that I wouldn't think of Lenka, so that I couldn't recall the exact shape of her nose. I ran for an hour and removed the harness. My eyes stung from the sweat, and my sweat reeked of whiskey. I made my way back to the Sleeping Chamber to wash off and change.

The creature was there, accompanied by the unusual odor. My clothing hung around its legs, as if it were a living coatrack; its face and one leg were buried in my closet, rummaging through, scratching.

"Stop," I said.

It turned around, its lips closed, eyes fidgeting between me and the contraband on its legs. The creature put my shirts and sweatpants back into the closet.

"I became so enthralled by the search that I forgot to monitor your movement. I am ashamed, skinny human."

"I thought you were gone. Cured by sleep."

"Do you intend for me to depart?"

"I don't know. What are you doing?"

"I am looking for it. The ash of your ancestor."

"You were...studying me again. I felt it."

"I apologize. I could not help myself. A researcher cannot escape his subject, can we agree? But I'd like your permission, skinny human. Permission to study you."

"What's in here doesn't belong to you. I don't want you to do it anymore."

Petr's voice sounded through the intercom. "We need to talk," he said with some distress.

I muttered gratitude for the interruption and left the creature behind, floating into the Lounge and strapping myself down in front of the Flat. I picked up Petr's call.

"Hey," he said, "people from PR are miffed about you canceling the video session. Lot of civilians lined up to talk to you."

"I couldn't do it. Not today."

"I told them I'd take the hit for it. With Lenka, and all. But there's something else—the air filters are detecting a foreign substance. Unable to determine what it is. Do you see anything unusual in Corridor 3? Or anywhere else?"

I glanced toward the filter shaft in the corridor, then at the creature floating toward the kitchen.

"Nope," I said.

"Okay, well, we're going to purify, as a safety measure. You know the drill."

I made my way to the lab. To avoid contamination of the samples, the room ran on a separate filter, and thus provided a safe haven during emergency cleansings. I passed the kitchen and saw the creature's face buried in the freezer, rifling through Popsicle packets. I considered whether I should give it a warning. Didn't it already know what was about to happen?

I closed the lab door and ran the filter analysis on my e-tablet.

No foreign substances found. I pulled up the call with Petr on the screen.

"Can I ask you for a favor?" I said.

"We're sealing you off. Cleaning in two. What?"

"Can you have someone track her down? I want to know she is safe."

"Minute and a half. Listen, I don't think that's such a good idea. She needs some time."

"Hell, I can't just not know where she is, what she's doing. She couldn't even stand to talk to me, Petr."

"Thirty seconds. I don't know, Jakub. Give it some time. Once we start poking around, people will talk. Before you know it, this is a scandal on the front pages of gutter magazines."

He was right, but being humiliated by the nation's notorious gossip rags seemed worth knowing how Lenka was doing. Why in the hell she had left me to wonder and agonize.

"I can't be up here without knowing anything. You need to figure something out for me."

I looked around the lab. On the left wall, drawers of Space dust particles already analyzed and cataloged, brought for comparison to the new dust gathered from Chopra. Highly processed pieces of the cosmos, containing H_2, magnesium, silicon, iron, carbon, silicon carbide, often mixed with asteroid and cometary dust, the latter always carrying hope, as comets are the universe's dumpster divers, vagrants pushing their carts of intergalactic junk tirelessly over the centuries. It was in those carts that we were most likely to discover new organic particles hinting at traces of other life within the universe, substances that would clarify the formation of planets and the structures of other solar systems, perhaps even a touch of what had occurred during the Big Bang. But all of these samples were old news, offered no stimuli for my imagination. On the right side of the room awaited empty glass and titanium containers, sterile, expertly shined, ready to be filled with the pieces of interstellar dust that had come to us from the unknown.

"Let me sleep on it," Petr said. "I can probably get the interior ministry on it. You need to regain your focus. You're flying on some serious currency. And the people are watching."

The familiar mist shot out of the filter vents, a slightly yellow substance. Bomba!, a revolution in home cleaning and mission sponsor. No more antibacterial wipes, no more Lysol. Once a week, the good housekeeper could place the blue square of Bomba! in the middle of his or her household. Activate, depart the house for five minutes. Meanwhile, the mist would spread around the house and eradicate 99.99993 percent of all bacteria, a ruthlessly efficient genocide. Afterward, the substance would transform itself into harmless nitrogen particles, leaving behind a pleasant citrus scent. Together with the creators of Bomba!, SPCR engineers had developed a new version of the substance to combat any known harmful particle an astronaut might encounter. *Bomba!*, the commercials cheered. *Now in Space!* I wondered whether the creature would be affected, whether I would find its dead body and drag it back to Earth. The mist grew thinner.

"All clear," Petr said. "No trace of foreign substances."

Behind me, a soft tap on the door.

"Great. Can I get off the grid?" I said.

"I need you stable, Kubo."

Kubo. What my mother used to call me.

"I get it. I'll pull it together. Just give me a break and try to find my wife."

Pause.

"I'll check on you in three hours," he said, and his face disappeared from the e-tablet screen.

Another tap. I opened the sealed door. The creature looked like schnitzel just before frying—its skin was covered in fine white powder, its hair dripping eggy yellow mucus. Its lips were a sickly blue. One of its legs was stuck in an empty jumbo jar of Nutella.

"You ate my dessert," I said.

"My apologies. I found no ova of the aviary type. I toured around the edges of your memory—only for a small amount of time, I promise—and I became what your kind calls *depressed*."

"I told you I didn't want you to do it," I said.

"Delicious, this spread of Nutella. Rich and creamy, like the Shtoma larvae back home. Crack them open, suck the fat."

"Are you hurt?" I asked.

"I do not blame you for your curiosity, skinny human. I experienced no pain in my encounter with Earth's cleaning liquids."

I swam toward it, wishing the creature wouldn't disappear. Its lips were closed, and I wondered what kind of cosmic evolution could lead to this species. Did my association of its body parts with Earth's animals signify a connection, or was I simply reaching desperately for familiarity? Perhaps I was a lunatic for having these thoughts in the first place. I sucked blood from my teeth and rubbed my sore eyes.

"I'm really not happy about the Nutella," I said. "I only have one jar left."

"I accept responsibility," the creature said, "though I do feel my excuse is valid. Your species considers the size of things around you in a comparative context. Things that are bigger than the reflective capacity of your brain terrify you. I found that fear uncomfortable, like sleeping on a bed made of empty Shtoma shells. It infected me. Along with you, I made love to your wife and stalked her as she urinated on pregnancy-detection devices. Along with you, I considered the thing you call death and the existential dread that comes with your ambition. Strange—the spread made of hazelnut felt sticky around my teeth, my stomachs were satiated, and this made my realizations seem less unpleasant. What pains me most, skinny human, is that I now share your fears, though I do not understand them. What will happen when I perish? Why ask such a question when, as the Elders of my tribe declare, certainty is impossible?"

A hallucination could not be full of thoughts that had never occurred to me, could it? Could not be dripping yolky cleaner and bringing on memories in a way that was nearly cinematic, lived in through frames and edges, as if I were at once in a theater seat and strolling around on the screen. Yes, fear was present, and I had no deities to call on for favors, but the sooner I brought on the moment of proof, the sooner I could bear the consequences of either discovering new life within the universe or finding that I had lost my mind.

I reached out my hand, one finger pointed. I could still turn back. Ideas, science, a future for the country, Tůma had said. What if I catch an extraterrestrial for you, senator? Will it inspire the national pride you hoped for? It could not be real. The lips, smoker's teeth, eyes, lack of genitals—what things could Kuřák's Freudian analysis reveal about this mosaic of my imagination? Yes, my mother had full lips, part of her movie star appeal. Yes, my father's teeth were often yellow. More likely, I would bring Tůma a new patient for Bohnice, Prague's finest establishment for the insane.

I touched the creature's leg, felt the motel carpet roughness of each individual hair, the steel solidity of bone underneath, the dry skin pulsing gently.

It was there. It was.

"You are here," I said.

"I am," it said.

I let go of the creature's leg and thrust myself backwards, pulling wildly on the wall handles.

"I wish I had the capacity to assist with your emotional distress, skinny human. I cannot offer you the solace of Nutella, for I have consumed it."

I needed to think, to digest, I needed a distraction from this touch. I left the creature and returned to the lab, where I inventoried old samples, manically trashed my logs and created brand-new ones, polished the glass, and reorganized the items strapped to my table: a lamp, sticky notes, silver pens, a notebook.

I hid in the lab for two hours. When I returned to the corridors, I heard a low snore. In the Lounge, the creature floated in the upper corner, all of its eyes closed, legs folded underneath its belly, forming a nearly perfect sphere. I knew what needed to be done.

I recovered a scalpel from the lab. What is a scientist to do when faced with impossible possibilities? A scientist gathers data and studies it in accordance with the scientific method. I pondered whether I could risk carving out a skin sample, or perhaps a scrape, and quickly come back to the lab before the creature realized what was happening. There was the safer option of collecting hair only. This was the way. If I put an item under the microscope and found real particles, I could be sure. Particles do not lie. Elements are truth tellers. For a moment, I considered simply plunging the scalpel into the creature's belly, spilling whatever insides it held all over the ship—there couldn't be more tangible proof than that. With an intense headache and shaking fingers, side effects of the sleep medication, I approached the alien creature, counted its exhales. I lifted the knife, deciding to go with the sound option of gathering hair.

With its eyes still closed, the creature said, "I would not follow your intentions here, skinny human."

I flinched. The sentence was a pure growl.

The eyes opened. Its legs did not move.

My eyelids pulsated, I couldn't swallow. There had to be a way. Something I could place underneath a microscope to affirm or refute my senses. At that moment, it seemed more important than stealing fire from Olympus or splitting the atom. What I did was inevitable.

I plunged the blade forward, toward the creature's back.

It caught the scalpel with one of its legs, while three others wrapped around my body. We flew upwards at a staggering speed, and it pressed its full weight against my chest, stomach, and groin. The pressure of the legs was like a trio of wandering snakes; I could not move a single body part below the neck.

"You refuse to be my subject, yet you subject me," the creature said. There seemed to be no anger, only a statement of fact. The scalpel flew toward the Lounge window.

"I'm sorry. I didn't want to hurt you."

"This I know, skinny human. But the body must not be violated. This is the greatest truth of the universe."

"You know this has been...unexpected. I have to know if you're here."

"Imagine my wonder when I discovered Earth," it said.

"It can't compare to all the other things you have seen."

It was silent.

"Give me a skin sample. A small one. So I can be sure. We can be subject to each other. Do you have a name? Something I can call you?"

More silence. Its grip loosened. The belly was warm, spread over me like a water bed mattress.

"Perhaps this was a mistake," the creature said. "Yes, I am certain of it." It let go of my torso and swiftly made its way through the corridors.

"It wasn't," I said. "Stay here."

I pulled myself forward on the railings, but I could not match the creature's speed. Soon it vanished out of sight. I looked inside the lab, my bunk, the kitchen, the bathroom, every corner of the Lounge. I shouted, pleaded for it to return. I promised to give it whatever it needed. I promised I would never consider violating it again. I promised it was simply too important.

There was no response.

Hours later, when I finally crawled inside the Womb and dimmed the lights, dripping twice the recommended dose of Sladké Sny onto my tongue, I again felt the pressure around my temples, witnessed an array of colored stains in my vision. My jaw ached from the infected molar. The creature probed on then, despite its absence. It was looking for a specific day. The day a stranger appeared in my life carrying an artifact belonging to my father. An iron shoe.

The Iron Shoe

Two days after my thirteenth birthday, I am bedridden with fever and stomachaches. Grandma checks on me every few hours as I read *Robinson Crusoe* and puke into the bucket usually used for pig blood. It is a rainy summer, and through the window I can see Grandpa, cursing the sky and squishing his boots in the mud as he stuffs hay inside the rabbit cages. Water captured by the gutters travels to a small tub from which Grandma draws to hydrate the houseplants. The chickens are sleeping inside the coop, their claws grasping at the wooden poles that serve as their beds. From the rooftop of the house, two black cats fall into the mud, hissing and screaming. I am not sure whether they are killing each other or mating, and I'm not sure whether the difference matters.

In my sweat I have lost track of days, unsure whether it is Sunday or Thursday, when a blue Nissan pulls up to our gate. A suited man exits the car, straightens out the creases in his jacket, and takes a purple backpack out of his trunk. His knock carries through the cold hallway. Grandma talks to him by the front door. I walk out of my room and try to hear their whispers.

"Go to sleep," Grandma says to me.

"So this is the boy," the stranger says. He speaks from the corner of his mouth, and despite the deep pox scars on his cheeks, he has the look of a movie actor—a defined jaw covered in stubble, his eyes cold, his hair slicked but not greasy.

Grandpa walks in from the yard, a cigarette between his teeth, a chunk of bulgur in his hand. He listens to the man.

"Jakub, bed," Grandpa says. He gestures for the stranger to follow him into the living room and shuts the door behind him. I count to sixty and walk over to the door. I slowly take the key out of its hole and peep through. Grandpa sits with a beer, while the stranger puts his wet backpack on the table and pulls out a rusty metal shoe, so large it could only fit a proper giant. Grandma waters her plants, her back turned to the men.

"Like I said, I was once, in a very specific way, closely tied to your son," the man says. "When we first met, he introduced me to the shoe you see on your table. He took me to an interrogation room in the secret police headquarters and he asked if I liked poetry."

"I will offer you a beer if you take your wet belongings off of my wife's table," Grandpa says.

"I apologize," the stranger says but keeps the shoe where it is. "I told him that I dabbled. I enjoyed the classics, like any other university student. William Blake, is what I told your son. He asked whether I wrote poetry too."

"Your time is wasted here," Grandpa says.

"I don't write poetry, Mr. Procházka. I like the stuff, but I'm no good at seeing the world in pictures. But your son was certain about my editorship of some international newsletter. A call to action. He was certain I wrote verse calling for a violent revolution, a tsarian slaughter of Party leadership and their families, opening the gates of our country to capitalists and once again enslaving the working class. He was so certain he put my feet inside these shoes. This is one of them, right here."

The man pats the shoe.

"You do know my son has passed," Grandpa says.

"Do your legs ever fall asleep? In a violent way, I mean. You try to stand up but you have no control, like someone severed the nerves and you are no longer in command of your own flesh. It's like that with these shoes. Your son was very gentle when he shaved my chest and placed the charges, right underneath my nipples. He coughed politely when he pushed my chair a little closer to the wall, so I could rest my head. Inserted a piece of cardboard in my mouth to bite on. He patted me on the shoulder, like a stranger telling someone they dropped a coin, before he pushed a button and watched as the galoshes circulated the charge through the marrow of my bones. You become a human light bulb. You piss yourself, you cry a little, and you take the pen and sign, you shout, *Oh yes, I did it all, I wrote poems*. But your son—I cannot speak for the other Party officers, but I can speak with every cell of my body about your son—he would not let me confess so soon. He lowered the charge and he described the average day in the life of my mother. Morning, he said, she has a roll with jam and Edam cheese. She brushes her teeth with Elmex while she listens to *dechovka* on the radio. She takes the A line to Old Town Square, where she works as a typist. For lunch, she makes a ham roll, except for Mondays, when she uses the schnitzel left over from Sunday, placing it between two slices of rye bread with a pickle. On her lunch break, she reads plays. She arrives home around four and watches television while she peels potatoes and cooks sauerkraut pork for dinner. This is when your son's face became very serious, Mr. Procházka, you see, because here he truly had me, and he was happy, but he could not show his sadistic pleasure. Your son, he had shame. He was very serious when he told me my mother copulated with my father on Wednesdays only, and she would never allow him to release inside of her, because she believed there would be another world war and the Americans would kill all of us, and why make more children only to watch them die? Like me, I'm sure you are wondering whether your son made these things up simply to terrorize me, or whether the Bolsheviks actually watched through their windows as my father and mother did or did not pleasure each other. I will always wonder, Mr. Procházka. What am I to do, ask my mother? I can see you are curious too. After this story, your son allowed my numb fingers to sign a paper, and he took that paper and he glowed like a little runt about to deliver the morning paper to its master. What do you think about that?"

Grandma stands still, looking out the window. Grandpa gets up from his chair, groans a little, and takes a moment to straighten his back. He walks to the refrigerator and takes out a beer. He puts it on the table, opens it, and drinks half of it in one gulp.

"Do you want me to apologize on his behalf?" Grandpa says. "Well, I can't. Because I can't be sure he would be sorry at this moment. I can't be sure if he would regret anything. He was a man of conviction."

"Aren't you curious how I got the shoe? I'm a wealthy man now, Mr. Procházka. The privatization has been kind to me. I dabble in iron, zinc. Some weapons contracts. I'm even looking into opening a couple fast-food stores downtown. I bought this shoe from a friend of mine at the police inventory. I know it is the one I had an intimate relationship with because the serial number burned itself onto my skin. Can you imagine? The prosecution was going to use it against your son, to shit on your name for the next ten generations, but he managed to depart before they could. I picture him crawling along the steel rope and cutting it himself, the coward he was. Do you think I traveled from Prague to hear an old man say he is sorry? Take your apology and go feed it to your swine."

Grandpa finishes the beer. He stands up and grabs the empty bottle by its neck. Grandma drops her spray bottle. The stranger scratches through his stubble, making the sound of a match struck on a matchbox. I wait for my grandfather to hurt the stranger, but he does not raise the bottle. His hand shakes. He sets the bottle down and breaks into a fit of smoker's cough, roars like a wounded bear until Grandma hands him a mint sucker and rubs his back.

SPACEMAN OF BOHEMIA

The stranger taps on the shoe with his finger to the rhythm of the rain. There is almost a politeness to it, as if he is giving his opponent a turn.

"That was rude," the stranger says. "I don't mean to insult your occupation or the wisdom of your age. But tell me, how could I stay away? There ought to be some rules in this universe. The Party gave your family rewards because your son was a good dog. Tell me I don't deserve justice. Convince me I shouldn't be here, and I will go, and never return."

"Are you a religious man?" Grandpa asks.

"No."

"Then go fuck yourself with justice. A car ran over one of our cats last week. Who should I go to for reparations? Men don't always pay for their mistakes."

"No. But if I can help it," the stranger says, stands up, and once again straightens out the creases on his jacket. "Anyway, this was a friendly introduction. You will be seeing me around. Maybe at the shop? The pub? I'll chat with your neighbors some. I own a cabin by the woods now. Lovely view."

"What is it you want?" Grandpa says. "Say it plain."

"I'm not sure yet," the stranger says, "but when I decide, I'll come see you again."

He picks up the shoe and slides it inside his backpack. Grandpa's shoulders sag and he stares out the window, overlooking the newly awakened chickens plucking at the leftovers of morning seed. I forget that I am not watching a movie. The man with the shoe opens the door and I fall backwards.

"Little Jakub," the stranger says.

I struggle to my feet. He extends a hand. I ignore it.

"What will you be when you grow up?"

"Astronaut," I say.

"A hero, then. Did you like your father?"

Grandpa takes the bottle again, runs toward us with the speed of a young man, and shouts "Shoo, scum. Begone!"

The stranger rushes out the door and out the gate while Šíma nips at his ankles. He drives off. Grandpa stands in front of the gate and breathes heavily. It is shortly before noon, and neighbors are walking in pairs and trios on the main road to pick up fresh rolls from the store. They pause to study the scene of the stranger's escape, surely enthusiastic to compose theories about the event later, during the evening's game of Mariáš.

"Did you hear us?" Grandpa asks when he comes back inside.

I nod.

"Are you feeling sick?"

I shake my head. Anger burns in my stomach, as if I'm about to belch, but I'm not sure whom to be angry with. I've never witnessed a threat of violence in front of me. It does not feel good or thrilling, like in books.

"Let's go skin a rabbit," Grandpa says.

"He has the flu," Grandma says.

"Give him a shot of slivovitz, then. He's been in the house for weeks. How is that healthy for a boy?"

I put on a raincoat and follow Grandpa to the rabbit cages. He reaches for Rost'a, a fat white buck cowering in the corner. Rost'a squeaks and thrashes around until Grandpa deals a swift blow to the back of his neck. The chickens gather around the compost and *bawk* upwards in ecstasy as Grandpa cuts Rost'a's throat and the blood pours over their beaks, thick and steamy.

Grandpa hangs Rost'a on two tree hooks, plucks the eyes out with the tip of his knife, and lets me feed them to the chickens. The sticky residue feels like snot on my fingers.

My father rarely spoke to me about his work. He said that while other people sat in hotel receptions or milked cows, cushy spots assigned by the state, he ensured that the truth and stability of the regime were not compromised by those without faith. People seemed to like him—they always said hello and smiled, although every year as I grew older and saw more, I noticed the insincerity of the gestures. Even after he had received his trial summons and the newspapers wrote about the likes of him, I didn't think my father could have hurt anyone who was innocent, anyone who was not out to destroy our way of life.

"Don't believe everything that man claims," Grandpa says as he slides the knife down Rost'a's belly.

"Do you know? If Dad could've been wrong to hurt him?"

"I don't know much more than you, Jakub. I know he did things I disagreed with. He thought he was carving a better world for you with his own two hands."

"Would he have gone to prison?"

"You know that the world is always trying to take us. This country, that country. We can't fight the whole world, the ten million of us, so we pick the people we think should be punished, and we make them suffer the best we can. In one book, your father is a hero. In another book, he is a monster. The men who don't have books written about them have it easier."

He gathers the liver, the heart, the kidneys. He slices off the legs and ribs, and leaves the skin hanging on the tree as we make our way back to the house. The fur will dry for a few days before Grandpa sells it. We peel chicken shit from our shoes with a butter knife, and while Grandpa washes the meat in the tub before packaging it for the freezer, I ask Grandma to make tea. On the living room table, a gigantic footprint disturbs a thin layer of dust. I wish the shoe was still there so I could touch it. At some point, my father had touched it, and perhaps a piece of him remained on it, a speck of dust, the smallest flake of skin composed of the same life as mine.

When I go to sleep that night, no longer with fever but still nause-ated, my grandparents speak in the kitchen, and there is one word I can safely recognize, repeated over and over: *Prague.*

A FEW DAYS LATER, I am well again. After school, I walk by the River Ohře stretching from Středa throughout the county, eventu-ally connecting to the Labe, the blue vein of Europe. Red catkins cover the river's surface. An occasional splash of fish interrupts the Sunday lunchtime silence of the main road. Everyone is at home eating potatoes and schnitzel, or potatoes and sausage, or potatoes with sour cream. They will watch the political debate shows where the newly found apostles of democracy spar with one another about how a free market should function and how severely communist collaborators should be punished under the humanist direction of President Havel's slogan: Love and truth prevail over hate and lies.

Up ahead, beneath a low-hanging leafy branch, a man is pissing against the trunk of a birch tree. He zips up and turns around. The stranger with the shoe.

"Little spaceman," he says, chewing.

"You're not supposed to talk to me."

"Charming places, these villages. Nice break from Prague. Too many Americans and Brits flowing in with their cameras after the fall of Moscow. Here, it's beer and rivers and soccer friendlies. Good place for a boy. Gum?"

He extends his hand. Images of apples and oranges decorate the packet. I've never had this gum and I badly want to reach for some—the scent coming from the man's mouth is as pleasant as that of cherry trees in the summer. But this man is not a friend. I slap the packet out of his hand and put my fists up, ready for him to strike. He laughs.

"Fighter! Good, good. Just don't take it too far. Every man these days fancies himself a fighter. Not all of us are. And that's okay. Just think: if the Americans had liberated us from Hitler before the Russians, we could've been free. Your father and I might've been great friends. You could've taken all the gum you wanted from me. I wonder. I always wonder."

Until this moment, I have never felt hated. Back in Prague, I had a rivalry with a boy named Jacko—we were both good at soccer and thus always competing for captain of the school team. We had fights in which we slapped each other, and almost always missed, and we both knew we would never cause real harm. We professed hatred for each other, but I kind of liked him, and I believe he liked me too. Jacko is now gone, everyone I knew in Prague is gone from my life, and now I miss him and the rules of our engagement, because there are no rules established with the man in front of me. He smirks as if he knows things. He has walked into my grandparents' house and made my grandfather, Grandpa the son of Perun, look weak. And now he is with me alone, and I recall all the news stories that make me sick to my stomach, the stories in which people of my age are dragged into the woods and killed by adults. I keep my fists up. Whatever he does to me, I won't let it be easy.

The man lights a cigarette and turns away. I feel as if I might fall to the ground. He makes his way up to the main road, then north, toward the vacation houses. I sit down and breathe, absorb the adrenaline, my thoughts regaining clarity. Next to me rests the stranger's packet of gum. I pick it up, rip off the wrapper, and place the pink contents on my tongue. It is sweet and sour, like berries with cream. I throw the gum in the river, as far as I can. While I walk home, I imagine the American tanks, decorated by the Allied silver star, rolling down our potato fields, and the girls of Bohemia lending their lips to the cut jaws and healthy bodies of boys raised on Marlboros and fudge sundaes instead of embracing the bare bones and starved chests of Soviet boys. What could've been.

For hours I walk the fields, throw pebbles at ducks, whistle tunes that do not exist outside my own mind, tease vicious dogs behind gates by poking at them with a stick. I feel childish, having never asked my father about his life. What I knew of our family while my father was alive came from hearsay and from the strange gestures of people around us, the way my friends cowered and catered to my every whim whenever we went outside (and now I wonder: What about Jacko? Why was he not afraid of me? Perhaps his parents failed to warn him, or maybe he was simply a maverick who didn't care about my family's status), or from how our neighbors ran into their apartments as my mother and I returned from the market so they wouldn't have to say hello to us. I search my mind for these moments now, careful not to make them up, but the distinction vanishes like morning mist stretching along the lake's surface. What I'm sure of now is that there is a stranger who sees my father in me and hates me for it. I am hated, and perhaps he wishes me harm, true harm. For a moment I wish to take it all back, the revolution, the fall of the Party. I want to be back at our big apartment in Prague, with my parents cooking together and tossing food at each other, the steam of the radiator fighting the annexation of winter. I don't care what reigns outside our house—capitalism, communism, or anything else—as long as my parents will return to me and keep me safe from men like the stranger. Yes, perhaps my father could even torture him a little. I would allow it. I would ask my father to torture the man until he stopped hating me.

I wipe my face on my shirt, look around to ensure no one witnessed my sobs.

At sunset, I walk back to the house. As I arrive, only half of the sun peeks over the horizon. On the solid brown wood of the gate, letters have been spray-painted in red:

Stalin's pigs, Oink Oink Oink.

Urine and spit drip to the grass below. I read the words repeatedly until it is dark and I can no longer see them. I enter the living room and Grandma looks at me from the newspaper. Wieners boil on the stove.

"What's on TV tonight?" I ask.

"A documentary about rock and roll in East Germany, before the wall fell. *Octopus*, a French gangster movie. Violent, but you can watch it."

I want to confess to Grandma. I'd like to tell her that I wish my father would return and hurt people for me. I'd like to tell her that I am afraid. Instead I eat wieners with hot mustard and watch the Frenchmen on the screen, their mouths out of sync with the Czech words they speak. Grandma applies her facial cream and I ask to sniff it from the bottle.

"Did Grandpa see the gate?" I ask.

"Yes. He went to the pub to calm his nerves."

Full and lazy, I lean back in the chair and place Šíma on my lap. Outside, I can hear Kuka, the village drunk, stumbling on the main road and singing about tits and rivers filled with Becherovka. The gate creaks open, and Šíma and I run to the door to greet Grandpa.

He sits down in a chair, blood dripping from his forehead onto both sides of his face. Šíma licks the salty spaces between Grandpa's toes while Grandma soaks a snotty handkerchief in peroxide and holds it to the wound. Grandpa's right cheek is black and swollen.

"It was Mládek and his little town friends," he says.

Mládek, the town cretin, body fed by a lifetime of pork consumption but mind fed only by misdirected rage. He swaggers around town like its appointed sheriff with his deputies of Prague vacationer teenagers, living on his parents' wages and drinking himself to an early death. He is the new breed of young Czech, the inadequacies that were both caused and subsidized by communism now rendering him useless to society. Of course Mládek finds his new cause in our family shame.

"Still had some red paint on his T-shirt, that fascist. All the new paint I have to buy. On this shitty retirement."

"At least it's not as shitty as it used to be," Grandma says.

"It's never enough," Grandpa says. "Different lords and the same shit for the commoner."

"Hold still."

"Did you hit them?" I ask.

Grandma gives me the same look she uses when I step on her plants or forget to feed Šíma.

"I did. You know I did, Jakub. You should see them, goddamn heathens, fascist shitfuckers. I grabbed Mládek by the rat tail and dipped his schnoz into the pavement."

"This is not how we wanted it," Grandma says quietly.

"It's all him. That shoe guy," Grandpa says. "No one seemed to care much before he came here and started running his mouth. We can always leave."

"We've done nothing," Grandma says. "Old Sedláková's son is in prison for touching a teenage boy, and what do you see on her gate? Nothing. Everyone trips over themselves to pat her shoulder, poor woman, giving birth to a monster—'Here, we made you strudel.' Why isn't she running? What makes us different?"

"Perverts didn't occupy the country for sixty years," Grandpa says.

"They've occupied the planet since the dawn of days," Grandma says.

She bandages the wound and gives him three shots of slivovitz for the pain, though his breath already stinks of rum and beer. Wordless, they retire to their bedroom and I slide under my covers. Šíma is not allowed on beds, but I pull him up anyway and bury my nose in his fur, the smell of Grandma's cooking and residue of flea shampoo. Usually, my grandfather snores loudly throughout the night, but today, aside from the apple tree branches scratching on the roof, the house is silent. For the first time since my parents' funeral, I can't sleep.

My father loved Elvis Presley. He bought his records from a blacklisted German actor who smuggled them in through the Berlin Wall. He would put the record on when he cooked, when my mother cooked, before bed, while on the toilet, while in the bath, while looking out the window at the cloned concrete housing projects, magnificent and dreadful in their efficiency. Women returned from work and threw wet dresses and bras over the clothing lines fastened to poles just outside their windows, lines of dripping rags expanding across the world like the sails of a haunted pirate ship, while men walked slowly and with their heads down, unsure whether to go to the pub and risk arrest for saying the wrong thing after too many beers, or go home and face the one-station television and the single-thought shelf of books, tools incapable of interrupting the silence of their lives. My father smoked and nodded his head to the music and it seemed as though everything was just the way he wanted it.

Don't tell anyone about Elvis, he would say at breakfast. His catchphrase. Those discovered listening to Western music were brought in for questioning, nothing too severe, as my father said (though I do wonder now: What did *nothing too severe* mean to him?), just a room with a small window and a casual comrade asking why the musical gifts from Mother Sovetia weren't enough to make the suspect happy.

One day, my mother found the box of records on the kitchen table, outside their usual hiding place in the pantry.

"You'd lose your job if someone took a photograph through the window," she said.

My father put his hand around her waist and caressed the edges of the records with his fingertip.

"They can take a thousand pictures," he said, "and here we're going to stay, drinking coffee and peeling potatoes. No one informs on the informer."

Two days later, I found my father holding a cup to the wall between our living room and the neighbors', his ear inside the hollow space. He put a finger to his lips and gestured for me to come over. He lowered the cup to my height and I listened. A sharp voice carried through static, announcing that a shortage of potatoes throughout the Soviet Union was just another sign of mismanagement by Moscow. Radio Free Europe, the cardinal sin, the enemy. My father went to his bedroom and dialed a number on the phone. About an hour later, shouting erupted in the hallway, and I cracked the door open to see Mr. Strezsman and his son, Staňek, being taken away by four police officers. I felt my father's breath on the back of my neck, and Mr. Strezsman, in a voice not dissimilar to the deadpan voice of the radio announcer, cursed in the direction of our door. "Collaborator cunt," he said. Over and over.

I wanted to question my father then. If only I could have strapped him down to a chair and set a hot teakettle on his lap until he told me about his workdays, his state secrets, told me who he was. He was so calm in his actions—setting the record player needle down, caressing my mother, picking up the phone, always straight-spined, letting out the smallest cough before he put on his official voice, the baritone of duty—that I couldn't see a life in which he wasn't the hero. He continued to play his records and I continued my silence.

Now I am here, watching a stray cat pierce a beetle with its unchecked claws on the windowsill as the sun rises, while my grandfather still does not snore, and I kick the heavy blanket off my body and the dust floats around in the thin rays of light, like the first pollen of the summer or star projections on the walls of a planetarium.

In the morning, Grandpa and I walk outside holding cups of tea. Overnight, more artists contributed to our gate. *Fascist*, *Marxfucker*, *Love and Truth Prevail* over *Fuck You*, and a simpler one: *Get Out.*

Eventually, the vandals gave up on spraying letters and instead created simple lines and crosses in red, blue, and white, the colors of the republic. Through my rose tea, I smell urine, so much of it. Grandpa gets on his bicycle to go buy paint. He returns in a couple of hours, so drunk that he cannot keep his left buttock on the seat.

Most of the children in the village never liked me—I am a city boy, will always be a city boy, and in this they assume I feel superior to them, with their village roots, though I have always regarded Středa as an equal home to Prague. Now their dislike turns hostile—they shout at me, chase me on their bicycles, and I make sure that I never find myself without adults around. The adults' hostility is more hidden. When I walk on the main road to buy ice cream, the women's hellos and how-are-yous are pointed accusations, as if to say that my well-being imposes on theirs. The men, young and old, are quietly aggressive, clenching their fists and flexing their forearms whenever they see me. The only person who does not act differently is my friend Bouďa. We have spent every summer vacation together since we were three, and now he has become my only friend and companion. He never speaks of my parents, doesn't mention my past. We simply walk to the Riviera, the village's version of a beach, and swim in the river when all the other children are away. We collect ants in soup cans, we try our first cigarette in the woods.

The rains pass and the world is now hot and inviting, but Grandma stops going to the store every day and Grandpa watches TV instead of going to the pub. Often, I catch him looking at the apartment section in the newspaper, circling places in Prague. He hides the paper when I come near and he won't talk. I don't want to think about moving from this house, this home. Though I grew up in Prague, Středa has always been a sanctuary, a place where my mother often smiled, taking me for hour-long walks, a place where my father spoke more, and never about work or politics, a place where no cars pass by at night and one can seek perfect darkness in the fields, away from street lamps and golden bulbs seeping from windows.

It is home, but we are no longer welcome. When my father the hero was lost, my father the nation's villain came to light. Those morning Elvis songs, mixed with his coffee slurps and the shuffling of newspapers (*The imperialists are killing the poor with drugs*, he would scoff), hum in my ears all night and into the morning, forbidding sleep.

Deep Surveillance

THE DISTANCES LIFE TRAVELS to find other life.

From the first prokaryote battling the wild seas of pre-historic Earth to hominids acquiring their first crude tools; from Neanderthals scratching the likeness of their world onto cave walls with red and yellow ochre to the first Russian satellite (weight: eighty-three kilograms) orbiting around *Terra* and pulsing its exhilarating beeps to Earth's radios; from the first Soviet phantom spacemen sent by the motherland to die nameless to the first men pinning flags to extraterrestrial surfaces (yes, these glowing rocks now belong to us); from the Hubble telescope photographing the first worlds beyond our own (could they ever be ours?) to the ecstasy of finding life's greatest bacteria sustainer, H_2O, on the surfaces of planets mercilessly teasing our imaginations; and finally to the first man-made *Voyager* exiting the cozy luxuries of our very own solar system. Life will always travel to find other life.

And there was me. Jakub Procházka, sole crew member of shuttle *JanHus1*, who could sweep these discoveries off the table as if they were merely the insignificant crumbs of a bygone era.

It had been six days and eighteen hours since I watched the creature flee. I found comfort in its mind visits, despite their invasiveness—the constant ache around my temples preserved my belief that I would see it again.

Earth was now a shining point deep within the heavens, a home reduced to a unit of punctuation. Once a day, I focused my telescope to remind myself of the blues and whites awaiting me upon my return, a planet willing to sustain me and those I knew. In comparison to these magnifications of my planet, Venus seemed quite dull and every bit as hostile as its never-ending thunderstorms and volcanic explosions, its surface a deceptively still malt of sand and rock. The planet was pale and static when viewed through the thick haze of cloud Chopra, still two weeks away and thus appearing motionless, though daily readings offered proof that the cloud was continuing to collapse on itself.

Every day now, my progress toward the cloud took over the news cycle, and the public relations frenzy over my mission was at its peak. The *New York Times* ran a six-page profile detailing the actions of my father, the regime's hero, the betrayer of the people. It was a fine essay on the history of the country (I wondered whether the *Times* had ever given my country the time of day before) combined with irrelevant and condescending comments on my life as a rags-to-riches boy from a small country with a big country's moxie. Media outlets all over the world took up the task to describe me to their respective populations as if they were describing a friend. A Norwegian starlet, touring Hollywood for a new major film, declared me her number one celebrity crush. My government PR team—most of whom I had never met, and who looked like they'd just obtained their real estate license—toured Europe to speak about my bravery, the importance of keeping Space exploration alive, and my preference regarding boxers versus briefs. Central forwarded emails from entertainment publicists in bulk, offering to represent me, to sell my life story rights to film producers, biographers, and the occasional desperate novelist.

It wasn't really so long ago that people had spit on my family's gate. Now they wanted to exchange money for what that name represented, perhaps offer the role of my father to an up-and-coming serious character actor looking to break into the major awards scene after portraying a series of multilayered, morally ambiguous white men in independent films.

Every day I continued to receive emails from Petr outlining the detailed schedule of tasks to complete before reaching my target. Filter testing, sensor cleaning, a more rigid exercise program to prepare me for possible emergency protocols, video chat events to satisfy the sense of ownership and pride of the taxpayers. I performed these tasks dutifully but without much excitement. All I could think about was the creature, its weight, its voice defying sound waves; or Lenka, Central's inability to find her, the silence, my resentment building up against her despite my best efforts. The pursuit of Chopra seemed ill-timed, perhaps even no longer worth the time and currency in the face of terrestrial intelligent life. But Chopra was ahead nevertheless, visible and life-altering to Earthlings, while the creature had vanished as quickly as it had appeared, and these mild headaches, the lingering proof of its presence, were beginning to feel self-inflicted. Both Lenka and the creature had abandoned me to my mission. My flesh attended to the menial tasks only with dry professionalism, while my mind wandered everywhere, anywhere, once manic and once passive, a buzzing fly making its way around a bedroom, torn between the freedom promised by sunlight seeping through a window and the endless buffet of crumbs scattered in dark corners.

Six days and eighteen hours after the creature's disappearance, when I settled into my lounge chair to check email before sleeping off two hours of television interviews, I found an email forwarded by Petr from the ministry of interior. The attachment was a text file titled *Lenka P.* The text of the email:

A gift from Senator Tůma. State security agent has eyes on Lenka 4 u.

P.

I opened the document.

The subject was first spotted while leaving the city hall building in Plzeň. In comparison to provided photograph #3, contrasts are immediately striking—hair cut short and dyed blood-orange red, some weight loss noted around cheekbones. Subject walked with confidence and a cell phone held to her ear. Phone records show the particular phone call was to her mother. Other calls have been made to a female friend in Prague and a male acquaintance in Plzeň. The male acquaintance will be followed up on shortly for possible involvement. The subject drove to a Hodovna supermarket, where she purchased half a kilo of lean ham, Camembert, three whole wheat rolls, two bottles of Cabernet Sauvignon, and a Bounty bar. It appears that the subject shops for only one meal at a time. The subject's evening activities were limited to watching reruns of The Simpsons, *consumption of purchased goods, and writing in a notebook the agent has not yet been able to access. It is of note that the subject consumed an entire bottle of red wine and smoked seven Marlboro menthol cigarettes before going to sleep. As the agent was asked for light detail, he abstained from observing the subject's bedroom activities, and did not enter the apartment. A view through the window revealed a neatly arranged living room with little furniture, no pictures or wall art, no books, a television placed upon a cheap table. The leather couch seems to be the only substantial piece of furniture in the house, suggesting the subject is not considering a permanent stay. Surveillance will resume...*

I closed the email. *Male acquaintance. Possible involvement.* Perhaps the surveillance was a terrible idea—the guilt was not worth the minimal relief it provided. But the guilt of spying on Lenka did not overpower the sudden thirst this report had created in me to know her every meal, every conversation, every sigh that could possibly be dedicated to me, perhaps a scent that reminded her we used to wake up to each other. Anything could be a clue to her return.

Thanks, I wrote to Petr, *this means everything.*

I rubbed my sore eyes and shut off the Lounge lights, a habit from home I could not shake, despite having limitless solar energy at my disposal. Somehow, not flicking a switch still seemed wasteful.

I made my way to the kitchen for a midnight snack, and recoiled at the sight.

The open refrigerator door was, along with the counters, covered in thin blotches of chocolate spread. A white lid floated across the room, cracked in two, and in front of me, suspended in midair, was the creature, two of its legs scratching along the inside of the Nutella jar. The creature blinked a few times, then extended the jar toward me.

"I am ashamed," it said. "I seem to have acquired an inability to resist impulses when it comes to Earth's hazelnut."

With a trembling hand, I recovered the jar. "You're back."

"After our unpleasant confrontation, I needed to meditate and reconsider. You must understand that our encounter is not a simple matter for me."

I approached the pantry and removed a package of tortillas. I spread the hazelnut miracle on the tortillas and rolled them up into anorexic burritos. The creature's legs quivered as it watched me, possibly a sign of excitement.

"I'm happy you're here," I said.

"Before my departure, you asked about a name. My kind has no need for distinguishing marks, identities. We simply are. Would it help you to call me by a name, skinny human?"

"It would."

"Call me by a smart human's name. The name of a philosopher king, or a great mathematician."

I revisited the catalog of great humans, the astonishing chronicle shining through the stained pages of history. There were so many—enough to convert anyone, briefly, to a perky optimist— but the correct one presented itself with absolution, as if the ghost of Adam's first naming were speaking through me. Once upon a time, Adam pointed at what then was nothing, and he declared, *Rabbit*. And thus *nothing* became a *rabbit*.

"Hanuš," I said.

And thus nothing became Hanuš.

"What has he done?" Hanuš asked.

I offered the burrito. With a grin, Hanuš accepted it between his teeth. He chewed with his lips and eyes closed, the bottom of his belly swinging from side to side as he emitted a low-pitched grumble resembling the sound of a large dog begging for treats. I was not sure why I had taken to calling him a he, as there was no sign of genitals.

"He constructed the astronomical clock in Prague. Orloj," I said. "Later the city hired thugs to stick hot iron rods in his eyes, so that he would never build another. With blood dripping from his sockets, Hanuš reached inside the clock and interrupted its functions with a single flick of his hand. No one could fix the clock for the next hundred years."

"He was an astronomer."

"Yes. An explorer. Like yourself."

"I will be called Hanuš."

The creature settled on the floor, suddenly unaffected by zero gravity. He extended a leg toward me, his lips spread into a wide smile, regaining their previous bright red color. I touched the pointed tip of the leg, felt the hard sleek shell beneath the hairs. The tip was hot, like a freshly poured cup of tea. I made two more burritos.

"Why did you choose me?" I asked Hanuš.

"I have surveyed Earth from its orbit, skinny human. I have studied your history and learned your languages. Yet, having accessed all knowledge, I do not seem to understand. My original intent was to study you for a day or two, observe your habits. But access into your memory trapped me. I wished to know more, always. The great human specimen, an ideal subject."

"If you say so."

"Your question, of course, is what you can receive from me."

"A hair sample. Blood sample. Anything you can give. The greatest gift would be for you to come to Earth."

"Humanry does not inspire the trust required," Hanuš said. "There is no benefit for my tribe. And I regret I cannot give you a piece of myself. The body cannot be violated. It is the law."

"Is there nothing we could exchange?"

"Let us begin with the two of us—the awareness of single beings—and see where our cohabitation takes us."

I nodded, and bit into the burrito. Could Hanuš presently read my thoughts of desperation? Czech astronaut discovers intelligent life in Space. The Czech president is the first world leader to shake hands with the extraterrestrial, and gives him a tour of the Prague Castle. State heads overwhelm the Prague airport with their aircrafts and stand in line to meet the new life-form. Hanuš agrees to noninvasive research by Czech scientists, and his organic functions lead to stunning advances in biology and medicine. The question of God's death is debated more hotly than ever. Atheists reaffirm his nonexistence; Catholics speak against the demon spreading Satan's deception. I am at the center of it all. Hanuš refuses to travel anywhere without my company.

"Do not hope for such things, skinny human," Hanuš said, "though I must ask—is it possible to share more of Earth's hazelnut?"

After making another wrap, I slid my hand inside the jar and the tortilla package to confirm that the ingredients I had used for Hanuš were truly vanishing. Madness remained an option, despite everything. That night, I slept without needing medication.

* * *

THE FOLLOWING DAY, I was scheduled to engage with selected citizens in a videoblog session. The first barrage of questions was business as usual — my religious beliefs, my opinion on wasting taxpayers' money on the mission, the workings of Space toilets. The last question of the day came from a young man, a university type, with thin-lensed eyeglasses and a lisp. His awkward throat-clearing reminded me of my old university friends, those manic beings racing through downtown Prague with backpacks and McDonald's sacks in hand, always frantic, always fidgeting, their hyperactive disorders a manifestation of sincere beliefs that they will, they must change the world. As soon as the young man asked his question, Petr's eyes widened in horror on the second screen. It was obvious that the young man had lied about his question during the prescreening. His inquiry was number one on Central's blacklist.

"How often do you think about dying due to mission failure?" he asked. "Does it make you feel anxious, or numb?"

I looked at Petr. He fondled his forehead and nodded weakly. The question had been posed, and cutting the live feed would only make it obvious to the nation that secrets were being kept, narratives manipulated, public perception controlled. No, in a democracy, a raised question resonates with a never-ending echo. I was to answer.

"When I think about death," I said, "I think of a sun-covered porch in the mountains. I take a sip of hot rum. I take a bite of cheesecake, and I ask the woman I love to sit on my lap. Then, death."

The ease with which I invented this false fantasy sent guilt aches into my head. The moderator announced the end of the session and the screen went dark, and I imagined the young man being roughly escorted outside the Central headquarters. Petr apologized, but I waved it off. My duties to the public were fulfilled for the day, and I'd stripped into my underpants and set out to find Hanuš.

"Other humans look up to you, skinny human," Hanuš noted over our next dinner session, "as if you are the Elder of your tribe."

TIME BECAME CHOPPY, like a scratched cassette tape. Tasks took longer to complete, I was always behind schedule, and lyrics from songs whose rhythm I had long forgotten returned to my mind and would not leave. It was as if the closer proximity to Venus was bringing about time warps, slowing my brain functions to a crawl while harvesting the most useless of memories—information that had no practical purpose, those simple pieces of living, like scraps of fabric that do not become part of the dress and are left littering the floor.

I checked email obsessively. Another update from the ministry arrived:

> ...*cannot determine whether subject is engaged in sexual relationship with male acquaintance, Zdeněk K., age 37, slightly overweight but good-natured and clean-faced with secure job as bank teller...*

> ...*apartment does not allow visual access to determine nature of meetings. Ministry is able to order deep surveillance, which would allow agent to access apartment when empty, gather evidence such as semen...*

> ...*subject purchased a package of peanuts and frozen stir-fry, resulting in a cleverly rigged kung pao...*

> ...*living a seemingly peaceful, ordinary life, as if she has taken on another identity...*

> ...*motives remain largely a mystery, deep surveillance recommended.*

I replied with *Deep surveillance a go, thanks.* I gave Hanuš the rest of my dinner, sick with shame. She had run off and begun living elsewhere, anonymous, or so she had hoped. I felt no happiness over her seeming satisfaction, her peace in solitude—my mind was filled only with vanity, a thirst for reassurance, guesses about what I had done to drive her away. Could I get Central to force her to communicate with me? But such imposed communication wouldn't be worth anything. No, I would have to be patient.

A FEW DAYS into our dinner tradition, Hanuš started following me around on my Chopra preparation tasks. As I ventured into the small chamber that contained Ferda, the cosmic dust collector and the crucial component of the Chopra mission, he asked whether he could assist. I unfastened the thick screws securing the outside shell of Ferda's grating and removed the layer of metal protecting the finer design of the filters inside the bulky cube. Hanuš's eyes traveled wildly between me and the grating I held, the tips of his legs touching the underside of his belly. He was always eager to help, to hold a piece of human technology. When I extended the grating toward him, with a smile he offered a leg as a temporary holder. I could see the filters now, pads covered in sticky silicone meant to capture particles, the pads themselves attached to rails that would eventually guide them back inside the ship for manual analysis.

"Skinny human, may I ask a question that could cause emotional distress?"

"You can always talk to me," I told Hanuš.

"Why do you wish so strongly for a human offspring? I have discovered from your fictional television programming about soap that your species does not always utilize sexual intercourse solely for breeding."

I removed the motherboard cover and it floated toward me like a heart still attached at the arteries.

"I guess it's insurance against being a nobody," I said.

"Who is a nobody?"

"Well, it's the opposite of being a somebody. Of having a body people can ask about."

"The written records of your language do not explain the word well. Is every human not a somebody?"

I plugged my tablet into the motherboard and ran diagnostics. Ferda's sensors and analytics were 100 percent functional. *Hooray*, Petr messaged via my e-tablet.

"It's about doing things that matter," I said. "It's about loving things and being loved in return. Acknowledged."

"It is love that counters your luxury of breeding by choice. I've had many pieces of offspring, skinny human. On every Eve, we shoot our seed into the vacuum, and wait to receive it as it showers down. The ceremony is law, and refusal to engage would mean death. One must shoot well into the distance to ensure one does not receive one's own seed. This would cause severe embarrassment. The entire galaxy glows on Eve. We carry the smaller me's until they hatch from inside our bellies. One does not miss an Eve. It is a very refreshing day. The consistency, the moisture, the solidity of seed. To you, an offspring is a choice, but the pleasure of this freedom is negated by the blackmail of love. If you love a partner, you crave to breed. Once you receive a human offspring, you are bound by love to care for its needs. Such attachments go against the concept of choice as defined by humanry, yet the planet of Earth is filled with these obligations. They define you."

I replaced the grating and fastened the screws. These tasks—tinkering with Ferda, the diagnostics coming back at 100 percent—were supposed to be the climax before the climax, the great pleasure of the mission as I anticipated the dust cloud and its possibilities. But without Lenka, my excitement for Chopra was muted.

"Someday, I'd like to see your Eve," I said.

"That won't be possible."

"Why not?"

Hanuš never answered. In fact, he ceased speaking entirely, and seemed to disappear from the ship altogether until the next morning.

FOUR DAYS UNTIL my arrival at Chopra, between my many video-blogs and interviews with the Czech media (Mr. Procházka, what do you think of the man behind your mission, Senator Tůma, becoming prime minister of the country? *Fantastic*, I told them, or something like it. Will your wife be present at the national screening event of your triumph, or will she watch from the comfort of your home? *Certainly, yes, she will be watching very closely,* I told them, or something like it. As you await the encounter, can you tell us— do you have time to watch football? What did you think about the country's performance in World Cup Latvia? *What is the polite version of "I don't give a shit about any of this, don't you see I can't say what I really want to say"?*), Hanuš said, "I have observed you dreaming of death. There is a pleasure to it. A sense of relief. Why is this, skinny human?"

In place of an answer, I brushed my teeth and opened yet another disposable towel. I regretted not having kept track of how many I had used since the beginning of the mission. The compost container holding the soiled towels was too full to count, with the towels not producing enough bacteria to properly dissolve along with my underwear.

The question followed me around. I was mostly silent during my dinner with Hanuš.

"What is troubling you, skinny human?" he asked.

"You keep asking questions," I said, "but you don't tell me anything. Where you come from. What you think, feel. Where your planet is, and all of your...tribe. Yet you get to browse my thoughts whenever you please. Is that not troubling?"

He left without an answer. I watched a video of Norman the Sloth visiting a cooking show. Norman dipped the tip of his finger into Alfredo sauce and curiously licked it. The studio broke out in laughter.

The dreams Hanuš had mentioned not only continued but intensified, until I lost the ability to sleep at all, even with the help of medication. As I sat in the Lounge, a newly minted insomniac, and played solitaire on the Flat (the simplicity of the game soothed me; I no longer wanted to play complicated computer games, watch complicated films, or read the news; it all pertained to Earth and Earth did not pertain to me; I was a telecommuter), a shadow passed by the observation window, an interruption to Venus's golden glow. I floated to the glass and again the object passed, this time so close I recognized a small canine snout, a white line leading up the dark forehead fur, ears perked up, black eyes wide-open and reflecting the blinking lights of infinity, a slim body bloated at the stomach, strapped into a thick harness.

I softly pulled the eyelid from my eyeball, felt a parting *pop*—a trick my grandmother taught me to determine whether I was conscious. I was awake, and this was real. It was her, the outcast of Moscow, the first living heroine of spaceflight, a street bandit transformed into a nation's pride.

It was Laika the dog. Her body preserved by the kindness of the vacuum, denying the erosive effects of oxygen. I thought about attempting a spacewalk to recover the body, but I was tired, and too close to Chopra to receive approval from Central. Why bring her home anyway, to rot in the ground or lie next to Lenin's embalmed corpse in Moscow's catacombs when here she was the eternal queen of her domain? The comrade engineers cried for her as she died in agony, and the nation built her a statue to repent for its sins. Earth could provide her with no further honors, while the cosmos gave her immortality. The dryness had evaporated most of the water in her body, leaving her skin pale, her ears perked up. The individual hairs of her fur waved back and forth, like sea reeds. With the biological decomposition suspended, Laika's body could float for millions of years, her physical form surpassing the species that had sentenced her to death. I thought of snapping a photo, sending it to Central, but we were not worthy of the honor of this witnessing. Laika's eternal flight was her own.

The body vanished. When I turned, Hanuš was with me. I asked him whether he had seen her too.

"Would you truly care to know?" he said.

ANOTHER EMAIL ARRIVED from the ministry of interior. I hesitated before reading.

> *... subject is not, I repeat, not currently engaged in a sexual relationship, at least not at her place. Analysis of bedsheets, sofa cover, bathroom towels ...*

> *... no traces of bodily fluids ...*

> *... in the afternoon, the subject engaged in a phone call with a journalist who had managed to track down her new phone number. The subject claimed that she was on simple holiday, and colorfully asked the journalist to cease his harassment. After hanging up, the subject recovered the photograph of J. P. from underneath the bed and briefly covered her face with her hand. After this episode, the subject ordered pad thai from a local ...*

> *... based on Zdeněk K.'s deeply intimate relations with another man outside the bar Kleo, it is clear the subject was not engaged with Zdeněk K. on any level other than friendly and platonic, and thus J. P. can rest easy knowing that he was not abandoned for another man, at least not this one ...*

... eight o'clock in the morning, the subject walked to a local ob-gyn office. Agent was not able to penetrate the building in a manner that would allow eavesdropping on the conversation between the subject and the healthcare provider, but another sweep of the subject's apartment revealed a positive pregnancy test wrapped in two Kleenex tissues. Might indicate subject is in the early stages of...

... agent sent urine sample for analysis to ensure it belongs to...

For a moment, I lost my vision. The black letters and white background spilled from the screen and coated my surroundings. I bent over and with a great force of will suppressed the bile building in my throat. I coughed and felt chunks of acidized tortilla at the tip of my tongue. Hanuš floated behind me.

"It doesn't make sense," I told Hanuš.

"The human cub could be yours, skinny human," Hanuš offered.

"She wouldn't be gone, then."

"As I have learned from all self-reflecting resources of humanry, your motives are not drawn as line segments."

"I don't understand anything," I said.

"The cloud of Chopra is days away, skinny human. All other things can be understood later."

I responded to the report: *Is the child mine? And can I get a picture of her?*

A response came almost immediately: *Will find out. What kind of picture?*

A nice one, I wrote.

I pressed my middle finger onto the screen and closed the browser. In the kitchen, I counted my remaining whiskey bottles. Three.

Damn Central and their regulations. Dr. Kuřák's asinine obsession with every human being as an alcoholic in training. The bottles were not enough, but I decided to drink properly instead of saving the goods to spread throughout the rest of the mission. Yes, wasn't this the way to live in modern times, to consume and forget the rest? Civilization could fall apart any day now.

As I opened the bottle, Hanuš appeared behind me.

"Want some of this?" I asked.

"Ah, Earth's spiritus frumenti. I have read much about its destructive effects."

"You must've skipped the chapters on healing."

I offered the bottle. Hanuš closed his eyes.

"I am afraid I have already sacrificed my impulses to hazelnut spread, skinny human. I do not desire further disruptions to my functioning."

"More for me," I said, and slurped.

"You grieve over your human love," he said.

"Can I ask you something? Or do you already know?"

"I may or may not, but do ask. Your speech comforts me."

"When I caught you in my room. Looking for the box."

"Yes. The ash of your ancestor."

"Why?"

Hanuš made his way out of the kitchen, and I followed him into the Lounge. There, he tapped on the computer screen, activating it.

"Please, do open the window," Hanuš said.

I pressed the command button for the window cover. Ahead of us, the universe opened.

"I am interested in human loss," Hanuš said. "It pertains to me and my tribe in a particular way."

"What are the particulars?"

Hanuš turned toward me, and for the first time, his eyes split in two different directions—the left half looking directly at me, the other staring absently into Space.

"I have deceived you, skinny human, but I cannot any longer. I do not approve of the physiological sensations associated with such actions. I will not be bringing the news of Earth to my Elders. I cannot."

Hanuš's form sagged toward the floor. He gazed out the window with longing, reminding me of those weeks I had searched for my parents, as if eyesight alone could penetrate space and time and the edges of mortality. His was the look of not knowing, a look that seemed to be shared and recognized by all species.

"I have traveled through galaxies," he said. "I have raced with meteor showers and I have painted the shapes of nebulas. I entered black holes, felt my physical form disintegrate with the chants of my tribe all around me, then appeared again, in the same world but an altered dimension. I traced the outlines of the universe and witnessed its expansion, a turn from something to nothing. I swam in dark matter. But never in my travels, or in the collective memory of my tribe, have I experienced a phenomenon as strange as your Earth. Your humanry. No, skinny human, you were not known to our tribe. I was not sent here by them. We considered ourselves the only spirits in the universe, privy to all of its secrets—but you were kept from us. As a human would say, I encountered you by pure coincidence. Not by mission."

I slurped at the whiskey. Zero gravity or not, the burn was the same: gut full of cotton, blood vessel dilation, bliss. "Go on," I said.

"Naturally, my curiosity led me to begin my research of humanry immediately. I have lived in your orbit for a decade of human years. I have visited a few astronauts, but all three either ignored me or prayed. The senseless chanting, I confess, repulsed me. I was content as a quiet observer until I learned of what you call comet Chopra."

I strapped myself into the Lounge chair to make my drinking easier. My calves were numb. Hanuš was truly speaking about himself for the first time. I felt justified to drink the entire bottle. What better response to such progress?

"You see, this comet, it comes from my home world. I was not sure before, but now I am certain. In a way, the dust of Chopra is tied to all of us, and to the Beginning. I must see it, skinny human. I must see it before certain events unravel. Before they come for me."

"Who? Please, tell me," I said.

"The Gorompeds will come. I cannot say more. Not yet."

The Flat monitor pinged. Another email from the ministry of interior, this time with an image attachment. I dropped the bottle, allowed it to travel, its contents spilling all across the Lounge, splashing over my technology, the window, Hanuš's belly.

I opened the email.

> *...physician agreed to provide confidential patient information for a sizable payment. It is confirmed that the test was a false positive, and the subject is not pregnant, nor has she been since beginning to visit Dr....*

> *...then confirmed that this was a case of so-called phantom pregnancy, in which the subject's body begins to react to the brain's certainty about conceiving...*

Of course. Miracles were nonsense, mere coping mechanisms. Despite the pain in my stomach, I was glad. Lenka would not have to face yet another complication in my absence. I'd left her with enough worry—it was best that growing a human being inside her body was not added to the list.

But I had hoped. I'd hoped that this was the reason for her leaving, that she needed to get away and think about the positive test, before returning and telling me that I was to be a father. It was a kind reassurance while it lasted.

I wished I could travel outside the ship and rip off the solar panels, along with their batteries, and hurl the container holding the water sourcing my oxygen out the door. I would shut off the lights, the hums, the view, and rest in darkness.

Think.

I studied the photograph of Lenka, taken in profile in the strange new bedroom as she prepared for bed. She wore black lace under-wear and her face was turned away slightly from the camera. Late sunshine seeping through the curtains outlined her cheekbones and melted the shadows of her curves. My lips were dry. I should have been outraged, outraged with myself for allowing this violation of her, some government goon peering at her through the windows, snapping photos to keep my dread at bay. But the pleasure of the image overwhelmed me. I recalled what it felt like when the black lace grazed my cheeks, what it tasted like between my teeth when I was too eager for her to take the time to remove it.

Why had she gone? I asked the picture. Where have you gone, why have you left me behind? No, wait, I was the one who'd done that. I begged the picture not to let me wander. From the pixels that formed the artificial flesh of my love, I received no answer.

The Burning of the Witches

THE LAST DAY OF April is the Day of the Witches, and for the first time my grandparents, leery of the growing hostility of neighbors, do not wish to attend the ceremonies. Witches is my favorite holiday and I beg and I plead, promise to be careful, and soon they agree to let me go. At the football field, a massive stack of wood rests underneath this year's witch, her body that of a scarecrow, made of long sticks tied together and clothed in an old army jacket, a teacher's skirt, and a cape. Rusting wire keeps a broomstick attached to her fingerless hand. The face is a plush pillow with two pieces of coal for eyes and a chili pepper for a nose, and a wad of rabbit turds form a wart at the nose's tip. The mouth is painted on, a crooked grin and blackened spaces for missing teeth. Boud'a and I each buy a sausage and sit on the benches, plotting to secure beer. I offer the girl at the counter an extra twenty crowns and swear secrecy, and she pours some Staropramen into a black cup.

Just as I get back to the bench the fire is set, and the witch wrinkles, her layers peeling away until her mannequin nudity is revealed. The chili pepper pops and its juice sizzles in the flames, and the witch's eyes become those of a demon, glowing steadily, burning red until the head finally collapses and the entire village cheers. The older boys start jumping over the fire while women throw old broomsticks into the flames and make a wish for better years ahead. My legs and arms feel numb, my stomach burdened with beer. I toss the emptied cup into the fire and others follow, until soon the fire is absorbing bottles, half-eaten bratwursts, a bandana, paper plates, a deflated soccer ball, whatever offerings we can find to satisfy the forces of good luck. No one is looking at me, no one appears to resent me in this moment, we are all beasts of tradition, slaves to ceremony. I slap Boud'a on the back and stumble across the field, toward the woods, where I unzip and drain the beer that has shot fiercely through me.

The sound of cracking sticks echoes behind me.

I don't realize it is Mládek until he pushes my face into the tree and something snaps inside my nose. I fall on my stomach and turn my head to see him, skull shaved in the front, messy curls in the back falling on his neck. Next to him is the boy from Prague wearing a Nike shirt and saggy jeans, his bangs drowned in gel. Mládek holds a weakly burning stick in his shaking hand. His eyebrows touch in a nervous scowl intended to be menacing.

"You like your old man?" he says.

"Only good for a fight with people strapped down," says the Prague boy.

I study the blood on my hand, my shirt, the moss underneath. The blood won't stop dripping. Mládek is blurry, everything is. I wonder where all the blood comes from, how it fills me to capacity and waits for the slightest reason to burst out. The Prague boy holds me down as I kick and scratch. His fingers push into the back of my skull, his knee lodged between my buttocks. Mládek rolls up my right pant leg and takes a deep breath. At first, the flame feels cold on my calf, but a second or two later the pain travels beyond my body, I smell my own searing flesh, my muscle seems to be melting into the ground and merging with dirt. Red patches shoot into my vision. The Prague boy has released me but I cannot move. My jaw muscles are cramped and I am no longer sure whether any sound is coming from my throat. The Prague boy runs away and Mládek drops the sizzling stick next to my face. His understanding of the history that brings us to this moment isn't any clearer than mine, meaning there is nothing we can say to each other. He is looking at my leg with his mouth agape.

"Oh that's big. Big, too big..." And he runs too, and I am alone.

Only the birds chirping above me know how long it takes before I regain control of my arms, and I dig my fingernails into the dirt and moss and pull myself forward, and again, and now I can push with my left leg too, but I have to wonder, did my right one catch on fire? Did it fall off? I don't dare look back to find out. I crawl out of the woods and back onto the football field, where the evening dew of manicured grass soaks into my lips. At last I feel my right leg again, a moment of relief brought on by the cool droplets before the real pain sets in, my scorched nerves no longer under the anesthesia of shock. The witch is buried somewhere inside the steadily burning pile of wood, and the celebration attendees are now more interested in alcohol and shouting. I crawl all the way to the pyre until finally their eyes turn toward me, and a wave of bodies runs in my direction. Mrs. Vlásková faints when she sees my leg. Men extend their hands toward me until I am airborne, steadied on broad shoulders. I shut my eyes and count. Count and wish my father could carry me now, wish he could apologize in every language of the world.

Two WEEKS LATER, I hobble to the mailbox and find a letter from the government. During this time of rest ordered by the doctor and intensely enforced by Grandma, these small trips for the mail are the highlight of my days. The envelope is standard mail size and contains a page folded thrice, with a stamp the size of my fist. My grandfather growls at the table as he finishes reading, then looks at me lying on the couch. I close my eyes, breathe deeply in pretense of sleep. My leg is sore and itchy beneath the bandaging, and the yellow antiseptic and plasma seep onto my fingertips whenever

I scratch it. I breathe through my mouth to avoid the smell of medicine and pus.

My grandfather stands up and walks over to the pantry. He takes out a gray plastic box and sets it on the living room table, glancing at me often. He removes his flintlock pistol from the box along with a vial of gunpowder and a bag of lead balls, scratches off a bit of rust with his fingernail, and blows into the barrel opening. Sliding the pistol under his belt, he pulls the bottom of his flannel shirt over it, and puts the ammunition in his front breast pocket. Šíma studies him with head tilted. Grandpa grabs his hiking stick and heads outside, steering off the main road and toward the vacation cabins by the lake. When he is out of view, I rise, slap my wound gently to ease the itching, and pick up my own hiking stick, the one Grandpa carved for me when I was six. Grandma will be in town buying books for a while longer, and so there is no one left to keep me on the couch. As I step outside, Šíma emits a subtle whine. He has never liked being alone.

Most people in Středa claim that the vacation cabins are their own village, as the cabin population has nothing in common with the people of the village. The houses stand far apart, each one surrounded by rich layers of trees, bushes, gardens. There must be at least two dozen of them by now, these new families having flowed in to embrace the weekend country life, teenage daughters tanning by inflatable pools, teenage sons hitting trees with sticks and fishing in the lake, fathers grilling with their legs spread wide apart and mothers drinking wine and reading on porches. The village kids say that Shoe Man's house is far away from the others, built at the edge of the forest, and that no one ever sees him arrive or depart—one day, he is simply there, and the next, the windows are shuttered and the heavy oak doors locked and secured. He does not purchase his goods in town, does not go to the pub, does not go for strolls on the main road.

Finally, I have caught up with my grandfather. He stalks through the front gate and stomps through the wildly overgrown grass covering the front lawn. A great cherry tree looms above the house, its products not yet ripe but already violated by bird pecks and weighing down the crown. The cabin itself is humble compared to the others— it is small, with a tin roof, and does not possess a satellite dish, porch, garage, or pool, the popular amenities of the other Prague weekenders. Judging from the faded texture of the wooden walls and a collapsed chimney, the cabin must have been here for a long time, perhaps decades, but I never saw it during the spying raids I took part in when some of the village children still tolerated me. The house has appeared before me as suddenly as Shoe Man and his backpack, a part of our lives that was always present but, until now, concealed.

I pause before the gate. Perhaps it would be best to allow my grandfather to do whatever he has come to do. What could the letter have said to make him place the gun under his belt? If he kills, we will lose him. It will be down to me, Grandma, and Šíma, a clan too small to amount to anything. We need Grandpa. I need his nightly coughing fits to fall asleep; I need the musk coming from his work shirts to feel I have a home.

I walk inside the house, the pain in my calf shooting into my knee, the tips of my fingers trembling. The front door creaks as I enter. The inside of the cabin is as sad and barren as the exterior—a plastic living room table with an empty beer bottle, a stove, shaggy carpet underneath a chair to my left on which my grandfather sits, the pistol in his lap. Across from him, Shoe Man leans back on a hideous orange couch, covered by a blanket. At his feet lies a black German shepherd, head resting on its paws, ears perked up. The space is so small that I could take two steps and touch any of them.

"Jakub, go back home," my grandfather says. "I won't tell you twice."

"No," I say.

"I take it knocking is not a part of your family's customs?" Shoe Man says, stretching out his right arm. He seems relaxed, pleasantly disheveled, as if he has just woken up from a nap.

"If I ever needed you to listen to me, it's now. Go home," Grandpa says.

I walk over to the chair next to Grandpa and take a seat. I can hear his dentures grinding. The dog watches me carefully.

"If you want me home, you'll have to drag me there," I say.

"I like him," Shoe Man says.

"You keep your mouth shut," Grandpa says.

"Yes, of course, I shouldn't speak inside my own house. What difference does it make whether the boy is here? You came here to talk, not to shoot, despite the show you're putting on. Besides, shouldn't the boy know what kind of blood flows through his veins? Don't shelter him from what he's bound to become."

"I'll shoot you in the knee," Grandpa hisses.

"My dog will rip out your throat."

I feel as though I'm breathing too loudly, and try to pace myself. But the more I try, the more fatigued my lungs become, until I am heaving and bending over. Grandpa puts his hand on my back.

"We can do this another time," Shoe Man says. "Or, we can speak calmly, without threats."

Grandpa pulls the crumpled letter from his pocket. "Will the dog pounce if I hand this to you?"

"I know what's in it," Shoe Man says.

"It tells me here that our house was confiscated by the Party from you in nineteen seventy-six, and given to my family as part of the redistribution of property to Party officials."

"Yes." Shoe Man doesn't seem amused by this, does not smile, or gloat. He has the solemn, neutral look of a weather anchor announcing an impending storm that might destroy a city or simply pass into the ocean.

"My great-grandfather built the house with his factory wages before the industrial revolution," Grandpa says. "This is a lie with a bureaucrat's stamp on it." He restlessly taps his finger on the pistol handle. A tic I have never seen, as my grandfather is not a nervous man. He wipes his sweaty palms on his shirt.

"And doesn't that get us right to the heart of the problem, Mr. Procházka? It doesn't matter. It doesn't matter that your great-grandfather dug the basement with his own bare hands, that the sun burned his forehead as he coated the roof. The document in your hand states that the house was stolen from me and given to you as reward for your son's work. So the state declares. You have two weeks to leave and hand the property over to its legal owner."

Grandpa reaches into his front pocket and pulls out a pack of cigarettes. As he lights one up, Shoe Man reaches for the thermos in front of him and pours a tall glass of milk.

"Sure, you can smoke in here," Shoe Man says. "No problem. Would you care for some milk? Jakub? It is still warm, fresh out of the udder."

For the first time in two weeks, I do not feel the pain of my wound. I feel no physical sensation whatsoever aside from the difficulty of breathing. How can we do it so effortlessly all day and all night? Five short breaths, one long. Three long, a dozen short. I count, tap my finger on my knee, and try to synchronize with Grandpa's tapping, focus all my brainpower on easing myself back into the classic inhale, exhale, one, two, but I am no longer the master of my own lungs.

"Don't talk to him," Grandpa whispers through clenched teeth, and I'm not sure whether he's telling me or Shoe Man. He rises and steps forward, and Shoe Man holds his snarling dog back by the neck skin.

"I've thought of this moment for years," Shoe Man says. "First, of course, when I did my time, four years in political prison. The food was salt and mush out of a can, Spam on Sundays, with hard rye bread and bleached water. My cellmate jacked off while he watched me sleep. He said that in the dark my jawline reminded him of his wife. He was some artist who'd painted genitalia into Brezhnev's eyebrows. This is where I decided I would come looking for your son someday. The Party moved my mother and father out of the apartment where they'd spent most of their lives, put them into one of those cramped studios with the other exiled families of political prisoners. When they found out we were of Hungarian heritage, they even considered putting them on a train to Budapest. They took most of our furniture and cut my parents' retirement. I can only be thankful I didn't have children—imagine what the Party would have done to them. Or to a wife. My life was taken from me by electrical currents and a signature on a statement of condemnation, Mr. Procházka. My family was banished so that yours could flourish. Now, I am the one with friends. I'm on the winning side."

The struggle to breathe leaves my throat hoarse. I crave Shoe Man's milk, but I can't accept it. Not ever. Grandpa lights a second cigarette while Shoe Man finishes his glass. I admire his resistance to lactose.

"You sent them to hurt Jakub," Grandpa says. "Is that part of settling accounts? Hurting little boys?"

"I'm not little."

"I deeply regret what happened to Jakub," Shoe Man says. "I've never been a proponent of using violence to achieve my goals, and I certainly never encouraged anyone to act against you. I've heard that the culprits were captured and punished?"

"Captured and let go," my grandfather sneers. "Jakub's word against theirs, they said. He must have tripped and fallen on the burning stick himself, they said. I wonder how Mládek's tractor-driving father managed to afford a fancy Prague lawyer."

"The other boy was from Prague, was he not? Listen, Mr.

Procházka, I haven't been sleeping much. I don't want you to think I take it lightly—my being here, posing a threat for you. The reason I haven't been sleeping is that I've wanted so badly to know what it is I want from you. What kind of reparations you can offer. It was after the attack on Jakub that I finally figured it out. Do you believe in fate? I don't. But sometimes my education and my books and my sense of chaos are overthrown by the pure force of coincidences we are handed. My punishment for you will also be your salvation. Banishment. You sell off some furniture, move somewhere far from here, where you can be anonymous, let Jakub grow up without the weight of your son's achievements. No one can hurt him anymore, he will not be a victim to the anger that has caused him harm. For now, it's the safest option. And your only one."

I wonder if the dog will bite me if I try to pet it. What is its name? In silence, Grandpa smokes a third cigarette, then crushes the empty packet under his foot. Finger upon the trigger.

The anger burning in my chest is not directed at Shoe Man, but at my father. My father should be the one sitting here, chain-smoking and losing his birth house. I want to apologize to the stranger. Kick him. Beg for the house my grandfather has held together for a life-time, attacking the summer mouse infestations with cats and poison, filling the cracks in the walls with concrete so that ice won't fill them and bust them apart. How many pigs have soaked the dirt with their blood, how many flowers have bloomed and withered in the garden under our watch?

"This is the acceptable reparation," Shoe Man says. "I want the house. I want you out. I can't get my justice from your son, but I will get something. Give it to me peacefully. Be dignified in your defeat."

Grandpa weighs the pistol in his hand. The dog raises its head to its master. There are no clocks in the room, I notice, no ticking, no rhythm—a perfect stillness.

"You will leave us alone if we go?" Grandpa says.

"Sure."

"Not good enough. I can fight this in court."

"On your retirement? Don't you realize I can get a judge to say no before you even file? You will be carried out of that house if you don't vacate."

"I could shoot you through the lungs." Grandpa grips the pistol handle. I remember the pistol's lead ball crushing through the pig's insides, that instant flow of blood mixing with the soil. Would a human shot with an old pistol bleed the same?

"You could. You will lose the home all the same. Jakub here can visit you in prison on Sundays."

Grandpa sits back down and rubs the root of his nose.

"What will happen to the house if I give it to you?"

"I'll renovate it. Rent it to some nice Prague folks. A museum of our relationship, a gravestone to mutual injustices. Tell you what. I'll even send you a cut of the rent, so you don't fall on hard times. A peace offering. This is not about money."

Grandpa stands up again. The dog lets out a baritone growl, and Shoe Man puts a hand on its head to calm it. The dog would kill me without hesitation, I realize, rip out my throat and chew it like a tennis ball. So be it. I will die by my grandfather's side.

"Let's go," Grandpa tells me.

I reach out a hand, and he takes it, pulls me to my feet. I lean on his shoulder to stop myself from falling.

"I trust you will vacate within the time specified in the letter."

"No," Grandpa says, and nothing more.

He leads me out of the cabin, past the gate, over the river bridge, back to the main road, and as we walk his *No* resonates, its tone weak and uncommitted, so unlike the declarative nature of my grandfather's usual speech, where every syllable is a truth not to be trifled with. A silent, humiliated *No* spoken by an entirely different man. A *No* that meant nothing.

"We're not leaving," I say once we've returned to the house.

"Go wash up. Grandma will be home soon. I'll boil up frankfurters."

"We're not leaving."

"No. We are not."

My grandparents speak somberly late into the night. I poke Šíma's tongue as I read *Robinson Crusoe* with a flashlight underneath the bedsheet.

The pub owner will no longer serve my grandfather. He drinks in the garage while sharpening his killing knives.

We find a gutted rat on our doormat. Most likely the cats.

We look into school transfers for me. I could wake up at 5 a.m. and take the bus to a school three villages away.

We take a train to the doctor in Louny and he spreads ointment on my wound. "Healing nicely," he says. "It will be the world's most interesting scar."

I pull newspapers from the trash. Prague apartments circled in green.

No.

I pass by Shoe Man's cabin three times. Its windows and doors are shuttered. A feral cat jumps at me from the top of the gate. I urinate onto the side of the house. Scratch tiny obscenities into the wood with a pocketknife.

The man who usually buys my grandfather's rabbit skins says he can't accept them anymore.

My grandmother is no longer welcome in the book club she founded. I catch her whispering to her plants early in the morning.

No.

My grandfather's hair seems terribly thin and gray, his eyelids sagging, like cave openings so small no human could breach them.

My grandmother's retirement check is lost in the mail. For two weeks, Grandpa has to take a job as overnight security in town to ensure we can pay the gas company. Every day for breakfast and dinner he eats cheap French fries from the rotisserie chicken stand across from work. Sometimes the cook takes pity and gives him the burnt wings that would otherwise be tossed. His breath and sweat smell of canola oil, and he spends what little time he has with us talking about his pigs, his land, food that fills the stomach to capacity without tearing at his intestinal lining. The lost check is never recovered, despite multiple filings with the government.

Five weeks have passed since Grandpa's *No*, and subconsciously we begin to pack our belongings. None of us has the strength to uphold the belief in our *No*. We are in agreement without needing to speak.

We leave so many things behind. We bring the great oak table my great-grandfather carved when he worked as a carpenter for the Austro-Hungarians. A painting from the seventeenth century of a crying redheaded girl who looks just like my grandmother. Pots, pans, and porcelain plates that survived world wars and great floods. We leave behind the double king bed under which my grandmother hid when sirens announced the possibility of bombings from the Luftwaffe. We leave the stove that has kept the house warm since the days of Franz Ferdinand. We leave the dozen stray cats living in the attic with a full bowl of milk in place of an apology. We leave the rabbits, the chickens, the small new Louda. The dozen hand-carved puppets with which my grandmother put on plays for schoolchildren. The outhouse with its arachnid families. We leave books that have escaped Austro-Hungarian burnings, German burnings, Stalinist burnings, books that have kept the language alive while regimes attempted to starve it out. We can bring only so much.

We leave Šíma in another village with our cousin Alois. He is too wild for the city, too fond of chasing little creatures and swimming in the river. It would not be fair to make him suffer the concrete and the noise of endless city cars. My grandmother and I cry for him as we ride the train from Alois's back to Středa. *Šíma.*

Throughout moving day, I clutch my copy of *Robinson Crusoe.* The marks of mice teeth pock the cover and the smell of mold clings to it, but the hard spine holds as strong as the gates of a fortress. After we are all loaded up, Grandpa insists on painting the gate before we leave. The movers, a couple of lanky Kazakhs with rum on their breath, smoke cigarettes and sigh with annoyance. I try to help, but he asks to do it alone. He has to break every few minutes because of the back pain, the strain in his deltoids and forearms. When we finally drive off, the gate is the color of fresh wooden logs that Grandpa and I would fetch from the forest during early spring, wood well-fed by morning rains and rich soil, wood that we'd have to leave out in the sun for months before it began to dry and lose its will to live. We leave the gate brown and solid for its new fate.

The apartment we have rented on Pařížská belonged to a Party official until 1989. After that, the new owner converted the entire floor into a French restaurant that went bankrupt within a year. Then a German entrepreneur bought the floor and split it into five apartments in the style of the New West, resulting in a plainness that makes it feel nothing like home. The sink is small and flimsy, the walls thin, the toilet seat plastic. Whenever a neighbor above us flushes, we hear the echo within the pipes. This is what we can afford on my grandparents' retirement, an apartment I would never bring a friend to, had I any left. There is no history here, no legacy—everything we now own or rent seems to be made of plastic or tin in a factory for a few coins paid to immigrant laborers. Even if Shoe Man was serious about sending money, I know that Grandpa would rather burn it and get a job in construction, if it comes down to it.

But all of this lies ahead. On the way to Prague I know nothing about the apartment, and as Grandpa follows the moving truck,

I spend my time in the backseat of the borrowed Škoda, deciding that I must be the biological carrier of my father's curse. It must rest within my bowels like a tapeworm. I am determined never to disappoint my grandparents, never to misbehave, for their lives will now be confined within the tight space of a city without soil because of something that is inherently a part of me. We drive over the cube bricks of Prague's Old Town, braking every few minutes for stray tourists standing in the middle of the road to take pictures of Gothic towers, old Jewish quarters, cemetery gates. The bakery where my father used to get *rakvičky*, or caskets—small pastries with tiramisu filling topped with whipped cream and chocolate shavings—is now a Kentucky Fried Chicken, and I yearn for a juicy thigh I could dip into mashed potatoes and gravy, but I have no right to make demands. I am the curse, and we don't have the money for Western takeout. Dinner will be potatoes and sour cream, the same dish that sustained my grandparents' families through the second war. We drive past the shopping malls and multiplexes rising from the ruins of old community centers, the places where Prague youths once gathered to watch educational films about doing their part for the Soviets and played football in red T-shirts. I don't recognize this city—its new, well-dressed explorers, its taxicabs and Tommy Hilfiger billboards. I don't know this free Prague, but I'd like to. So many luxuries are now within reach, and I cannot afford any of them.

Just as we park in front of the building and Grandpa instructs the movers, Elvis's "Jailhouse Rock" comes on the radio. I reach over and switch to a different station. Grandma doesn't say a word. The sound of flutes, bassoons, and a harp. The soprano of a woman calling for something, reminding me of an owl seeking the return of sound waves through the middle of a black night. I ask Grandma what this is, and she smiles.

"*Rusalka*," she says. "It's an opera."

"Have you seen it?" I ask.

"It was your mother's favorite. She and I saw it together soon after she married your father."

"Are you angry with him? For all of this."

The station's signal vanishes, and the song morphs into static. Grandma ignores it and looks directly ahead. The static reminds me of a toothache. Finally, Grandma turns down the volume, gathers her things, and speaks upwards, as if making a declaration to a crowd, via microphone.

"*No,*" she says, sounding just like my grandfather.

Rusalka

THE CIGAR BOX was made of solid cedar and weighed exactly two kilograms and thirty grams. For the past few nights, after Hanuš and I finished our conversation and he nestled in his usual corner, just outside my sleeping chamber, I had removed it from the storage chest and run my hands over its matte yellow cover hailing *Partagas—Hecho en Cuba*. I would slide the cover off and pull out the silk pouch holding the ashes of my grandfather. I allowed the pouch to float around the cabin for a while, like a mother guiding her child on a first swim.

I couldn't help but think of my grandfather's actual body and how it would fare in Space, his short legs, stout enough to support a belly holding sixty full years of enthusiasm for brew, his thick arms tattooed with a blue jay and a fading cowboy, his bullish face covered with gray stubble and his thin hair permanently plagued with dandruff, all of this mass suspended in the air and calmly measuring the universe outside, occasionally wheezing and roaring with smoker's cough and asking for a Marlboro to soothe it. I knew he would've liked the peace and quiet of Space to read the newspaper and write in his journals, but his hands would crave livestock and gardening in the midst of all the idleness, the waiting. No, I supposed, my grandfather would not have the patience for stargazing and matter expansion. He was not a man who could stare into darkness and wonder. Yet, I had brought him with me, hoping at last to discover his final resting place after having held on to the box containing his ashes for years. Every day, after breakfast and again before sleep, I wished to put the box into the dispenser and shoot it out into the cosmos. Every day, I could not bring myself to do it. Today was the day. Venus was so close now it made up the majority of the panorama. Within hours, I would make contact with cloud Chopra.

I returned to the Lounge, where Hanuš witnessed the approaching dust storm through the observation window. Over the past few hours, the patterns photographed by *JanHus1*'s lenses had been analyzed by Central, and Petr's team had concluded that the cloud's seemingly calm demeanor was a disguise for a storm raging within its borders, as if the thicker core held gravitational powers causing the dust to swirl around it, like a cyclone. The concerns about my safety were unspoken but clear on Petr's face during our video calls.

Hanuš's legs hung loosely beneath him. He was all shadow against the explosions of light ahead. A thick cloud of purple tainted the map of dying stars in front of us, like a swarm of buzzards raiding a can of paint. Over the course of my mission, the cloud had shrunk to half its original size, but it had not moved an inch, establishing a baffling relationship with Venus's gravitational influence. I was so close now I could see the movement of its particles, snowflakes inside a freshly shaken globe. The swarming dust was phosphorescent, glowing around the edges and darkening until reaching the purple core, a mass so thick I could not see through it. The speed of the particles as measured by photographic analysis was deemed safe enough for entry. The excitement for the mission that I had lost now loomed around the edges of my mind again. Whatever Hanuš was, he wasn't mine to possess, not even mine to understand. His presence was soothing, but his existence incomprehensible. The cloud ahead, however—behaving in a way we'd never seen a phenomenon of its kind behave, measurable, unable to run—was mine to own. The cloud ahead could be put under a microscope. It could be understood.

Hanuš turned toward me. Black liquid dripped from the corner of his mouth and formed miniature bubbles dancing around the Lounge.

"When I was young I caught these grains on my tongue, skinny human. This dust holds the beginning to all things."

"It's impossible to know where things began," I said.

"Yet you want to believe so badly. I insist, skinny human—these grains were present when the universe exploded into being. They were the first to Be and they will be the last."

Hanuš grinned as widely as I had ever seen. Central's call came from the Flat. I strapped myself down, ran my hand over my freshly shaved skull, and accepted the call.

On the screen appeared the main operations room of the Space Institute, a U-shaped auditorium stuffed with monitors and bodies. The crew of this room, thirty engineers with Petr in the lead, was responsible for the entire mission, from running the automatic functions of *JanHus1* to analyzing my stool. Today the room was hosting a much bigger sampling of the country's finest, along with bottles of champagne, cocktail servers, and tables holding shrimp and tea sandwiches. Next to Petr stood Dr. Kuřák, a notebook in his hand ready for note-taking, along with members of the board of trustees, CEOs of partner companies, Senator Tůma (tanned, slim, ready to become prime minister) with other members of the House I'd seen on television, and, ahead of them all, President Vančura himself. These important men and women, together with the members of the press loyally snapping pictures and recording video, formed the core of a larger circle of the institute's employees, engineers and bureaucrats alike, all applauding for me. Behind the Flat monitor, out of view of the camera transmitting my likeness to Earth, was Hanuš. The greatest discovery in human history was about five feet away from becoming a reality to the rest of Earthlings. My role was to sit and pretend he wasn't there.

The sound of gentle flutes filled the hollow spaces of *JanHus1*, followed by English horns. This was the cue.

"What is this sound, skinny human?" Hanuš asked.

"*Rusalka*," I replied. "It's an opera. I chose it to announce this moment."

Hanuš nodded, and already Petr had begun to perform the rehearsed lines that public relations had given us:

"*JanHus1*, confirm functionality of filtering systems. Countdown to contact begins: twenty-nine minutes, three seconds. Report..."

I tuned in to TV Nova's live stream of the Petřín Hill festivities, and here, on the hill where the nation had witnessed my ascent four months earlier, the people once again gathered with brews and fast food in hand. This time their attention was turned toward a magnificent IMAX screen installed on top of the hill, courtesy of Tonbon, major operator of the country's largest cinemas and mission sponsor. A trio of streams appeared on the display: one of my face, its imperfections processed by airbrushing wizards, so large that I saw the sweat upon my earlobes; one that cut between the main operations room, containing the politicians and scientists responsible for the triumph, and Czech actors, singers, and reality stars giving interviews from their own exclusive podium on Petřín Hill; and a third showing the footage captured by *JanHus1*, which closely resembled what Hanuš and I were seeing from the observation window, with the contrast adjusted and some kind of special effects glow added to emphasize a science fiction experience. All three streams were intercut for internationally televised programming interrupted briefly by commercials from all mission sponsors. If only there were a way to contact the mysterious government agent now, ask him to run over to Lenka's apartment and peek through her window, see if she was glued to the television, eager to partake in my triumph.

It was nighttime in Prague, and though the massive stadium

lights surrounding the hill massacred much of the horizon, on the crowd's screen Chopra announced itself in the form of a watercolor hue melting into the atmosphere. But on my screen, the coloring, so distant and so foreign, looked like an ominous stain. It seemed much more befitting that cloud Chopra would attach itself to Venus and remain there forever, keep away from our home and cease to alter the comforting nighttime darkness that humans had embraced for centuries. Panic seized me. I looked around the Flat panel, seeking the button that would instantly parachute me back to Earth, directly to my bed four or five years ago, when stipend cash was enough to pay for spaghetti, and Lenka and I had little but our sex and our books and a small world that seemed knowable and kind. A time when the universe was black and glossy on the pages of overpriced textbooks.

Rusalka continued to play, a series of violins and horns, reminding me of the gentle comfort of music playing on elevators, inside shopping malls, hotel lobbies. I touched the sleek material of the desk before me, tightened my chair straps such that I could truly feel the support pushing into my back. Panic gave way to momentary bliss. The megalomania of the possible discoveries that lay ahead, even the simple act of witnessing, overshadowed everything else. I had leaped over the canyon on a motorcycle. I was about to land, and the rush of blood into my ears and eyes blocked out the audience, strangers and loved ones, their applause and chants, the explosive piping of eagles flying above our heads, the roar of a teased engine and the crashing of my bones against gravity, it gave me three, four, five seconds of complete detachment from what the world asks and what it provides, making the fact of living purely physical, a soaring of the body through the elements. I was grateful.

The cloud would make contact any minute now.

"Last remote analytic data coming in," Petr said. A close-up of his face split my screen in two, taking attention away from the festive panorama of chattering politicians. "You are at one hundred percent, *JanHus1*." He paused to chew on his mustache. "Jakub, are you ready?"

Ready. What a question. A smooth American astronaut would have given a thumbs-up and shown a row of bleached teeth. I closed my eyes and exhaled and nodded.

"I have never experienced humanry being this quiet, skinny human," Hanuš said. "For the first time, I cannot hear the hum of Earth."

Hanuš and I observed the collision quietly. I saw the images of the cloud reflected in the eyes of Petr. The politicians grew mute, newly filled glasses of Bohemia Sekt suspended in midair. For a moment, I wondered whether they had all forgotten that I existed. Hanuš too turned his attention away from me, did not search my mind for reactions, his body rising and falling in front of the observation glass.

What else rested within the contours of ever-expanding matter? What mysteries other than bamboo-legged extraterrestrials and volatile clouds of intergalactic gas and debris awaited me? Rusalka sang her joys and sorrows. Petr and his engineers and politicians gazed upon their many screens. (I had to wonder whether any of these men and women felt jealousy — as children, we had all wanted to be here, lone spacemen upon a distant planet, yet they ended up wearing ties and making promises they couldn't keep for a living. I also couldn't help but speculate about whether my mentor from university, Dr. Bivoj, was watching from the village house to which he had retired, whether he was ecstatic or enraged that his pupil had surpassed by light-years his most significant accomplishments.) Hanuš focused all of his eyes — thirty-four, as I had recently counted — on the cloud as if he too had never seen anything so unfamiliar. The fact that my extraterrestrial companion could still be in awe of these purple particles confirmed that whatever other life flourished in the universe had some level of cluelessness and thus a capacity to be genuinely curious. A trait proudly claimed by humans that could, in fact, be universal.

I held on to the restraints cutting into my chest and stomach, took a few deep breaths. Hanuš stirred. Petr finally turned his attention back to me, wiping sweat from his forehead. The dust particles rolled past in waves, poured over the observation window like shavings of wood flying off a chain saw blade. The contact was soundless, but *JanHus1* trembled nonetheless. The trajectory of the spacecraft changed left to right, up and down, as its burning fuel struggled against Chopra's chaotic influence. Petr instructed me to shut off the engines, and I did, now simply gliding along the rotating patterns around the thick core. On Earth, the Petřín Hill crowds raised their Staropramens and cheered the old adage: *The golden Czech hands!* I embraced the kitsch. Those raised beers were all for me.

How would Jan Hus feel about this encounter? Would he take it as a reaffirmation of his all-powerful deity? I wanted to think that his brilliant mind would embrace it as a token of complexity of the universe, a clue that the definition of *deity* goes beyond the abstract definitions of scripture.

"We are here," I would tell Hus, "the only humans. Every time we venture out farther in thought or time or space (and isn't it all the same, master?), we are giving your God a steel-bound handshake. You did it and now I did it too, even if my God is the microscope."

I ran my fingertips along the panel and activated Ferda the dust collector. The control interface displayed the filter as it slid out of its protective shell and began to collect the dust particles. No, the belly of my ship would not go hungry. Already Ferda's scanners displayed the structure of the crystals it had gathered. Lapping them all up like a dog's thirsty tongue.

"The core is bringing you in," Petr said. "It looks like it has its own mild gravitational influence. Feeling good up there?"

"Feeling great. How much time before I reach the core?"

"At this pace, about twenty minutes. Let's allow ten more for collection, then activate the propulsion engines and shoot you out of there. We'll stabilize your trajectory back to Earth remotely. After that, you get those golden hands in the lab."

"Roger."

I looked around and realized Hanuš had gone away. I did not feel his presence in my temples. An echo of sandpaper scratching upon metal spread through the ship. I listened to locate its source, but it seemed to be everywhere, a merciless grinding. The speed at which I spun was increasing quickly. The core seemed too close. Solid, like a piece of rock. Impenetrable.

The lights above me flickered, as did the Flat monitor. A rush of cool air chilled my shoulders.

"Something funny with your power source," Petr said.

The scratching turned into a steady hiss. The lights flickered at more prolonged intervals. The ship was no longer merely trembling—massive vibrations rocked it back and forth, and the purple dust crashing against my window had become so thick that I could no longer see Venus.

"It's speeding up," Petr said, his voice cracking. He pinched his beard and pulled a few hairs out.

Senator Tůma stood next to him, a foolish smile frozen on his face, champagne glass now empty. The hired help all watched the screens, mouths agape.

The light bulbs above me exploded, their tiny, sharp pieces crashing against the protective plastic ensuring the shards wouldn't float around the cabin. The blue emergency lights kicked in, powered by a generator disconnected from the main circulation, the same generator powering the Flat. A sharp emergency ring interrupted the gentle symphony of *Rusalka*. I focused all of my thoughts on Hanuš, hoping he would come back.

"Jakub, the mainframe is down. Visual diagnostics?"

I unstrapped from the chair and pulled myself toward the Corridors, relieved to be free of the rough vibrations now that I wasn't attached to any surface. All seemed normal in zero gravity. Just as I was about to leave the Lounge to inspect the mainframe, I noticed a few purple grains making their way in between the thin bars of a filter vent. I leaped back toward the Flat.

"The dust is penetrating the ship," I told Petr.

"Fuck, what?" he said. Seconds later, the video feed to the IMAX screen on Petřín Hill faded, leaving a paralyzed herd of onlookers squinting at the crude stadium lighting. Secret service agents ushered the politicians and journalists outside the Control Room while Petr barked orders at his engineers.

"All right, we're calling it. Run the propulsion engines. Get the hell out of that thing."

I checked the Ferda collection levels. Only about 6 percent filled—not nearly enough. "Another minute," I said, "just one more."

"The dust is eating through your ship, Jakub. The electrical cables are already eroded. Get out. I'd override your controls if it still worked."

"I need just another minute," I said.

"Do as you're told. Propulsion in three—"

"I've spent four goddamn months," I said. "My tooth is rotting, my wife left me, and now he's gone too. One more minute."

"Who's 'he'?"

"Just a bit of time, Petr."

I took out my earpiece. A bit of time. I figured it would make me wiser, that one minute. Make me understand something about the universe, or myself. Perhaps I believed Hanuš that Chopra held the key to the beginning. Perhaps I was daring myself to die. See what the fuss was about.

Wisdom did not arrive at the minute's conclusion. Within thirty seconds, the blue emergency lights melted into darkness, as did the Flat.

I hadn't realized just how loud *JanHus1* was when operating. Without the hum of filters and air-conditioning and screens, all I could hear was the ceaseless grinding. The purple phosphorescence provided only a fragment of light. I heard a quiet voice and felt around the desk for the earpiece.

"...ammit, *JanHus1*, respond, fuck..."

"Petr?" I said.

"Jakub. I can't see you. Report."

The vibrations ceased. The vision of the core covered the rest of my universe. It seemed I was so close that I could touch it. The layer of the cloud I found myself in was free of dust, free of any debris, like an atmosphere that had rejected everything else but me. The core no longer pulled. *JanHus1* was perfectly still within this sphere of nothingness.

"I'm close," I said, "but the gravitational influence has weakened."

"Comms are the only thing that's working. Not a single sensor in the ship is functional."

Something landed on my cheek. I wiped it with my finger and found purple smeared on my fingertip. The flakes surrounded me now, falling from crevices in the ceiling. The air was stale and hard to breathe.

"Petr," I said.

"Yeah."

"I think the oxygen tank is out."

I recovered a flashlight from the desk drawer and made my way through the Corridors. The electronic door panel leading to the mechanical bay was not functional, and I had to pull the levers and push with all my strength to open the hatch. I passed the engine control bay and entered the oxygen room, where a trio of massive gray barrels rested on the floor. As long as an electrical current ran through these tanks, allowing them to separate hydrogen and oxygen, they were perhaps the most crucial parts of the ship. Now they were simply three useless water towers tossed on their bellies like pigs about to be slaughtered. No fresh oxygen was being pumped into my world, just as the carbon dioxide was not being filtered out.

I informed Petr.

"Tell me when you start to feel dizzy," he said. "And get your ass to the mainframe panel. Let's fix this. Let's get you out."

I took comfort in his orders. Someone was in charge. As long as Petr was providing clear steps to follow, things could still be okay. I didn't need to think about anything else.

I turned off the earpiece. "Hanuš!" I shouted into the Corridors. "Hanuš!"

The mainframe panel was cold and dark. At Petr's instructions, I removed the panel cover and checked the wires inside. They were untouched, disturbingly clean just as they were when the ship was assembled. I took the panel apart, looking for burned-out motherboards, misplaced plugs. Everything was just as it should've been. I gave Petr a chance to say it before I did, but he was silent.

"Either the solar panel wiring got eaten through," I said, "or the solar panels are gone."

"Go put your suit on," Petr said.

"The suit?"

"I don't want you fainting when the oxygen drops. Put it on. I have to...I have to brief the people upstairs."

The line went quiet.

I dressed first in the cooling garment, a sophisticated onesie that circulated water through a hose system to regulate body temperature, then pulled the thick mass of my space suit over my body. It smelled faintly of thrift stores and burning coal. On Earth, tens, perhaps hundreds of millions of humans were gasping at their televisions, obsessively refreshing the front pages of media blogs, their minds attuned to a single thought: what would become of their spaceman? Yes, it was more than likely that my journey on *JanHus1* had captivated the imagination of all of humanity, well beyond my countrymen standing on Petřín Hill and groaning at the dark screen ahead. Show must go on, even when it is not seen.

While I trapped myself inside the suit, I did not worry, as the task of living remained methodical—pulling at straps, placing the Life Support System on my back, securing the helmet, greedily inhaling fresh oxygen. My toothache pulsed brutally along the right side of my jaw, now that my senses were renewed. Once the suit was on, however, I found myself without tasks. I shone the flashlight into the ship's dark corners, almost expecting a daddy longlegs to crawl out.

I made my way into the Sleeping Chamber and I reached inside a drawer, feeling around underneath the sweatpants and under-wear. I removed the cigar box and slid it inside the pocket of my suit. More than likely, this was the end, and I had to keep my grand-father close. Briefly, I considered hiding inside the spacebag, using the same invisibility cloak that had protected me from monsters in the night when I was a boy. I did not.

The Life Support System on my back was to give me three hours of oxygen, and those hours seemed like a lifetime. So much could be done. Within three hours, wars could be declared, cities anni-hilated, future world leaders planted within their mothers' wombs, deadly diseases contracted, religious faiths obtained or lost. I returned to the mainframe and tugged at cables, kicked at the dead panels, saliva dripping from the corner of my mouth and soiling my helmet glass. Finally, a voice came back to me, but it was not Petr's.

"Jakub," Senator Tůma said. "Can you hear my words?"

"Yes," I said.

"I'm speaking to you on behalf of the president and your country.

I have taken this unfair burden from Petr. I sent you on the mission, Jakub. It is only right that we have this conversation together."

"You sound calm," I said.

"I am not. Maybe what you hear is how much I believe in your mission. In your sacrifice. Do you still believe?"

"I think so. It's hard to think about a higher purpose during decompression. You're a diver. You know the strange ache in your lungs."

Tůma told me that sensor readings captured seconds before the ship's power source had failed showed twenty different points of damage in the ship's internal wiring, and two of four solar panels were disabled. The dust had cut through them like a saw. "Do you understand what I'm saying?" he finished.

I let go of the mainframe cables and hung my arms loosely along my body. "Yes."

Replacing all the damaged wiring would take approximately twenty hours, he said, for which I had neither the oxygen nor the supplies. And more damage could have been done after the ship had shut down. Comms could fail at any minute — the independent battery powering it was also damaged and wouldn't last much longer. "Do you understand?" he repeated.

"Senator. Of course I understand."

My chest felt hollow. It was a strange sensation, the opposite of anxiety or fear, which to me was always heavy, like chugging asphalt. Now I was a cadaver in waiting. With death so near, the body looks forward to its eternal rest without the pesky soul. So simple, this body. Pulsing and secreting and creaking along, one beat, two beats, filling up one hour after another. The body is the worker and the soul the oppressor. *Free the proles*, I could hear my father saying. I almost cackled. Tůma breathed quietly. *Don't lose it on me now*, I heard from a distance.

"Jakub. I could not be more sorry."

"Senator. What happens now?"

"Tell me what it feels like up there, Jakub."

"Is my wife there, senator?"

"She is not, Jakub. I'm sure she's thinking of you. She will be there when I declare you the nation's hero. She will be there when I establish a holiday in your name, along with scholarships for brilliant young scientists." His words were interrupted now and then by echoes, scratching, an occasional mute pause. "I will make sure these people don't forget your name for the next thousand years, Jakub. Tell me what it's like up there. Pretend I'm a friend and you're telling me about a dream you can't forget."

Tůma's voice was terribly nice, I decided. Like silk wrapped around a stone. A soothing timbre that could break empires. Not bad to die to. Yes, the word at last came out. *Die die die die*, I whispered. Tůma ignored it.

I made my way to the observation window. In front of the purple core floated a torso of fur and sagging legs. Like a worshipper kneeling at the stairs of a shrine, begging for entry. He looked back at me, all thirty-four eyes glowing. His irises did not change when illuminated by the flashlight.

"It reminds me of a time I almost drowned," I said. "I looked up through the murky water and saw the sun. And I thought, I am drowning, and yet the star of light and warmth is burning itself up to keep me alive. Now I'm thinking the sun too looked purple back then. But who knows?"

"That sounds good, Jakub. I'll tell it to all the people outside who wish they could hear from you."

"Tell it to Lenka. Tell her how glad I am that I didn't drown back then. So I could go on living and meet her in the square."

"Go to...Sleeping Chamber. I need...give...thing," the senator said. The transmission was so weak now that I could hear only every other word.

I floated into the Sleeping Chamber, wound up the flashlight lever, and shone it into the corners, expecting to find something new.

"...emove...sleep...small hook..."

I removed the sleeping bag from its hinges and let it float away. I would not be in need of sleep anymore. There, just as Tůma had said, a seemingly random hook was placed in the midst of the sleek wall, an apparent design flaw. I pulled at it, and a book-size box slid out.

"...bite down...immediate..." Tůma said.

I opened the box. A clear packet containing two black pills entered free zero gravity space, along with a small printed leaflet issuing a stern warning: *Consumption strictly forbidden without permission from Central.*

I gave a loud exaggerated laugh to ensure Tůma heard me. "Thank you, senator. I have a better way."

The communication stream faded. I wasn't sure whether Tůma had heard my last words. Outside the Sleeping Chamber, Hanuš awaited, his eyes turned toward me in anticipation. Yes, there was a better way. I would have to breathe pure oxygen for another hour to eliminate all nitrogen in my body. I imagined the gas bubbles inside of me dissolving like a sodium tablet in a glass of water. After the hour, I would join Hanuš in Deep Space, and hand the ashes of my grandfather over to the cosmos before I too would be consumed. I floated to the kitchen, removed the last remaining jar of Nutella, and put it inside my pocket. The hour would be long. I waited, thinking of the first days at the Space Institute, the weight loss, the constant chewing of gum, the pain.

These faint memories of spacewalk training brought back my old sour stomach, like a fingernail probing its way around my abdomen.

My body trapped by a heavy underwater suit, my mouth stuffed with an oxygen propellant, the training pool stinking of bleach and illuminated by azure bulbs. Along its one-mile circumference paced men who recorded my progress in yellow notepads. The first time I retched, the mask slipped out of my mouth and I released bile and peanuts into the water, immediately gasping for breath and receiving in exchange a liter of pool water in my throat. Coming up for air felt like rock climbing, muscles and veins fat with blood, the surface concealed by the play of shadows.

We tried many things—antinausea medication, different masks, relaxation exercises, a multitude of diets—but every training session had the same ending. It wasn't that I feared enclosed spaces. Mine was a unique breed of claustrophobia. The training pool wasn't a dark closet, it was thousands of dark closets lined up, with no door one could open to escape. I could only swim, and swim, and swim, with every foot the same silence and loneliness, the same sense of abandonment. I couldn't take it. Or, perhaps, I got sick simply because of the physical strain of diving. We couldn't be sure. In the end, after rapid weight loss and a decrease in my cardio performance, we ended the spacewalk training a week early. It was extremely unlikely that I would go outside anyway, they said. I was okay with it.

I wondered now why I still feared these endless closets, the vacuum outside that would remind me of those bleached diving pools. It was all to end there. But no one was watching anymore, no one would think worse of me. The end was up to me, and yet the nausea held on.

Hanuš interrupted these thoughts. "You are to join me soon," he said.

"It looks that way."

"Your tribe has abandoned you."

"Something like that."

"Do not worry, skinny human. I am an accomplished explorer. Together we shall explore the Beginning."

I let go of the flashlight and floated to the air lock door, located below Corridor 4. I did this slowly, patting the walls of *JanHus1*, memorizing its dead, lightless crevices and feeling guilt, as if I had somehow drained the life out of this spacecraft entrusted to me. The incubator that had carried me and kept me warm, fed, clean, and entertained for four months was now a shell of useless materials. An overpriced casket. But it had gotten me to Chopra and I could not fault it for failing against the unknowable forces of other worlds. I closed the compression door behind me. I opened the hatch leading into the universe.

My tether slid along the side of the ship as I shifted outside, and the unfiltered vacuum tightened around me like bathwater. In the distance, Hanuš was a silhouette within the purple storm. I was not afraid of anything except the silence. My suit was built to eliminate the hiss of oxygen release, and thus all I heard were the faint vibrations of my own lungs and heart. The noise of thought seemed sufficient in theory, but it offered no comfort in physical reality. Without the background racket of air conditioners, the hum of distant engines, the creaks of old houses, the murmur of refrigerators, the silence of nothingness became real enough to make any self-professed nihilist shit his pants.

I waited to reach the length of the tether before detaching from the ship, if only to tell the cosmos I remained a believer in small odds. The chance of rescue, be it *JanHus1* miraculously coming back to life or a top secret American drone swooping in to carry me home, was astronomically low, and yet there was some chance, and where there was a chance there remained a desire to gamble. At last I unsnapped the tether and I was free, floating toward Hanuš. Like him, I was now a piece of debris sailing through Space until meeting its end, as most things do, inside a black hole or the burning core of a sun. I could reach into the darkness of eternity and grasp at nothing.

My Maximal Absorption Garment moistened. Cool water soothed my skin. I was thirsty. I felt discomfort around my abdomen, but the nausea hadn't arrived yet. Ahead loomed the menacing haze of Venus, blood seeping through its craters, and I was grateful that I would not come any closer. The Chopra core rested over it like a calm, dedicated moon. Everywhere around me raged the sandstorm of dust, but the ring in which I made my way toward Hanuš offered the simplicity of vacuum. Floating through it wasn't much different than spending the night in a long field, away from city lights—a latitude of darkness, with sparkling photographs of overwhelmingly plentiful dead stars. Only there was no hard soil under me, no grass, no dung beetles pushing their feces along like Sisyphus. Ending my existence here would be so simple. I would leave no flesh behind, nothing for hazmat cleaners to dispose of. There would be no funerals, no heavy stones with generous lies inflicted upon them in golden lettering. My body would simply vanish, burn out in Venus's atmosphere, cause the smallest belch of an eruption. And along with my body would go everything else—the sensations, pleasures, and worries that I could not stop from unfolding in my mind: people I have loved, breakfasts served as dinners and dinner cocktails served as breakfasts, changes in weather patterns, fresh chocolate cake, my hair growing gray, Sunday crosswords, science fiction films, an awareness of the world consumed by financial collapse or environmental disaster or a flu named after yet another harmless animal. Death would be so much easier to dance with if it weren't surrounded by the clutter of civilization. I reached Hanuš.

"Skinny human," he said, "I wish to experience the ash of your ancestor."

I felt the outline of the cigar box inside my pocket. This was the time. Nothing could make it clearer but the universe speaking it aloud. I removed the box from my pocket and opened it and looked inside the silk pouch. There rested the powdered calcium of bones that once held my grandfather together, along with bits of magnesium and salt, the very last chemical remnants of a body that had farmed and drunk beer and thrown punches with the verve of a Slavic god. Behind me, Hanuš studied the powder with all of his eyes.

"May I?" he asked.

"Yes."

He delicately reached a leg over my shoulder and submerged the sharp tip inside the pouch.

"The magic of fire," he said. "A human mystery I find difficult to understand. How do you feel about this, skinny human? Are you fond of fire?"

"It releases us from the constraints of the body."

"We do not view bodies as prisons."

"That's magic too," I said.

Hanuš removed his leg. I turned the pouch inside out and watched the immortal powder slip out, the specks divided and floating in all directions until they created a new pretend galaxy, the first one made by man, the first one made of man. A tomb worthy of Emil Procházka, perhaps the last Great Man of Earth, who, were he present to witness this dispersion of his own remains, would light a cigarette and shake his head and say, *Jakub, all this foolishness, should've just put me in the ground so the worms could have a snack,* but I knew that he would love me for it, that he would understand my need for the grand gesture. An honest good-bye. What kind of resting place purchased on Earth with my hero's salary could ever match the silence and dignity of Space? The grains of dust floated toward the purple core until they vanished.

"This is the Beginning," I told Hanuš.

"It is the Beginning I know," he said. "Perhaps there was one before it, perhaps not."

"Are we headed there?"

"Yes. But ask the question that is on your mind first."

"*Rusalka*. Can you find it?"

Hanuš closed his eyes, and a faint, popping sound of the opera resonated within my mind. Occasionally, the recording was interrupted by random voices, snippets of pop music, the deep, dark voices of demons, the sighs of copulating lovers, sirens, dial-up modems, but Hanuš kept the recording clean enough to soothe my nausea, and to give me the kind of peace experienced on a Sunday morning among soft sheets and drawn curtains.

"What is it like, your death?" I said.

"Sooner or later, the Gorompeds of Death consume all. They have come for me."

He lifted one of his legs. In the space where the leg attached to his torso, there were enormous transparent blisters, diseased and foreign. They were filled with a phosphorescent yellow liquid in which swarms of what looked like ticks floated from one side to another in perfect synchrony. There must have been thousands of them. One of the blisters popped, and the liquid leaked onto Hanuš's belly as the miniature critters scattered into his pores.

"Soon," he said, "they will weaken me enough to consume my flesh. But I will not let them. I will enter the Beginning with you, skinny human. Death cannot reach us there."

"You're dying?"

"Yes. I have been for some time now."

"Hanuš. Does it hurt?"

"I feel it, this fear of yours. I hesitate to depart. If our Elders knew, they would strike me down with sharongu spears. To fear a truth! Blasphemy! Alas, fear is what I've found, here within the brilliance of Earthlings."

"There's nothing to fear anymore."

I saw myself there, a boy in an itchy tuxedo, my rat tail cut off for the occasion, sitting on a red seat inside the State Opera, consuming the mint suckers my grandmother had snuck in. Three years after the death of my parents, not long after we move to Prague, we go to see the opera on my mother's birthday, purchasing an additional empty seat next to us. I am hopelessly in love with this Rusalka, a wild-haired beauty dressed in the muted colors of the forest. She is a water nymph in love with a prince, and she gladly drinks the witch's potion to become human and capture his attention. The prince takes Rusalka to his castle, but of course, as I guessed, the square-jawed scumbag betrays her, casts my Rusalka aside for a foreign princess. I wish the opera would never end, I am captivated, I wipe the snot off my upper lip. During the third act all seems to be lost. The echoing voices of the forest spirits sing sad songs for Rusalka, who, abandoned by the prince, is now forever destined to lure young men to the lake, let them use her body, then drown them and keep their souls in porcelain cups. I want to jump onstage and save her, carry her away, this lovesick ghost trapped within the confines of a lake made of papier-mâché and a kiddie pool. In my future, there would be only one other woman I'd love as much as Rusalka.

"Yes. I feel it with you, skinny human."

Through the echoes and through the darkness, the prince rides looking once again for Rusalka, realizing now that he cannot live without her. He calls, and she appears, and he asks for a kiss, knowing that touching Rusalka will cost him his soul. The lovers kiss, and the prince collapses on the stage. Now Rusalka's father, the feared water goblin, emerges from his pool, and his voice soars: *All sacrifices are futile.*

Hanuš sang it. He sang the line and for the first time in my life, I understood it, just as it came out of the alien's mouth.

"It is not yet the end," Hanuš said.

"No."

Rusalka weeps with gratitude, for she now knows human love. She gathers the prince's soul, and instead of adding it to her father's cup collection, she releases it to God, allows it to ascend to the heavens. Both lovers are now apart but free. As a child, I found this to be a bad ending. The prince, in heaven or not, was still dead, and Rusalka was alone, left with her beastly father and a chorus of whiny forest ghosts. Love didn't seem worth all this trouble, especially if in the end the lovers were torn apart. But now, hearing *Rusalka* in Space for one last time, I saw that the water goblin's declaration was wrong. There was no futility in me, in Hanuš, in Lenka, in the SPCR, in the stubborn human eye always looking beyond, under, next to, below. In the atoms composing air and planets and buildings and bodies, puttering around and holding up an entire dynasty of life and anti-life. Futility nowhere to be found.

I looked ahead to the core. There was something to it after all. Perhaps my death would mean more than my life. I couldn't come up with anything else I had to offer the universe. I was a selfish husband. I had not produced a genius child, given the world peace, or fed the poor. Perhaps I was among the men who needed to die to make anything of life.

"This is not a bad place to end things," I said.

Unaccountably, I found myself wondering where Shoe Man was, and whether he was well. Whether he would remember me if he saw a story in the newspaper—*Astronaut dies for country, body lost in Space*. He would put down his newspaper and announce to no one in particular: "Little spaceman." He would finally stuff the repugnant old shoe inside the garbage can, where it had always belonged, and allow it to rot on the heaps of landfill trash with all the other useless artifacts of human memory. Cruel images invaded my brain. I saw Shoe Man in my bedroom, sliding his tongue along Lenka's light stomach fuzz, his fingers pushing gently on the inside of her thighs. While the iron shoe rests on our living room table, freshly shined, he turns Lenka around and she looks straight at me as she comes, silently, suffocating her screams in a pillow that still smells of my hair and saliva. Age has not affected the hairline or skin of Shoe Man over the years, but he has grown a thick black beard, and from the beard, black ink, or blood, or simply some liquid evil drips onto our cream-colored sheets, seeps into them like petroleum. As Lenka falls asleep, overwhelmed by the intensity of the superior orgasm this stranger has given her, the man looks at me, a silent observer, and pours himself a glass of steaming milk. As he drinks, the milk turns the color of licorice, and I wait for the ink to make its way through his blood, to poison his heart, rip it to shreds. He sets the empty glass down and goes back to bed. Lenka wraps her thighs around him.

Perhaps Shoe Man did not exist at all anymore. Or perhaps, with my father's line now extinguished, he would drop dead and dissolve as soon as I died.

I opened my wrist panel and checked the oxygen level gauge. The clock's hand quivered in the same way my grandfather's clock used to when he smoked cigarettes in front of it. In its generous approximation, I had forty-two minutes to live.

Hanuš offered one of his legs. I held it. Together we entered the core of cloud Chopra.

Prague in Spring

IT IS IMPOSSIBLE to state precisely when my grandfather's lungs begin to fail, but Grandma swears that he took his very last breath during the twenty-seventh and twenty-eighth seconds of the sixteenth minute of the third morning hour of the second day of the last week in spring. I'm staying at my grandparents' apartment for the weekend, trading KFC lunches and the funk of a broken sewage pump at the graduate student dorms for pillows expertly fluffed by my grandmother's hands and noodles baked with lard and ham. My grandmother wakes me and I rush into their bedroom to find my grandfather convulsing and heaving, his head firmly planted in Grandma's lap. She asks me to get some water. I cannot remember where any of the glasses are, how to turn on the faucet, how to turn it off, how to walk with only one foot at a time, how to open the door, and again I am standing in my grandparents' bedroom extending the glass, not sure how I got there, and my grandfather is dead. I stand there motionless, still offering the glass, until strange men in uniform enter the apartment and Grandma takes the glass from my hand.

A week later, I ride Prague's B train and crave the breakfast sandwich I saw in a commercial before leaving the apartment. The smell of morning breath and commuter armpit sweat spreading through the train reminds me of rancid sausage. At least I'm sitting. Guiltily, though: an old woman stands a few inches away from me, fixing the frizz in her white hair with a trembling hand.

At last it is spring, and blooming trees canvas the city in white and red, though the season also plunges Prague into a perpetual state of sexual frustration as young men and women, citizens and tourists alike, become minimalist in their wardrobe choices and eyefuck each other across store aisles, buses, streets. We are a hub of tanned stomachs, muscled arms, full lips clinching cigarettes, there among the sweating seniors dragging their groceries and the bulge-gutted beer lovers stuffed into suits, those apostles of capitalism with their clean-shaven chins buried in the business sections of newspapers. I wonder which group I belong to. Can I be with the youth, the hedonists turning Prague into a playground of the Old Continent? Or does my destination, the science department of Univerzita Karlova, put me in with that other dreaded group, the adults, those who get up in the morning and know exactly how their day will unravel, those who live on the exchange system of work, awaiting their grave with quiet politeness?

My body is young, but today I feel old. Too old to become exceptional. I've spent the past week listening to my grandmother weep over loud television, episodes of *Walker, Texas Ranger* pitched at ear-splitting levels, with Chuck Norris dubbed by an actor who used to be an avid Party member. I've spent the week boiling water for tea and apologizing to my grandmother over and over again about nothing in particular.

It is hard to see why we are here, inside a tin *machina* carrying us toward whatever places we have chosen. It is hard to see why we are here until we are not. I wish I could make sense of these thoughts and whisper them to the old woman with frizzy hair, who has seen history unfold from one day to the next and who must know so much about grief and about asking the gods for a sign.

I arrive at the offices of the university's science department and walk into Dr. Bivoj's office. Before I set my backpack down, I reach inside to ensure the cigar box is still there. Dr. Bivoj is at his desk, bending over one of his books and eating an apple like a rabbit, using his front teeth to shave off tiny bits. I don't take outside lunches during my workdays because watching him eat delights me—his unawareness, the generosity with which he presents his childish features despite being a man well into his fifties.

He looks up at me with a bit of apple skin caught on his mustache. "Ah, you are here. Truthfully, I don't know what to say to you."

I remove the cigar box from my bag. Before my father traveled to Cuba as a representative of the Party to demonstrate Czechoslovakia's solidarity with Castro's struggle against the Imperialist, he asked my grandfather to name the most exotic gift he could think of. "A Cuban monkey," Grandpa said, his first choice. "We can get it a job in government." My father did not laugh. "Hell, ask the bearded lunatic for some cigars" went over much better. Grandpa would smoke the cigars while he fed his chickens, slaughtered pigs. He would bring them to the pub and blow smoke in the faces of his poker foes. Once the contents ran out, he kept the empty box underneath his bed, and on several occasions I caught him sniffing the inside.

Grandma and I could not afford an urn. The box seems like the next best alternative to contain my grandfather. For now.

"He's in here," I say. "I touched it last night. It's softer than campfire ash."

"You know you can take the day off."

"I've nothing to do."

On my desk, significantly smaller than Dr. Bivoj's, is a pile of astrophysics journals to read, most of them in English. On Tuesdays, I go through the journals and write out any passages that may be related to our research of cosmic dust. I have created dozens of scrapbooks filled with data, cutout photos, graphs. I capture events indiscriminately, anything related to our field, significant or not, and at night I like to think that what I have assembled is the most elaborate and complete collection of its kind in Europe, if not the world.

On Wednesdays and Thursdays, I catalog the cosmic dust samples sent to us by European universities, by private collectors, and by a few companies contracted by our modest departmental budget. I unpack the samples and store them in glass slides until Dr. Bivoj moves his enormous behind onto the slight laboratory stool and gathers his instruments. Often, he invites me to look through the lens of his microscope, but I am not allowed to touch. You can replace me on this chair someday, he says, but it will not be until I am demented or dead.

On Fridays, Dr. Bivoj takes out his bottle of slivovitz and pours for two, leans back on his creaking chair, pulls on the suspenders cutting into his soft academic belly, and loudly fantasizes about placing his future Nobel Prize on a handcrafted shelf he will order from an Austrian carpenter.

Though Dr. Bivoj is one of the most respected experts in a field that I would, someday, like to become the king of, I cannot call him my hero. His belief in the work has overshadowed everything else in his life, and the peace of his soul depends entirely on success or failure in science, a field more unpredictable than the moods of Olympian gods. Dr. Bivoj's lifelong obsession with cosmic dust is unbreakable, a cult of one. He is convinced that he can find new life within it, organic matter carried as a result of dissolving, far-away stars, meteors, and comets. His entire life has been about these journals crowding my desk, publishing in them and going to conferences where colleagues will buy him shots and some impressed intern—male, female, he isn't picky—will blow him in the bathroom because his wife "doesn't do that anymore." Day by day, Dr. Bivoj sits in this office, lurks and farts and eats schnitzel sandwiches, his faithful chair sagging more and more every day under the weight of his self-neglect. He reads, he takes notes, he types his findings into an ancient document on a dusty Macintosh with a cracked screen. Twice a day he lumbers to the classroom one floor above and teaches future masters and doctors about galaxies and rotational patterns—a tribute, this teaching, the dues he must pay to keep the office and the Macintosh. Dr. Bivoj is convinced that before he dies, he will discover alien cells of life within the dust specks we study. His genius is humble and methodical. He takes no issue with the darkness of his office, the stale air, the hum of an old computer. When he returns home from work, his idea of relaxation is more work or, in rare moments of intellectual sloth, watching the Discovery Channel. He is the rare man whose work discipline single-handedly sustains him through life. He makes no further demands. This is what I know about him.

Worst-case scenario, I hope to be there when and if Dr. Bivoj makes this breakthrough, a trusty assistant who can use the credentials to jump-start a brilliant career of his own. Best-case scenario, I will fulfill the ancient cliché of a student dominating his teacher, and make the discoveries he failed to achieve on my own. But these days in his office are the key to the future I need. I did not take the job for the measly stipend or the glamour of grading freshman science papers that make the professor "bloated and existentially desolate." I took it because, like Dr. Bivoj, I want my obsession with the particles of the universe—the small clues to the very origin of Everything—to become my lifelong work.

"He was a good one, your grandfather?" Dr. Bivoj asks.

"Yes. He was good."

"Was he proud?"

"Of me?"

"In general."

"He was proud of loving the same woman for fifty years. Proud of working with his hands. Made great rabbit stew."

Dr. Bivoj opens his slivovitz drawer. I expect the usual blue label, but instead he holds an unmarked bottle filled with yellow liquid. Small black particles float around as he pours. "I have a cabin in Paka," he says, "a small village in the mountains. I go whenever I can. A man lives there who has no teeth and keeps chickens in his living room. He makes this apple brandy in his backyard from the rotten apples that fall on his property. He hands it out to his neighbors every summer. They've actually turned the whole thing into an event, a party to welcome the fall. They roast potatoes and sausage while they drink themselves stupid with this stuff."

"I didn't know you took vacations," I say. "You're always here."

"Weekends are for freedom and chaos. Of my weekends, you know nothing, Jakub. You only know my routines of the week. My academic grind."

I swallow the liquor and feel snot melt inside my sinuses and drip down my nostrils. The brandy tastes like tonic water mixed with vinegar and dirt. I hold my glass out for more.

"I went to the spring celebration a few years back," Dr. Bivoj says. "I could see the stars, dew on the grass, and I felt an irresistible urge to remove my shoes. A woman I didn't know kissed me on the cheek. I'm telling you this because I imagine that by knowing these people, I also knew your grandfather. People who have a different idea of ambition. Of building houses with their own hands and living off simpler things. They made me realize that the way I viewed ambition had been a cancer, killing me since the day I was born. Do you want your name to be known, Jakub? I used to. I wanted people to pronounce it in classrooms after my death. I've made myself unhappy most of my life so a professor could write my name on the blackboard and punish students for not memorizing it. Isn't that something?"

He drinks. And again. And again. The liquor smells sour on his breath.

"Ah, I am rambling. Your grandfather was a happy man, Jakub.

I know it. I never told you about my relationship with President Havel. Would you like to hear it?"

"Havel? You knew him?"

"Yes I did. We used to run in the same dissident circles, back when all of us were followed by the secret police and could only congregate with each other. Havel, he was a writer to the core, he was never happier than when he could hide away in his country house and type, morning to night, left alone by people and the larger problems of the world. But he couldn't help himself—he wanted the world to be better, and so he got involved with the Charter, wrote letters to the wrong people, and his arrest established him as the face of the regime's enemies. He was so unhappy about this, Jakub. He didn't want to be in the spotlight. But we got our happy ending. We overthrew the Party, he was elected, and what I don't tell people often, Jakub—please, keep it to yourself, I must be able to trust my assistant, right?—I was to be a part of his cabinet. I was to be a politician, to help build a democratic Czechoslovakia from the ground up. We arrived at the Prague Castle after New Year's Eve, hungover as all hell, and we had to make phone calls to get inside, as none of us even had the key. And when inside, Jakub—and this isn't known to history—when inside, Havel's face turned the color of the dead, and he sat on the ground in the middle of those never-ending halls, with fifteen million people waiting for him to say what's *next*, and he knew he would never get to sit alone and type away in that country house again. He was known, the face of the nation, and there would never again be rest, peace, comfort. His every move, every decision—from his breakfast to his love of cigarettes to his foreign policy—would be ripped apart, glued back together, then ripped again. I resigned immediately. I have been in this office since. My own castle, suited to my own needs."

He laughs, and seems to mean it.

"And you are happy here," I say.

"I love science. I have never truly loved anything else. Why pretend otherwise? Václav Havel lost his typewriter; I won't let them take my microscope."

"I want to do big things," I say, "things that are tangible, like the big discoverers. Tesla, Niels Bohr, Salk. No one cares for the names of the people shaping things anymore. The people who found out that the expansion of the universe is accelerating? You could walk out on the street and ask strangers all day long, but no one could tell you their names."

"But one has to ask: why do the big things at such a high cost? I chose the quiet life. I like the idea of being recognized by my field and no one else. This way I have a purpose, one I believe in, but I'm not burdened by the constant idea of putting on a public image, a view of myself the masses can accept. Nobody cares whether I am fat or cheat on my taxes. It is not the only right kind of life, of course, but it is the honest life for me. What I'm saying is, I make the right choices for myself. Being of use to the world doesn't always mean having your name in the papers. Politicians, movie stars...You know, I keep waiting for someone to say, 'Those Czechs, impressive people! Only ten million of them and look at how they shape the world.' Not because we have beautiful models or talented football players, but because we have advanced the civilization in a real way, a way that doesn't interest the paparazzi. My plea to you is, think beyond celebrity. Do you think Tesla cared if he had his picture taken? Think of whether you're any good to anyone, truly."

His voice is gruff but quiet, uncharacteristic for this usually boisterous man. I figure it must be the brandy, and thanks to the brandy, I almost tell him about my father, about the curse of my family, about my desire to become the very definition of good to everyone, and to carry my family name back to the favorable side. One week ago, three uniformed men carried my grandfather's body out of the apartment and my grandmother took a glass full of water out of my hand. She asked if potatoes with sour cream were okay for lunch. I have to be a person. These words accompany me to bed and wake me from pleasant dreams. I don't know the difference between coming up short or becoming too much of a person and ruining my life with the ambition Dr. Bivoj warns about. Was Havel truly unhappy at the end of his life? He'd changed so many destinies. Some hated him but most adored him. There had to be happiness in that, somewhere.

"Tesla," Dr. Bivoj murmurs, "never got laid and never got a good night's sleep. A man to aspire to." He stares at his glass and soon his eyes begin to close.

I take my place at my desk and I study the latest journals, distracting myself with thoughts of how I might differentiate myself from Dr. Bivoj. Is he, after all, of any good to anyone? A lecturer with a toxic addiction to food. Is his commitment to his own satisfaction wise, or selfish, or simply impossible to categorize? I think of the photographs I've seen from those dissident days. Rebels with long hair, penning revolutionary essays and changing the course of a nation by day, drinking and fucking and dancing by night. Beaten, interrogated, imprisoned, alive, so goddamn alive every day, though they would probably scoff at me for glorifying the struggle. And now here is Bivoj, in the chair that will surrender to his growing mass any day. Breathing frantically through his mouth, working up a snore. The choice between remaining a person from those photos or becoming the modern Dr. Bivoj seems clear. Does he doubt his choices, does he weep over them in the shower? He could've been president by now. Or maybe he did exactly what he should have. Kept to small pleasures and daily routines of work.

At four in the afternoon he staggers out of the office as he whispers that he has to take a piss and go home to nap. He turns the light off on his way out as though he's already forgotten that I am there. I take another swig from his bottle and the burn brings on an idea. In the booze drawer I find two full bottles of slivovitz along with the dirty moonshine. I open the office minifridge, a territory extremely off-limits to anyone but Dr. Bivoj. There rest three schnitzel and pickle sandwiches wrapped in foil, an entire roll of salami, and a brick of blue cheese—to Bivoj, about two lunches' worth of provisions. I take all of it, and stuff the bottles and food inside my bag. No more potatoes and sour cream. Grandma will eat like a queen tonight.

I walk outside. I feel an unbidden impulse to know my city, to put my ear to its chest. To be with its people in a place they are all forced to congregate in against their will, a fallout of all great human cities. In a place where the city's contradictions meet and create an entire new biosphere in which one must acquire previously unknown survival skills. I take the metro to Wenceslas Square.

Burnt sausage, air-conditioned linen stench of clothing stores, police car exhaust, the rancid diapers of toddlers in designer strollers, street waffles with salmonella whipped cream, whiskey spilled between the cracks of ancient brick roads, coffee, newspapers just unpacked at tobacco stands, stray marijuana smoke seeping from one of the windows above a Gap, the sneakily abandoned waste from dogs, grease sizzling off the exposed bicycle chains, Windex dripping down the freshly washed office windows, a faint spring breeze barely penetrating the connected buildings lining the square—this chemical anarchy of scents placed in the cradle of every Prague child early on welcomes us home every time, and in this native knowledge we all simply refer to it as "Wenceslas."

It has been almost a year since I last visited, I realize, while the antibodies inside my olfactory system fight off the invasion of smog. I hold my breath. All around me lives the assurance of our sprint toward capitalism. Few things remain from the old days of the Soviet reign—the only significant remainder being the nineteenth-century statue of Saint Wenceslas, the postcard hero trudging above the masses, green and stone-faced on his trusty horse, the animal's majestic thighs and ass generously caked with pigeon shit. French teenage tourists, unaware of any history around them, thumb through their phones and catcall women as they surround the statue's base. Food vendors offer hot dogs and burgers and alcohol illegally sold at significant markup, making a fortune on underage tourists eager for the true alcoholic Prague experience. Alcohol sales keep the vendors in competition with the McDonald's, the KFC, the Subway, those invaders seducing the populace with the sweet breath of air-conditioning, restrooms free of the toilet paper charge, hot food injected with chemical pleasure. Both tourists and natives face the daily struggle of giving in to the addictive delights of sizzling fats and the Western unity offered by those neon sign giants, or handing themselves over to the old-school exoticism of a slightly burnt sausage served by a man who doesn't waste words or offer a customer comment card.

I approach one of the vendors, a pale man with an honest black mustache, and ask if he sells whiskey.

Without acknowledgment of my presence, he reaches into the depths of his cart and produces a black plastic cup. "Hundredandeighty," he says.

I hand the money over and ask for a sausage, horseradish, spicy mustard.

This is Wenceslas Square almost thirteen years after the revolution. The place where we took our nation back. Where the heart of the Czech resistance launched its assault on the Nazis, building barricades and running at the German soldiers to rip the weapons out of their hands while Soviet liberator tanks were still a world away. Where in 1989 women and men shook their keys as the headless-chicken corpse of the Soviet-installed government pleaded with Moscow to order their tanks to shoot, for Chrissake, shoot these people before they establish a democracy.

The cube bricks that form the road and oblique rooftops, once witness to thronging crowds of revolutionaries, to bullets, to heads cracked by police batons, now provide a historical feel to a shopping experience. Clothing stores, cafés, strip clubs. Promoters stand in front of the shiny entrances and hand out colorful flyers with pictures of girls and happy hour specials. It is four thirty in the afternoon and already these campaigners of sin stand in the trenches, their chins stinking of vodka from the previous night.

I drink the whiskey and wonder if the square isn't a bit colorless despite the neon, perhaps ripe for another climax of history. Will we ever again march on these bricks in national unity, fighting yet another threat to Europe's beating heart, or will this new Prague become an architecturally brilliant strip mall?

My sausage is ready and I order another whiskey.

Then, I smell perfume.

"Vodka and sausage," a woman says.

The vendor denies her.

I turn. Her hair is short and dark, her thin lips emphasized, not enlarged, by a line of dark red lipstick. A gray dress fits tightly around her hips. She is small, so very small, but she doesn't wear heels to position herself higher, nor does she look in any way anxious while speaking to the broad man in front of her. In fact, she doesn't even lift her chin. She meets the vendor's eyes with her own, as if suggesting that she has nothing to apologize for and that, if anything, he should be shorter to accommodate her. She seems a presence unaffected by the square's chaos and hostility, like one of the surly statues of saints and warriors who'd been there when Prague was still barely a trading post. She invites love. Right away I want good things to happen for her.

"Why not?" she asks.

"No sausages, no alcohol. He cleaned me out for the night," the vendor says.

She looks at me and the evidence of my crimes, the plate heavy with sausage in my left hand and a freshly poured cup in my right.

"My fucking luck," she says.

I extend both arms toward her, peace offerings. She measures up the shaking plate and smirks.

"I'll take the whiskey if you're really offering," she says.

I nod.

"Is he mute?" she asks the vendor, who cuts his thumb while slicing an onion.

"Bag of dicks," he roars.

I give her the whiskey. "You can have a bite," I say.

"A gentleman," she says.

The vendor starts kicking the cart while blood drips onto his utensils. The cart shakes and seems as though it could fall over at any minute. Already witnesses are gathering around for photos, and a skinny policeman strolls over at a leisurely pace, munching on chicken nuggets.

The woman in the gray dress gestures toward some benches across the street, then walks off without looking back to see if I'm following. She sits, crosses her legs, and downs the entire cup of whiskey in one gulp, finishing up with a soft belch. She appraises me as I consider sitting down beside her. Finally, the vendor upends his cart, and the buns and condiments spill on the sidewalk. The policeman tosses his chicken nuggets aside and pulls out a baton, whereupon the vendor points a pair of tongs at him.

"Well, sit down, share the food," the woman says. "Let's enjoy the show."

"I'm Jakub," I tell her as I obey.

"Lenka," she says. "Thanks, I needed a drink."

The vendor snaps at the policeman with his tongs, like an emaciated crab leg, and the policeman backs away, switching his baton for a Taser.

"That's what happens when you force people into lives they hate," Lenka says. "They snap. Come at you with kitchenware."

"How do you know he was forced into anything?" I say.

"Do you think he'd be frying pork in this tourist trap if he had better choices?"

Reinforcements arrive. Four officers circle the crazed vendor now, hands on their pistols. Spectators mumble with delight. At last the vendor hurls the tongs into the air, and falls to his knees, right in the pool of ketchup and mustard. He dips his hand into it, and smiles, drawing shapes, like a child playing with crayons. The cops and bystanders all look on, uncertainly.

"I feel like this is our fault," I say.

"It is possible our demands ruined the man's life," she says.

"He must've been craving this kind of self-destruction for a long time now."

"I don't blame him. I feel like self-destructing today too."

"Bad day on the job?"

"Funny thing," she says. "The other day, a man on TV said that unemployment makes people unhappy because they lose meaning in their lives. He went on to say that jobs are a source of meaningful pleasure. Who is this guy? Coffee is pleasure. Vodka melon balls and theater. Waking up with a strand of your lover's hair in your mouth. Those are pleasures. Tell me, if robots did all of our work for us, do you think we'd all plunge into depression and form suicide pacts? If we could all pay attention to art, spend our days climbing mountains or diving into oceans, all of us wealthy and satiated because our robots have things covered, would the world be overrun with maniacs shooting at each other because their lives lack meaning? Dignity is attached to money, they say. So, a person with a decent job making decent money is supposed to have reached nirvana. According to this man's theory, I'm supposed to have dignity because I pick up the phone in hotel reception. Well, here I am, dignity nowhere to be seen, rambling drunkenly to a stranger. Let me have a bite."

She pulls her hair behind her ear as horseradish and black grease spread on her chin. She chews and checks her watch.

"So, what's your deal?" she says. "Drunk at six, bumming around the square."

"I want to know more about your theory. This robotic communism."

"Let me guess," she says. "You go to university. You're determined to deconstruct my ramblings, to align me with a theory. And you are so clean-shaven. All you student boys shave so carefully, yet your idols were all bearded men!"

"I study astrophysics. Though, today, I'm not sure why."

"A good day to ask questions," she says, and finishes the sausage.

The policemen have at last nabbed the vendor, and they load him into the back of a police car. They leave, ignoring the overturned cart, the mess, until soon it becomes just a part of the evening crowd frenzy, pedestrians stepping over without a second thought about its origin.

"I'm still hungry," Lenka says.

I open my bag and remove Bivoj's schnitzel sandwich along with a bottle of dirty moonshine. "And thirsty?" I say.

"You are a resourceful man."

We eat, though I ensure that there's plenty left for Grandma's dinner feast. The neon burns the eyes now, drowning out the soft beauty of the Gothic street lamps. We sit for twenty minutes or so, not saying much of anything, until I decide I haven't much to lose. I ask whether I can see her again, whether we can share more food and more drink, because there has been a clamor inside my head drowning out everything else, but when she speaks, I can hear clearly, and I listen with pleasure. She agrees to meet for coffee on Friday, and we part.

And on Friday we sip cappuccino on Kampa Island. And the following week we go to the Matějská fair and shoot laser guns. She visits me every day on breaks between classes and brings strudel and beer. Lenka. The name comes from Helena, meaning *torch* or *light*. Jakub comes from the Hebrew for *holder of the heel*. My name destines me for always walking upon the Earth, attached to dirt and pavement, while hers destines her for burning and rising into the skies. This makes no difference. We move together like we've always known we'd be here someday. We are loners, and thus the fact that we are deciding to be with each other over the safe cradle of solitude says everything we need to know.

Three weeks after our introduction, I tell her about my grandfather's death, and she insists I must see a place that is important to her. A secret place that could become important to me too.

When we meet, once again by our bench in Wenceslas Square, she's smoking a cigarette and wearing, for the first time, the yellow summer dress with dandelions, the same dress she will later wear for our last night together on Earth. She does not waste time with a hello.

"Let's go," she says.

"Where?"

"To the moon, of course. Is school making you this dense?"

Briskly, we fight a path through the thick cloud of bodies, kicking shopping bags and elbowing the heads of children as we go. I hear a hiss behind us. The light evening breeze coming all the way from the Atlantic, trapped between these hills of Bohemia, is a stark contrast to the recent scorching days. Everyone is layered tonight, mysterious. The sounds of Jay Z, flowing from the boom box of some resting break-dancers, clash with the orchestra of clarinets and flutes spitting awful folk music at old-school pubs. We take a turn into Provaznická, and the sudden silence causes my ears to pop.

The lines of apartment buildings ahead have been untouched by time, war, and regimes. Some blue, some brown, all crowded underneath fading red tiled roofs. Many of these Old Town apartments used to be the bounty of Party officials. Now they belong to citizens with fat wallets. Change is relative. I am six blocks away from the apartment I grew up in, secured by my father's loyal work.

Lenka leads me to a yellow building, where she presses eight different doorbells. A man's voice barks a question over the intercom. We are quiet. She rings more doorbells, until the door buzzes and we hurry inside.

"Can't believe that worked," I say.

"There is always a person expecting someone who won't come."

We make our way up the twisting stairwell, dodging a man who is missing a nose and a woman dragging two fat Dalmatians. These strangers must think of us already as a couple—the revelation hastens my steps. Is Lenka taking me to her apartment? Impossible, otherwise she would have the keys. Is this a trap? She stumbles into me, whispering an apology, my fingertips graze her exposed thigh and she grabs my side for support. At last, we face the attic access, a battered door leaking light around the edges. She jerks the knob and I grimace at the hysterical creak. The attic has all the expected signs of neglect: hesitant light seeping through small windows, migrating globs of dust, a bicycle belonging to a dead child, boxes. A black curtain separates one of the far corners. Lenka leads me to it.

"Are you going to sacrifice me to Satan?" I ask.

"Would that be okay?"

"If it's you who does it, yes."

She pulls down all the window shades until I can see nothing but the silhouette of her curves. With the scent of apricot and powder in tow, she passes me and casts the black curtain aside, inviting me in, and she turns on a small lamp in the corner, its shade covered in black sheer fabric. On black wallpaper, shapes of stars and moons shine in gold. Above us hangs a papier-mâché moon, its craters and creases emphasized with a pencil. At our feet rest Jupiter, Saturn,

Venus, a cutout of the Milky Way, *Apollo 1*, the *Millennium Falcon*, faded gum packets, and a disemboweled rat.

Lenka kicks the rat aside and bends over and reaches underneath the gum wrappers. She holds up a figurine of a saluting NASA astronaut. "What do you think?" she says.

"I think I'd like to live here."

"I used to come here as a kid and play with my best friend. We would take all this bubble gum up here and see who could chew the most. Petra, she made the moon. All her. It's lucky people don't pay attention to these attics, isn't it? They throw their junk in here and forget about it. I haven't been here for what, twelve years? Thirteen? So, I said to myself: Jakub, my astrophysicist, I'll take him and see if my universe still exists. If it does, he can see it, and maybe it'll make up for my silence over his grief, because grief is something I run from. And perhaps I won't protest if he tries to kiss me, because I have not been in love for a while. Here we are. Things are unchanged, all these years later. I'm in my only hiding place. With you."

Solar flares occur when magnetic energy is converted into kinetic energy—thus, the attraction of one element to another turns into a movement. What exactly causes this process, we are not sure. Be it the ejection of electrons, ions, and atoms into the universe, or a cocktail of pheromones infiltrating the olfactory receptors of a future lover, some of the most essential functions of reality remain a mystery. Lenka's breath smells of cigarettes and Juicy Fruit. We lean gently against the wall and I thumb the outline of the cigar box, which I still carry in my bag. The bag slides off my shoulder. She takes my face in her hands and studies it, while I take a breath, take two important seconds to realize I am in love and living will never feel as it did before. The alteration to my future, a whole new fate stands here in the form of a slightly drunk beauty who has invited me to the greatest place I've seen. So much we can tell from a single surficial eruption. A flare to tear the sun apart. The flares are my fingertips feeling the inside of her thighs, her breath on my neck, her hands pulling up the hem of her dress, her eyes searching for my reaction to what I see underneath. The universe assigned the tasks of speaking and kissing to the lips because there is never a need to do both at the same time. We do not speak for hours. Soon most of the room is covered in our clothes. Our bodies pleasantly battered from the wooden floorboards.

Exhausted, we sit among the planets and talk about the foods we'd like to eat. She wants spaghetti; I crave an old-fashioned Spanish bird—thin beef rolled around bacon, egg, and a pickle. We concur that our best plan of action is to drink and walk well into the night.

Do my grandfather's ashes belong here? Can I leave the box behind and feel happier once I walk out the door, or will I forever wonder whether the same cat that murdered the rodent will eat the contents of the box? Lenka asks what I'm thinking about. Everything. How to leave it behind. I carry my father's curse and my grandfather's dust. She does not understand what this means, not yet, and she doesn't ask.

Instead, she tells me of her own father, who went to America before the revolution to work on a car assembly line in Detroit. A true worker's paradise, he wrote back, declaring that Detroit would become the city of the future, a hub of industry and wealth. Each summer, he was supposed to arrive home, smuggle Lenka and her mother through the Berlin Wall, and take them to this new world. Each summer, instead he wrote that it wasn't the right time, that he'd wait for another promotion, another bump in pay, so he could welcome his "queen and princess" with a mansion, an American car. By 1989, his letters came only biannually, coarse and bereft of affection or detail. When Lenka's mother wrote to him that the country was free, that they could cross the newly opened borders in daylight, among the people, and come to him immediately, she received no response. With her father lost to her, Lenka often retreated to the attic, keeping clear of her mother's devastation, the empty wine boxes collecting by the door. Only when the Internet began to connect disjointed lives around the globe did Lenka find a photo of her father. He stood on a Florida beach, beaming at the camera, one arm around his new son, the other around a new wife, a fully stocked cooler of some blue American beer at their feet. Lenka never spoke to her mother about this, and wasn't sure whether her mother ever found out. They lived on.

I ask Lenka what she feels now. Rage?

No. Not here in the attic.

"When I was a child," I say, "I used to sit in a car and pretend it was a spaceship. The cassette player was my deck computer. I wanted to turn the radio knob and blast off—fly away. But I didn't know much about being alone back then."

"Would you fly away now?" she says.

"Not anymore. Now that you're here."

"Now that *we're* here. In our hiding place."

In exactly two years, we will return. The attic won't change—we will simply dip our feet into thicker dust. We will hide behind the curtain and I will ask her to marry me, voice shaking, knees so heavy I'll wonder if the floor might collapse beneath us. At the wedding, my grandmother will dance like a woman half her age, telling me at the end of the night that she stayed alive to see me and Lenka on this day.

And my grandfather's ashes will rest inside the cigar box in our closet, thought of with devotion, until I leave them at the mercy of the cosmos, a reminder that most everything dear to us is bound to become powder.

The Claw

I PASSED THROUGH the knot of time like sand slipping away inside an hourglass, grain by grain, atom by atom.

Time was not a line, but an awareness. I was no longer a body, but a series of pieces whistling as they bonded. I felt every cell within me. I could count them, name them, kill them, and resurrect them. Within the core, I was a tower made of fossil fragments. I could be disassembled and reassembled. If only someone knew the correct pressure point, I would turn into a pile of elements running off to find another bond, like seasonal farmhands journeying from East to West.

This is what elements do. They leap into darkness until something else catches hold of them. Energy has no consciousness. Force plots no schemes. Things crash into one another, form alliances until physics rips them apart and sends them in opposite directions.

The core offered no wisdom. It took away my senses. It made me live inside my own body, truly, made me a flash of matter without the power of reflection. I wasn't a human. I was a stream of dust. *What did you expect?* the core asked me. No, I asked that of myself. Another projection. My desperation to ascribe personality and will to capricious outcomes of chaos. The true kings of the world, elements and particles, had no agenda except movement.

I regained sight just as the core ejected me, then my wits as I passed the core's calm atmosphere and collided with the storm of raging dust. The core had ejected me back into the world at the speed of a launching shuttle. The spiraling dust particles cut into my gloves and chest, forced cracks into my visor. I set my hands upon the helmet's lock, considering a swifter end.

Death in Space would be a brief affair. For ten seconds, I would remain conscious. During this time, gases in my lungs and digestive system would cause a painful expansion of organs, leading to a rupture of my lungs and the release of oxygen into my circulatory system. Muscles would bloat to twice their current size, causing stretch marks and bruising. The sun would burn blisters into my cheeks and forehead. Saliva would boil off my tongue. After these ten seconds of agony, my brain would asphyxiate and my consciousness would melt into the surrounding darkness. Cyanosis would turn my skin blue, my blood would boil, my mouth and nasal cavities would freeze until finally, the heart would cease to function, rendering me an exquisite corpse, a dry, gaseous Smurf at the altar of the Milky Way.

I was ready for this quick passage when I felt a tap on my back. Hanuš was soaring with me, his skin gray and shriveled, like a potato cooked in hot ashes. A blister appeared above his right lip. We were to move on together. I removed my hands from the helmet. Soon enough, the dust would cut through the suit far enough to depressurize it, and I could still have a cosmic death. I would use my ten seconds to remove the suit and follow the example set by Laika — allow for the vacuum to embalm me and preserve me as a wax figurine for future generations of explorers.

"The Beginning has rejected us," Hanuš said.

"It seems that way."

"We did not belong," he said.

"You love your riddles."

The terrorizing fury of Chopra's dust turned to nothingness. We shot out of the cloud completely, once again subjects to the Zen of Deep Space. There could not be much time left now, but I refused to check my suit, refused to check the oxygen count. I focused on my friend. Suddenly, I feared boredom more than death. If my friend died before me, what was there to do with the rest of my time? With the entirety of the universe in front of me, without his voice I would have nothing to guide me as I choked. I reached for one of his legs and offered the jar of Nutella from my pocket.

"Yes, this will do," he said.

I struggled to find words that were profound, some famous deathbed babble, but if existence could be so simply played out by language, why would we spend our lives trying to justify our right to breathe?

I changed my mind.

My words should not be profound. Instead, I called back to the quick village wisdom of my grandfather's drinking buddies, eight liters of beer in, their heads closer to the table's surface with each passing minute. Wisdom about chickens faring so well without heads, or about Grandmother's strudel always having too many raisins and not enough apples, or about giving the middle finger to God's hands so horny to grab the soul, or about Icelandic songs always sounding as though they were composed on whispering ships sailing through ice, or about the inside of the very planet we occupy burning as hotly as the surface of the sun yet here we complain about a scorching summer day, or about being so afraid to ask girls to dance as boys while being too brazen, even rude, to ask girls to dance as adults, the unifying postcoital feeling of thirst, when two spent bodies stinking and leaking with nature crave bread and, greedily, another orgasm to reaffirm the fragile chemistry of love. Had the pub closed and taken away this only method of socialization, these village miners and butchers would surely have taken to traveling the Earth like old-school philosophers, exchanging barfly wisdom for pork chops. How could I contribute to this phenomenon? Perhaps with the greatest wisecrack of them all, one that could keep me awake for so many nights—energy cannot be annihilated, and thus matter cannot be annihilated, and thus all we burn and destroy remains with us and within us. We are living dumpsters. We have run out of antimatter, and now the eternal game is one of Tetris—how do we organize the self so as not to choke? I laughed. Hanuš understood.

In the distance, flashes of red. Was the universe on fire? Was it all to end now, with me the fresh pub dialectician? A lovely thought. From the distance and the darkness, a dragon soared, its sharp nose sniffing for easy flesh. Perhaps this was death. I knocked on the hard plate covering my chest, felt the echo of the vibration in my lungs. If it was not death, and the last living dragon was slain by Saint Jiří so many lifetimes ago, there was only one other option. The nose belonged to a space shuttle, headed for me like the bayonet of a mad soldier. Its beacons saturated the universe like bordello light bulbs, flickering hellishly and seductively, tirelessly to a beat. I was an island, a bastard floating the river in a poorly woven basket, my umbilical cord having been crudely sliced with a pair of rusty shears. Surely, the colors of the spacecraft and the flag singed into its side along with a proud name were a fata morgana, a vision to keep me distracted upon the hour of my death.

"Do you see them?" I asked Hanuš.

"Rescuers," he said.

NashaSlava1. The words rested next to the stripes of white, blue, and red painted onto its side. Russia. Hell. The grinning chancre of my history.

Instinctively, I swam forward, attempting to get away. Impossible. The ship approached silently and swiftly, easing its speed as it came near.

"You do not welcome the rescue," Hanuš said.

"I want to be here. With you."

A hangar door along the ship's fat midsection opened, and

something loomed in its darkness. A robotic arm slid out of its lair, smooth with the movement of muscle and joint. A cybernetic octopus seeking me with its eyeless gaze, as its fingers quivered like wheat awns in storm winds. As a child, I had run from my grandfather whenever he mowed the lawn, putting as much distance between me and the spinning blade as I could. I hid in the wooden shed, between stacks of freshly cut firewood, inhaling its sweetness and pulling splinters from my fingers. Now I had no earth to run on, no structures between which to hide. How I longed for firm ground, for the strain of muscle pulling resolutely toward the center of something, anything.

"You may live," Hanuš said weakly. "Why do you resist?"

"I'm tired, Hanuš."

At last I looked at the oxygen gauge, which showed three minutes of remaining oxygen. The ship's claw was no longer erect. It had bent into position, ready to pick me up, or perhaps to penetrate me—what was the difference? They would save me in time unless I removed my helmet. I did not want to be saved. By anyone, but especially not by Them. Those who had engineered my father, had given him the power that transformed him into what they needed him to be. This was the one thing my grandfather and I had never agreed on. He insisted that the blame should be placed on the person, not the circumstances. My father, he felt, was bound to make the same kinds of mistakes under any regime. I couldn't accept this. I couldn't accept that without the arrival of the Rus, without Moscow's puppets in Czechoslovakia waving rewards and promises in front of my father's desire for a better life, he would still be capable of inflicting the same pain. We do not live outside history. Not ever. And here I was, another Procházka forced to capitulate to the occupier.

As I checked the oxygen gauge again, I recounted the number of people who owed me explanations, who owed me looks and kindness and life. There was Lenka. Somewhere out there she existed, outside the picture sent to me as consolation, and the simple temptation that her hands might once again touch my sore back seemed reason enough to consider breathing the expiring O_2.

What kind of carpet did Emil Hácha feel underneath his feet inside Hitler's office as he pondered whether the Czechs would fight against invasion and be slaughtered, or concede and lose dignity? After making the old man wait until the morning hours while he watched movies with his posse, Hitler spit in Hácha's face as he recounted the various ways in which a country could be raped, in which children and women could be bled, in which the king towers of Prague could be bombarded, shot, burned, stomped into a fine powder, and soaked in the piss of the Gestapo. How close was Hácha to exercising stupid heroism, to asking Hitler to go fuck a herring, thereby earning himself a bullet in the cheek and slaughter for his nation? He too was a bastard in a basket, an old man of ill health who had replaced the president in exile after Hitler's machinations picked the republic apart. The country had been sold to the highest bidder at the Munich Betrayal, where, without our presence, Chamberlain/Daladier/Mussolini/Der Führer shook hands, ate tea sandwiches, and agreed that a wee Czechoslovakia was a small price to pay for world peace. How close was Hácha to unleashing the Great Genocide of the Czechs and Slovaks? How much easier might it have been simply to die at the Führer's hand and allow for someone else to deal with the greater questions? Hácha chose life, and shame. His reward was seeing the nation survive, witnessing the capital emerge from the war unscathed, unlike the beautiful towers of Warsaw and Berlin. After Hitler's abuse, Hácha fainted. The Nazi royalty helped him to his feet shortly before he signed the country over into protective occupation by Germany. This coward who saved the nation by giving it up along with his pride.

Two minutes of life remained and I held on to my friend. When I gripped one of his legs more tightly it fell from his body like a leech, trailing bubbles of gray juice. His lips and belly fur were sticky with chocolate and hazelnut. And then I saw them: Hanuš's Gorompeds, those little ovum parasites that lived in his blisters, crawling onto my suit and finding their way underneath it. They swarmed between my armpit hairs. I kicked, pulled both Hanuš and me away from the Russian ship to buy just a bit more time before the rescue. The Claw was so near my legs I felt goose bumps at the anticipation of its touch.

I saw what would have happened if Hácha had decided to die for principle. He would have gotten his bullet to the head, and the Aryans thirsty to claim their Slav slaves would have overrun the fighters of our nation, whose Bohemian bodies would have turned the Vltava red as they floated West, small gifts to Chamberlain and his naïveté. I saw Prague burning; the castle that had served the most magnificent of European kings pillaged by the greedy hands of hate-filled German boys; beautiful village girls with freckles hiding under their beds from the entitled hands of sour-breathed captains; the Moravian grapevines flattened under tank belts; the pure creeks and hills of Šumava soiled by guts and deforested by hand grenades. Hácha had made his decision. Death was too easy.

The Claw caught my ankle, as gently as a mother tugging on a newborn. It pulled.

"I wish you could come with me," I told Hanuš.

I felt him shrink. Another leg left us.

"Not much longer now," he said.

"You have saved me," I said.

"Would you feel better if I wasn't real?"

"No."

"What are your regrets?" Hanuš said.

"Now that I know I'll live, I have millions."

"Odd."

"I don't know if I want to go back. To divide life into mornings and nights. To walk upright, attached at the foot."

"Do not leave, then, skinny human."

The grip of the Claw tightened. Did the Russians see the friend in my embrace?

"I want to die within you," Hanuš said. "Take me to a good place. I too will show you where I come from. Home."

A Goromped crawled across my cheek, evoking the sensation of a sticker that Lenka had once attached to it. I remembered the pain then as I had pulled the sticker from my beard, removing a small patch of hair in the process.

This would be my final gift to Hanuš. I did not cower from his invasion. For the first time I felt the heaviness and despair of death that he had learned from me, a dull pain in my abdomen. My dry tongue encountered a new sore on my gums and my head was battered by the pressure building at the back of my skull. In these last moments, Hanuš was welcome to every last bit of my lifetime. I craved to see his home.

What came to me was an afternoon in May. A beautiful month. Lenka and I used to read Karel Hynek Mácha together. He wrote a famous romantic poem about May, and all of us had to learn it in school, rolling our eyes at its sentiments, not yet understanding how easily pleasures led to poetry. There is a section I can hear Lenka read as if she were here now, as she was back then inside our tent in the forest, lying naked with her hair tucked behind her ears, sweat glistening on the white fuzz of her belly button:

In shadowy woods the burnished lake
Darkly complained a secret pain,
By circling shores embraced again;
And heaven's clear sun leaned down to take

A road astray in azure deeps,
Like burning tears the lover weeps.

This is what I wanted Hanuš to hear now.

Together we traveled to that May morning. Hanuš of the cosmos, an alien but overpoweringly human friend. Jakub Procházka of Earth, the first Spaceman of Bohemia. I choked. The oxygen had run out, all soaked up by the greedy sponges inside my chest. Despite the hold the Claw had on me, the ship seemed far away. Death was near.

May

L ENKA AND I WALK along the edges of the Karlův Bridge, across the untamed width of the Vltava, the river vein of Bohemia that divides our city. We have just visited my grandmother at the hospital, finding her in great spirits as she happily slurped on the hospital cabbage soup even though we had brought her sandwiches, and asked whether we were planning to give her a grandchild. With my grandmother's warmth and seamless recovery from the stroke putting us at ease, we wander. Around us, the languages of the world mix into the usual hum of spring. A notorious bridge artist draws crude caricatures of clueless tourists. He picks at the fleas in his beard and drinks wine out of a leather jug as he grins at the platinum faces of the Swedish couple shifting on his stool, then adds a goat udder below the man's chin and gives the woman a Victorian mustache. I've seen his shenanigans a thousand times — often the tourists simply get up and walk away, and he yells at them in his own invented language. But once in a while, their visitors' guilt overpowers them, and they pay for his nonsense. He is a comforting sight against the backdrop of the statues of patron saints guarding the bridge, with a rather grim portrayal of crucified Jesus leading the entourage. Without the painters, pickpockets, and strolling couples, the bridge would be a cold, terrifying reminder of Gothic overindulgence. But here we are, the winos and leather-clad Eurotourists and Prague lovebirds eager for a Sunday beer buzz and a stroll along the water, providing the bridge with the humor and gentleness it needs. In exchange, the bridge makes us feel like our history goes back beyond the day we signed up for a bank account.

We leave the bridge and walk through one of the many Vietnamese markets, where children chase each other with laser guns, adults gloomily smoke Petras, and their knockoff Adidas and Nike merchandise flutters in the wind like a nation's flag. Frowning men scoop a mixture of eggplant and chicken into foam containers. Muscular white men in baseball hats—likely policemen staking out illegal sales—lurk about clumsily. Child scouts let their parents know with elaborate whistles whenever a fashionable customer is coming, so they can quickly display their fake designer dresses before hiding them again from the poorly dressed policemen. The inner workings of the market.

A little boy knocks a little girl on the nose with his laser gun and disappears between the windswept tents. The little girl sobs until Lenka, my sweet Lenka, takes her by the hand.

"Boys play rough," Lenka says. "You have to play rough too. Next time you see him, knock him over his own melon."

The girl stares at us, tight-lipped, her own laser gun still in hand. She pulls Lenka forward and leads us three tents down, where a woman snoozes in a lawn chair. The girl extends a yellow T-shirt toward Lenka and nods with a devious smile.

"You want me to have this?" Lenka asks.

"Sixty. Discount," the girl says.

"Sixty crowns?"

The girl nods, a savvy saleswoman. It is obvious that she means to keep the money to herself, and not to share with her mother—if she is even related to the sleeping woman at all.

There is no turning back. Lenka's compassion flagged us as weak, and she hands the money over and pats the girl on the head.

"You told her to play rough," I say, "so she's playing rough."

"Good. Let her be an entrepreneur."

Lenka unrolls the shirt. Over the yellow background of the cotton, a cartoon sun holds a pint of beer in one hand and a bottle of sunblock in the other. It squints its right eye in a drunken stupor, while its left eye studies the obscene curves of nude men and women tanning on the beach below (nudity beyond nudity, with a double line for every crevice, thick pubic hair, massive breasts and erections). The sun grins creepily as it squeezes liters of creamy sunblock onto these unsuspecting bodies.

The girl smirks as we explore the cartoon. "Nice for summer," she says.

"You are naughty," Lenka tells her.

"Sixty crowns!" she squeals as she disappears between the tents just as quickly as the boy who hurt her, clutching the hard-earned bills. The snoozing woman wakes up and looks at the T-shirt.

"Eighty crowns," she says, hand outstretched.

Lenka and I cannot contain our laughter as we give her more of our cash.

"You realize you have to wear this now, right?" I ask Lenka.

"Are you mental?"

"Law of the universe. You rolled over and exposed your neck as the enemy bared her teeth. You were presented with a simple Darwinian challenge, and you failed."

"You sound like a hopeless academic."

I point at the shirt and frown with insistence. She sighs, but the half smile she betrays does not escape me. This is what we need. Teasing. Humor. Something unexpected. After months and months of me sweating on top of her without pleasure, praying to reinforce my sperm as she sends positive vibes toward her *aureus ovarii*; after piles of pregnancy test boxes crowding the bathroom trash can; after failure upon failure, and my retreat between the halls of the university, where I stay late to "grade papers" and "attend committee meetings" while really just snacking in my office and playing

Snake on my phone, this day could be our chance at finding a new way forward, at once again fusing our emotional and neurological chemistry instead of seeing each other merely as the owner of a potentially defunct baby-making orifice or appendage.

Lenka pulls the T-shirt on over her shoulders, and I nod with approval. She kisses me and presses the large round *S* sticker from the shirt against my beard.

"Now we both look like idiots," she says.

Witness my most joyous moments, skinny human. I will show you where I come from. Hanuš interrupts the memory of Prague, takes me elsewhere. I see his world, once upon a time.

Millions of eggs circumvent a small green planet. Above the ovum ring hover members of Hanuš's tribe, a collective hum of their speech announcing that the time is right. The eggs begin to crack, tips of thin arachnid tarsi pushing through membrane and shell. Among the thousands of newborns I see Hanuš, I recognize his hum as slightly different from the others. He studies his own legs as they poke at the smooth, furless skin of his body. The shell fragments float around, create an entire dust cloud of their own, and the young and old members of the tribe circle one another. At last the Elders, a council of twenty, their legs short and contorted like the roots of trees, order the tribe to cease motion. The tribe's laws are passed on to the children:

The body must not be violated.
Truths must not be feared.

Now the newborns separate from the herd and descend upon their green planet. Its surface is rock and crystal, its caves lead into underground tunnels. Shtoma worms—the size of a human child, fat and eyeless and pink as boiled pig skin—flee into these tunnels as the tribe's children chase after them. A storm gathers within seconds above the planet, blue and red lightning bites into its rock, the surface cracks and reveals the worms slithering underground. Hanuš lands on a worm and plunges his legs into its back. He tears through the worm's skin and the white insides, thick and pasty like lard, spill upwards. The storm cannot be heard, and yet the wind rages on the planet's surface, sweeps away the emptied membranes that used to be Shtoma. The Elders hum the melody of a celebration song, the storm weakens, the overfed children slowly retreat into their caves to digest. Hanuš opens his memory without limit—I become him. In this moment, as hair begins to grow on his body and for the first time he knows the gift of food, he is absolutely certain. About the universe, all of its secrets, about his place within the tribe, about his laws. I am unable to comprehend the happiness that comes with his certainty. All is as it should be until the Gorompeds of Death arrive, whether tomorrow or in two million years.

Satiated and knowing, young Hanuš rests. Not yet aware of the last secret of the universe kept from his tribe: humans, their Earth, and the horror of their fears.

I wish I could've been there, Hanuš. To hunt with you in the storm, to know your siblings.

Lenka and I leave the bridge, pick up boiled chestnuts and grog from a vendor cart, and sit in Old Town Square, waiting for the Orloj clock to ring in the hour as awestruck tourists gather with digital cameras in hand. I feel drowsy in the warmth, and the sweet scent of chestnuts lingers around Lenka's lips. I kiss her, tangle my fingers in her beautifully frizzed hair, pull. She bites down on my lip.

The Orloj rings, and the Procession of the Apostles begins—the wooden figurines appear one after another in the window above the clock: Paul with a sword and a book, Matthew with an ax, the rest of the gang holding either weapons or symbols of wisdom. Fixed statues that are not part of the processional permanently stare visitors down from around the clock: Death ringing a bell, a Turk shaking his head at the infidel apostles, a Miser holding his bag of gold, and Vanity looking at himself in a mirror. The clock itself shows the position of the moon and the sun, along with the rotations of the stars. Is it art, or a piece of magnificent engineering, or a tourist trap? It's as if the Orloj can't decide and thus takes on the identity of all. Children squeak as the mechanical rooster crows, and the show ends with the Turk again shaking his head in disbelief at this Christian nonsense.

Lenka finishes her beer and stands up. She takes my hand and guides me through the background noise of the dispersing crowd. We approach the Orloj entrance, tug on the heavy wooden door. The attendant booth is empty, with a scribbled note stuck to the glass: *Lunch break*. We walk up the narrow stairwell, Lenka stumbling a bit, overpowered by warmth and alcohol. The last time I was inside the Orloj was on a school field trip, and elderly guards stood in corners to supervise the nation's monument. Now the corners are empty—perhaps the dust and the musky smell of stale ocean so prevalent in any abandoned place swallowed them whole, or they simply died and no youths wanted to replace them, though government cuts are the likelier reason for their absence.

Lenka climbs the ladder leading to the restricted upper levels, tugs on my shirt collar when I hesitate. I follow, listening to the creak of gears, the genius design that Master Hanuš lost his eyesight for. This is the oldest working astronomical clock on the planet, yet who has need of its services? Satellites photograph the planets, the sun, the stars, the moons, Cosmic Depths Beyond Comprehension with drone-like precision; lone rovers scout the surfaces of other planets, performing alchemy within their bellies; any human can spend nights zooming above virtual continents with Google Earth. How much longer can the Orloj captivate the attention of tourists with its mystery and puppet show, how long can its entertainment value, its appeal to the retro-fetishism of the human mind, overshadow its tragic impracticality? Lenka and I reach the apostle room, where the wooden guardians rest, lined up in a circle and queued for their next show. She sits inside the window nook, dangerously close to Saint Andrew and his large wooden cross. She pulls on my chest hair and bites into my neck, and I collapse to my knees and bury my nose, eyes, chin in her underwear, rip them off and fling them across the room.

This is what we need, pleasure, abandon, not scheduled mating, not calendars and tests and doctors asking about our "sex angles." My scalp burns from her nails digging into my skull. This is the pain we've been looking for. My jaw is numb, I cannot breathe, and I decide that this is how I would like to die someday, smothered in her lap, her body trembling with lust under my fingertips. Lenka pulls me up and unbuttons my jeans, encourages me with whispered begging, and in our fury we stumble to the side and bump into poor Saint Andrew. With the cross still tightly clutched to his chest, the apostle plummets from his grid, and after he crashes to the stone ground, his head rolls off into the distance. Andrew has withstood centuries featuring the Black Death, the Crusades, two world wars, termite assaults, communism, capitalism, and reality television, but he is no match for two clumsy lovers. But as Lenka spreads my cum over her inner thigh, an act of rebellion against the purpose of the cloudy substance, I do not grieve for having defaced a national treasure. We've made our mark on history, done what no woman or man has done before, proved that we are here to live before death, and to have a bit of fun while doing so.

They killed them all, skinny human. If I do not show you, there will be no witness left. They came to eradicate us. This is the Gorompeds' only purpose. Our destruction.

Hanuš is now fully grown, his body exactly as I know it. A new ring of eggs circles the green planet, not nearly as plentiful as during Hanuš's birth. Along with his kin, Hanuš patrols the ring. On the horizon, a swarm appears. An army the size of an asteroid. Hanuš asks his Elders for guidance, for help, as do all the others of his tribe. For the first time, the Elders are silent.

They run, leaving the young behind. The Gorompeds crack the shells of the tribe's future, feasting greedily on the embryos. Hanuš runs across galaxies and the swarm follows, a black hole swallowing everything in its path. The Elders are slow and falling behind, and the siblings who stay to protect them are doomed. *Run*, the Elders order, *run and never stop, you might be the last of us*, and soon Hanuš does not look back, he simply flies through the gates of the cosmos as quickly as his body allows, and the hiss of the swarm weakens along with the collective hum of his siblings, until at last he looks back and sees that no sibling remains. The world feels empty, he is alone, and so he stops and waits for the Gorompeds to find him, as there is no life without his tribe. But the Gorompeds do not come, and Hanuš sleeps from exhaustion and again wakes in a place he has not encountered before, a place known by its inhabitants as the Milky Way, and he is alive, alive though he knows the Gorompeds are bound to find him, whether tomorrow or in two million years. The certainty given to him as a birthright begins to vanish just as he hears the first echoes of voices and minds occupying planet Earth. He understands nothing.

Stay with Lenka and me, Hanuš. Only good thoughts now.

Lenka and I will always remember this moment—she slides to the floor, her back against the cool stone wall, hair tangled in her mouth, and I follow. Neither of us is concerned with the smell, the sweat covering our faces and limbs. We believe that we can fix our marriage. We know that the world operates on a whim, a system of coincidences. There are two basic coping mechanisms. One consists of dreading the chaos, fighting it and abusing oneself after losing, building a structured life of work/marriage/gym/reunions/ children/depression/affair/divorce/alcoholism/recovery/heart attack, in which every decision is a reaction against the fear of the worst (make children to avoid being forgotten, fuck someone at the reunion in case the opportunity never comes again, and the Holy Grail of paradoxes: marry to combat loneliness, then plunge into that constant marital desire to be alone). This is the life that cannot be won, but it does offer the comforts of battle — the human heart is content when distracted by war.

The second mechanism is an across-the-board acceptance of the absurd all around us. Everything that exists, from consciousness to the digestive workings of the human body to sound waves and bladeless fans, is magnificently unlikely. It seems so much likelier that things would not exist at all and yet the world shows up to class every morning as the cosmos takes attendance. Why combat the unlikeliness? This is the way to survive in this world, to wake up in the morning and receive a cancer diagnosis, discover that a man has murdered forty children, discover that the milk has gone sour, and exclaim, "How unlikely! Yet here we are," and have a laugh, and swim in the chaos, swim without fear, swim without expectation but always with an appreciation of every whim, the beauty of screwball twists and jerks that pump blood through our emaciated veins.

I want to share these thoughts with Lenka but I'm afraid of the noise of words. *I am happy you can see her, Hanuš, because I could hardly describe it.* She looks at me as if I am the first thing in the world she has ever seen. Is it possible I am misreading her adoration, or romanticizing a normal postcoital look of carnal satisfaction? I don't think so. I think that at this moment Lenka's physical capacity for love has reached its apex. Dopamine crashes its way through her frontal cortex, breaking down its membrane walls. Norepinephrine overwhelms the chamber of her cerebellum, burns it down, and feeds on the ashes. Her brain is soaked with blood, it has become a love sponge, an organ of complete biological devotion—this brain of hers, the most beautiful thing I've ever known to exist. I feel the same as she does. This moment will never be cheapened, as other moments are after love fades. It will always be perfect. We will always be fools.

We are more than our ability to conceive a viable fetus. We are lovers. We are the greatest contradiction of the universe. We go against it all. We live for the pleasure of living, not for the sake of evolutionary legacy. Today, at least, we'd like to think so.

And there, Hanuš, is where I want to leave you. Hold the moment. I feel you slipping away. Are you still here? Feel it, Hanuš. Feel the afternoon in May, with the sunrays peeking through and the smell of sex sharp in the air. Hanuš?

How unlikely! Hanuš said. *Yet here we are.*

Then he was gone.

A VERY BRIEF
INTERMISSION

MASTER JAN HUS did not burn to death. In fact, he spent his last days in the warm bed of a widow, his thoughts at peace with God and love.

Hanuš unearthed these truths in a long-abandoned archive sealed by the keepers of history. Thirty-two days into his imprisonment and torture, Hus received a guilty visit from King Sigismund, who offered a pardon under a simple condition. Hus would travel secretly to the edge of the Christian lands, where no one could recognize him, and live out the rest of his life in exile. At first, Hus refused. He predicted that his public death would cause the desired uprising in the Bohemian lands. This was to be his part in God's plan for Europe's rebellion against the Catholic Church.

Then entered the widow. She ran her fingers along the bruises and cuts on Hus's ribs, cheeks, hands—those he had received from his tormenters. She said she saw the love of God in him. She said that one of God's sons had already died and caused the world a great sorrow. Soon, Hus and the widow were on their way to a quiet Moldavian village. They baked bread, bathed with each other, began to sleep with each other as husband and wife. Hus no longer felt compelled to preach. The torture had broken him—after the suffering, he was ready to die or to take on another life. A simple life—one that did not force him to become a symbol.

Of course, the necessity for symbols did not disappear with Hus. The king hoped that the master's crimes would simply be forgiven, but the church leaders would not let go of the despised heretic, and demanded his return. They smelled blood and spectacle. The king sent three dozen of his best men to seek a villager who resembled Hus. They found a few, and of these few, a man dying of consumption agreed to take on the role of Hus. In return, the wife and child he left behind would benefit from the king's generous coin. The man grew out his beard and took a few beatings to look even more like his doppelgänger before marching onto the platform and burning at the stake. The mob, blind with rage, could not tell the difference. Neither could the church leaders celebrating the death of their dissident.

Following Hus's death, the people of Bohemia rebelled and a civil war broke out between the Hussites, avengers of their beloved philosopher, and the monarchs, representatives of the dreaded church. Hus told the news of the impending conflict to his widow over tea with milk—calmly, as if the wars were happening in a world he'd never visited. The widow asked him whether he would go back and fight alongside his countrymen. Hus declined.

His death, whether it was his or someone else's, had unleashed the revolution Bohemia needed to free itself. No amount of fighting he could have done as a living man would have achieved the impact of his death at the stake. He had served his part in history.

Now, Hus could truly live.

PART TWO

FALL

Astronaut Dies for Country

Hanuš slipped from my hands. His legs detached, one by one, and dropped into the universe as if they had business of their own. He was nothing more than a small sack of skin whirring with the vibrations of the feeding Gorompeds, his eyes dead, his lips dark. Only after he had floated away did I realize that the Gorompeds, having leaked from his pores, were swarming around my arm, my shoulder, my helmet—and suddenly they were inside my suit, biting into the flesh of my armpit and groin. Hanuš was gone.

I screamed in pain as the gates of the Russian ship opened and from the inside emerged an astronaut clad in a suit so finely cut and fitting it must have been tailored to order. He grabbed me and pulled while the Claw retreated into its lair. The fierce biting around my privates ceased, but I felt the burn of the inflicted wounds. As the crawling sensation around my body faded, I looked at the finger of my glove, where a few Gorompeds exited the suit and disappeared as I tried to grab them. I allowed the astronaut to carry me, to push me wherever he liked. The chute closed and the decontamination fans hummed. I was sick with fever, nausea, my lungs burned at the exposure to fresh oxygen. The fashionable astronaut brought me out of the chamber, between sleek gray corridor walls showing no cables, no control panels, no guts of the ship, as if the vessel sailed on faith alone. Another astronaut approached, suit cut to match wide hips and short legs. Together they brought me into a small, dark room with a single sleeping bag, and unfastened my helmet. Greedily, I breathed, sweat pouring into my mouth.

"*Ty menya slyshis?*" a female voice inquired.

I tried to speak but couldn't make a sound. I nodded.

"*Ty govorish po russki?*"

I shook my head.

"Do you speak English?"

I nodded.

The lights dimmed even more, the darkness became a grain, and some frames skipped, until I could see nothing at all. I tried to shout. I waved my arms, felt my back pushed firmly into the wall, my hands tied down, another set of straps pulled over my shoulder.

"Do you feel thirst?" the woman asked.

Desperately, I tried again to answer in speech, but no trembles resonated through my dry throat. I nodded angrily.

A straw scratched my lips, and I sucked and sucked. My suit was stripped from me, peeled from my scorching skin, and I drank all the while, until not a drop was left and I lost the strength to stay awake.

A tap on the shoulder. Her voice was robotic, distant, meaning she was speaking to me through her suit's microphone. I was not awake enough to comprehend her words. She held something cold to my cheek. There was a sudden pressure in my mouth, my cheeks filled up, followed by the flavor of pasta, canned beef, and tomato sauce along my teeth and tongue. I chewed, swallowed, felt the heaviness of my eardrums.

"...real...food...toast...three days...do you know?" Her voice was in and out.

I tried to speak, and lost consciousness again.

When I opened my eyes, blurry shapes crept around the room. I could not feel my tongue. Something wet and substantial rested in my Maximal Absorption Garment.

Two thick silhouettes materialized in the doorway.

"Are you awake?" she said, still through her suit's microphone.

I nodded.

They approached. I looked down to see that my starved body was clothed in nothing but a blue T-shirt and a diaper.

"You are ill. We don't know what it is. Do you?" she asked.

I observed her companion through the visor of his helmet, broad-shouldered, with a round jawline shaved too cleanly and fat eyebrows merged into one by his insistent frown. I shook my head.

"We don't know if it can spread to us. That is why we keep quarantine. Is this okay?" she said.

I lifted my hand and scratched air letters with an imaginary pen. She nodded and looked at the man. He left for a few minutes and returned with a notepad and pencil. The woman unstrapped my hands.

Home? I wrote.

"Yes, home. We are setting course for Earth now."

My shuttle?

"Gone, in the cloud. We barely made it out ourselves. The dust, it finds its way under."

Only the two of you?

"We have a third. But he rarely leaves his chamber. There has been...an incident."

She looked down at my diaper, smiled awkwardly, and took the writing pad away. She placed it in the front pocket of my sleeping bag.

"You must rest," she said, and floated back to the man waiting by the doorway. They drew sticks out of a box. The man drew the shorter stick. The woman left.

He unzipped my sleeping bag, leaving fastened the constraints that held my body to the wall. He pulled off the safety Velcro straps of my diaper, and began sliding it down. I put my hands on his shoulders in protest, but he pushed them away. I took the notepad and wrote furiously: *Don't, I can do*

He shook his head and began to remove the diaper with a disgusted grimace. I slapped the top of his helmet. He grabbed my arm, thrust it to the side, and strapped it to the wall, then did the same with my left. The notepad and pen floated away. When I looked down at the straps on my chest and stomach, I realized that all of them were secured by a miniature padlock. I wasn't too surprised — of course they had to quarantine me by force, in case I decided to take a tour of the ship during my feverish hallucinations. Whatever bacteria I might contaminate the corridors with would mutate unpredictably in the zero gravity environment, causing possible disaster for both the crew and the structural integrity of the vessel. Yet this confinement brought on unprecedented terror in me. I tried to scream, wriggled in my chains, turned my hips to the side, but nothing could end the violation. With flared nostrils, the man wrapped plastic around the diaper to prevent its contents from flowing around. He tied the bag three times and unwrapped four towels, which he used to wipe my groin, my thighs, and my rectum. I closed my eyes, counted, wished I could produce an auditory expression of my rage and shame, but I could do nothing. The man left without looking at me, as if he were somehow the punished dog.

I had no way to tell how long the Russians left me in solitary. I tried to count, but by the fifth minute, all numbers seemed alike, thirty the same as a thousand, and I could not guess how long a second lasted. Throughout these hours in the darkened room serving as my holding cell, I had only one thing to hold on to: the reality of my return to Earth, the possibility of living. Because if all that had happened had really happened — from the moment I stared into the fire as the Velvet Revolution sent my father and, eventually, the rest of us on the course of our punishment, through the time I first spotted the iron shoe in its monstrous efficiency, through the time

I met Lenka by a sausage cart and a senator proposed that I fly to Space—if all was true (and I couldn't be sure about anything in this room, not life or death, not dream or reality), then I was really on my way home, on my way to all the other futures I could create. The vision slowly returned to my right eye, and the burning around my forehead and chest subsided.

Home. I focused on the concept intensely so my thoughts would not wander to questions I may not want answered. For instance, why a Russian ship had come to cloud Chopra without anyone knowing. Or whether Gorompeds bred somewhere inside me, bound to consume me from within as they had with Hanuš.

Hanuš. His body slipping away. The ache around my temples I would never feel again.

The female astronaut came to me in the midst of these thoughts, bearing another tube of spaghetti. She allowed me to feed myself. I grunted without shame, lapped at the tomato sauce like a feral dog, ignoring the excruciating pain of my rotted tooth. I studied her through the visor. Her sunken eyes, brown with golden nebulas shooting from the middle, indicated a lack of sleep, and a thick scar snaked along her round cheek.

When I was done with the meal, she took the empty tube and handed me an e-tablet.

"Your obituary," she said, and smiled.

I looked at the date and time of the article, which had been written by Tůma and published a few hours after Central lost contact with *JanHus1*:

In the search for brilliance, sovereignty, and a better future for its children, every country must occasionally face a dark hour. One of these moments descends upon our hearts today, as we mourn the loss of a man who accepted the most significant mission our country has ever embarked on. Though books could—and will—be written on this man's service and role in advancing both our humanity and our technology, we are all already familiar with Jakub Procházka the Hero. What I'd like to write about now is Jakub Procházka the Human.

Jakub's father chose to align himself with a specific current of history, one he considered righteous but which turned out to be monstrous. Jakub's willingness and determination to overcome this...

My hand trembled. I became aware of my lachrymal ducts—dried out, burning, empty.

...his last moments, before we lost contact, Jakub told me a story of a time he almost drowned, and the symbolism of a burning sun...

...so as a great personal friend of Jakub's, I feel deep sorrow in my every cell, and consider it a small but significant consolation that he expired without pain, fulfilling a lifelong dream...

Without pain. A barefaced lie.

The service will be held at the Prague Castle, and the nation is invited to join the procession that will travel to a service organized in the St. Vitus Cathedral, and conclude outside the castle walls, where vendors will provide free food and beverages to celebrate Jakub's life. Arrive early, as the event is expected to become one of the biggest mass gatherings...

...and to go against what I set out to do earlier, I would like, once again, to return to Jakub Procházka the Hero, and remind us all of the famous words of a poet who captured the meaning of the Chopra mission: "With JanHusl *lie our hopes of new sovereignty and*

*prosperity, for we now belong among the explorers of the universe,
the guardians of the frontier. We look away from our past..."*

I handed the tablet over.

"You want to see pictures of funeral?" she asked.

No. Maybe later. How long has it been?

"A week. They are building statue. There are many candles still
in this square, and pictures of you. Paintings."

What is your name?

"Klara. Your fever is coming down. We fear superbacteria. That
is why there is quarantine. But you seem better."

Yes. Better. Why are you here?

She studied something on my forehead. The silence felt long,
even excruciating.

"We are part of phantom program. Have you heard of this?"

Myth, I thought?

"A myth, yes. No one knows exactly how many have died being
shot into Space quietly. At least technology makes odds bigger
now. We are a phantom mission. There was one before us, shortly
after cloud appeared, even before Germans sent the monkey. It was
one-man mission, like yours, and the man—Sergei, I knew him well,
good person—he never returned. And so we come, bigger ship, more
crew, we launched couple of weeks before you but came off course
when Vasily...well, there was the incident. And so we arrive late, after
you, and you were a floating man. I am telling you this because you
have to know, Jakub, that my government will never admit to phantom programs, especially now that we have Chopra dust, we have this
advantage, what world wants. And if we do not exist, then your rescue
does not exist. You do not exist. Do you understand?"

You gathered it? Chopra?

"Yes, we have dust. But do not think of it anymore. You will never
see it."

I looked away. She apologized under her breath and I waved her off. She too was a soldier. Home felt much less certain now. What could the future of a rescued phantom dead man be? Life under surveillance in a Belarusian village? A Russian prison? Would they hold me until the fact of my rescue could somehow be used to political advantage, or until a whistle-blower agile enough to penetrate a century of state-sanctioned lies revealed that the phantom program of the USSR was alive and well, a wild conspiracy theory sure to kill at any cocktail party?

You said incident? With your third?

"Yes, Vasily. He hasn't been himself."

What happened?

She studied the strap on her glove, quiet, frowning.

You don't have to say

"I will tell you because it is nice to talk. These two with me, they will not talk. Do you know what it is like when you speak and no one listens? You do, Jakub. They sent you all on your own, your people. It was three months into our mission. Vasily looked into my bunk, pale, breathing heavy. Yuraj and I, we asked him for two hours, what is wrong? And he said nothing, only drank the milk and looked into distance. And then, finally, he put his hands like this" — she crossed her arms on her chest — "and said, I hear monster. It speaks in darkness, like a dog's growl, and it scratches on walls. And this monster, he said, it spoke inside his head, asked about Earth, asked about Russia. And he just sat, his hands like that, saying like, C'mon, *druz'ya*, you tell me I'm wrong, I won't agree, I know what I heard. We never told him anything, never said, Vasily, you are probably little crazy from Space. Still he always put his hands like that, like we wanted to take the truth away from him. We reported what he said to *tsentr*, but they never told us what they did, if anyone talked to him. And so, after that day, he does research on his own, and he eats his meals on his own, and we are worried, but what can we do? We are tired too. We too can't be taking care of someone's head."

I tapped the pen on my forearm.

A monster

"Yes. A dog's or wolf's growl."

Could I talk to Vasily?

"Maybe if you get better and he agrees to come here. We cannot let you out of room."

How much longer?

"We are expected to be on Earth in three months."

Are you scared?

"Of?"

Going home

She took the pad from my hands and slid it back inside the front pocket of my sleeping bag, then zipped me up to the neck, and rested the forefinger of her glove on my cheek. "You should sleep," she said. "Fever is coming down — maybe we can unstrap you soon, if you promise to not come out to the ship."

She floated away, stopped in the entry, but did not turn around.

"Silence drives us crazy," she said. "But we are afraid we will miss the silence. *Bozhe*, it is hostile up here, but it is easy. Routines and computers and food in plastic. Yes, I wonder, can I ever share life with people again. I think about refilling my car with oil and I want to be sick to my stomach."

She left.

I pulled the cocoon of the sleeping bag over my head so I would not hear the subtle creaks of the ship. Even the most sophisticated structures cannot avoid the sighs of life. Materials copulate, clash, grasp for air. I felt strong, the blood flowing through my extremities, and thus I slept. Once, I caught myself stretching my fingers toward the rabbit's eyes so I could drop them to the quarreling chickens. Rain escaped through holes in the gutter and woke cats snoozing on the bench. The modest sandals of the doppelgänger Jan Hus struck the cobblestone path as he was led to his trial, and he grunted quietly as he was hoisted onto the wooden platform where he was to burn.

I have never been clear on my first memory. It could be one of my father holding me nude on his bare chest, my clumsy hands grabbing at his curled chest hair. But it could also be that this is no real memory at all, that I wish so desperately to remember this moment because of the ragged black-and-white photo my mother kept on her nightstand. My father's jaw was still fleshy with youthful fat, not yet sharpened by age and unfulfilled desires. I knew nothing except this man's warm hands nearly as big as my body, his odor that would one day become mine, the warmth, the light. Is the question of whether I remember this moment more important than the empirical evidence proving it actually happened? I hope the memory is real. I hope the sensation, the phantom of my father holding me that closely, isn't manufactured, but is based in the animalistic instinct of grasping at those moments in which we are protected. The instinct in the animal named Jakub.

I DIDN'T KNOW how long I had slept after the last feeding break when Klara and Yuraj came to unstrap me. Klara told me that three weeks had passed and the quarantine was over. I floated around the room, stretching out my muscles, my joints, smiling at the pleasure of motion. My voice had come back to me, at first a hoarse whisper, then a guttural tone I didn't recognize. My throat still ached whenever I spoke more than one short sentence. I studied Klara, who was no longer cautious around me, only kind. Even Yuraj shot me a quick smile, though he maintained an air of masculine indifference. They had laid out the rules: I'd promise not to leave the room under any circumstances without being accompanied, and in exchange they would uncover the small window. I agreed. When I asked about my future, about their instructions from Russia, they became tight-lipped and irritated, and so I ceased to inquire about the matter altogether. I was too happy to have human companions, to hear language travel through its usual channels, to smell someone else's sweat. We were headed to Earth. I missed Hanuš, more than I could attempt to describe, yet I could not speak of him at all.

Klara seemed to like talking to me, especially now that I was healthy and thus offered no bacterial threat. She would come into my room without her space suit, sometimes with her hair braided, revealing a slender neck I could not avert my eyes from, other times with her hair untamed and frizzed, a lion's mane surrounding her cranium. Eventually, I couldn't prevent thoughts of kissing her slender neck, of zipping the two of us inside my spacebag and feeling the touch of human skin along mine. Perhaps strangely, these thoughts never arrived outside our conversations. Her insights and her memories rekindled the seemingly dead impulses within me, the impulses I had pledged to forever limit to Lenka. I made no indication of my lust to Klara. I wanted her to keep coming back. The simple comfort of her companionship as the dreaded day of our return to Earth approached was worth more than any physical gratification.

"I have been reading about you," she said once over our lunch, "about your father. Not too many things left around the ship to do, so I think, I will know more about our guest."

"Okay."

"Did you love him?"

"Of course," I said. "It's the curse of family."

"I hoped you'd say this. Have you heard of Dasha Sergijovna?"

"I haven't."

"She was my mother. She too was phantom. Is this surprising?"

She wore a sports bra and loose sweatpants, the postworkout sweat staining the smooth edges of her clavicle, belly button, lip line. She seemed as comfortable as a human being could be, and I envied her.

"It is."

"When I was small, the military people told me that she went to be spy at British embassy, and was killed by this imperial diplomat. Three bullets to her back, *bam*, they said, by West. But when I entered the air force, they finally told me some of this truth. A heavy brown file. She was second woman to travel to Space, ever, with another cosmonaut. The space program thought they could make it to moon and back, but this was so far before such things were possible, only one year after Gagarin. The Party was thirsty to do everything before the Americans. And so my mother went up, with this man, and I was told SSP lost hearing two hours into the mission. Probably, they made it to the moon and crashed, or they choked because of oxygen coming out. Either way, this death was quick and like heroes, they said."

"Kind assurance," I said.

The room was hot. A malfunction caused by the Chopra dust that couldn't be fixed, Klara had told me. At night, I would wake, thinking I had a high fever, and at last I was to die. But then Klara would arrive in the morning to deliver breakfast, and I was glad for another day.

"Well," she said, "then this man from ministry of interior fell in love with me, and I suppose I wanted to see how things go. And one evening, after we went to *kino* and he was drunk, he told me that he could get this file in secret for me—a file containing truths. I made love to him that night from the excitement of possibility. I thought my mother's heroism would, at last, take good shape. And so he brought the file, and I read it under candlelight on night when electric went out."

She wasn't looking at me now. She stretched out her fingertips, as if the file still rested there, and she was feeling along its edges.

"And the truth was different," I said.

"Yes. The mission was suicide from beginning. The SSP wanted to see if a new vehicle could make full distance to Mars, unbroken, while keeping life. My mother knew this, the man knew this, and they volunteered, and they kissed their different children good-bye and they went off forever. Two hours into the mission, all is well, and suddenly, her partner starts to speak crazy. He said he could hear God in waves of universe, and he knew the world would end soon. And this God of waves was sending him and my mother to Mars to become new Adam and Eve, to begin again on different planet. He was certain this was their fate. My mother tried to talk with him, the engineers talk to him, even Khrushchev stopped by to tell him some words before complete crisis. But the man would not stop raving, and he was looking at my mother like some beast, and so she took a can opener and she sticked him somewhere, maybe throat, she would not tell *tsentr*, SSP, but they heard the man chok-ing on blood, and so they guessed. After this, my mother spoke of the things she could see. She asked why so many things in whole universe were circles. Planets and stardust and atoms and aster-oids. A softness to so many things. Then she choked to death. They recorded it on manuscripts. She choked so far away from Mars, still so close to Earth. Do you know how they wrote this? For this man she killed, he choked as this: *kchakchakchachchchchch*, and so on. Sudden bursts, like heartbeats, you know. But my mother, hers was more slow: *eghougheghougheghough*. They really paid attention to how many times she did this. Of course, her ship crashed, or per-haps it is still out in universe somewhere, who knows. And that was phantom mission number two."

"But here you are. An astronaut."

"I haven't had to kill a man. Not yet."

"You think of her often."

"I think about what made her go, and what made me go. I decide this brand of madness must be in the blood. Do you ask? I bet what brings you to the sky was same duty as your father's: that final—no, that terminal decision to serve. I find comforting there. The idea of being, I don't know, like there is no choice, you have to be a certain person, the instinct put into DNA. It seems honest."

I imagined Klara's mother, the two of them perfect look-alikes, and her wonder at her crewmate's blood spilling out like soap bubbles. The first murder of the cosmos. Perhaps she killed the man and then anticipated redemption on Mars. An alien creature assuring her, "You did what had to be done."

Wasn't all life a form of phantom being, given its involuntary origin in the womb? No one could guarantee a happy life, a safe life, a life free of violations, external or eternal. Yet we exited birth canals at unsustainable speeds, eager to live, floating away to Mars at the mercy of Spartan technology or living simpler lives on Earth at the mercy of chance. We lived regardless of who observed us, who recorded us, who cared where we went.

"It is hot," I told Klara.

"Yes."

Quietly, we ate.

DURING THE LAST MONTH of our journey, the crew of *NashaSlava1* blessed me with magnificent meals. It turned out that the spaghetti I had initially been fed during my illness was the worst food on board, something they were willing to waste on a potentially dying man. Now that it was clear I would live, they brought different meals every day. General Tso's chicken, borscht, beef stroganoff topped with sour cream, tiramisu, and bacon—that glorious memento of Lenka. These were all microwaved meals, but to a man starved down to nearly two-thirds of his original size, it didn't matter.

Klara explained that these meals were meant as weekly treats for the crew, small interruptions to their otherwise impeccably healthy diets. Since the food reserves were too plentiful for three people and Vasily refused to eat any of the cheat meals, Klara and Yuraj had decided to make the remainder of the mission a celebration of gluttony, and had challenged themselves to empty the reserves as we reached Earth. I was happy to help, so happy that the constant pain of an infected tooth crippling half my face presented no challenge to my newfound appetite—for the food, for the Japanese tea, for the bottles of American bourbon, of Russian vodka, of Japanese beer. I spent the week eating, breathing, and looking out the observation window, making a list of everything I wanted from life. Of everything I felt I was owed.

I wanted to see the hairy belly of my friend one last time, a legless corpse.

I wanted to see God touch the universe, reach his hand through the black curtain and shake the strings on which the planets loom. A proof.

I wanted to witness giant cosmic lovers, two larger-than-life figures holding hands, picnicking on the surface of Mars, in love with craters and barren landscapes. They were so made for each other that they looked exactly alike, their sexes blurred out, indistinct.

I wanted to see Earth crack at its core, split into shards, and confirm my theory—that it is simply too fragile to earn its keep. A proof.

I wanted to see the dead bodies of all phantom astronauts. To bring them back to Earth and keep them embalmed in glass cases inside Lenin's mausoleum.

I wanted Valkyries to soar through dimensions and caress the dead souls of African orphans. I wanted all the mythical beasts the human mind has created to pile on top of one another and fuck and give birth to a hybrid so perverse it would unite us all. I wanted the basic needs of human existence—satiation of hunger, good health, love—to take on the shapes of small fruits we could plant and harvest. But who would be the plantation owners, and who the harvesters? I wanted cosmic dust to gather around clay nests with the aggression of hornets, to breed and evolve and merge and form its own planet occupied by its own humanlike figures driving their own carlike cars. Perhaps if such a world of gray shadows existed— a reflection, a mimicry of the entire human experiment—we could finally watch and learn. A proof.

I wanted someone to tell me they know what they're doing. I wanted someone to claim authority. I wanted to leap into the Vltava and taste its toxicity, to recognize that somewhere along the slush of runoff there was real water. I wanted to live on both sides. I wanted to touch every cube brick on France's roads. I wanted to drink English tea without milk. I wanted to enter the filthiest American diner in the dustiest city and order a burger and a milk shake. The way the word rolls off the tongue—*buRrRgeRrR*. I wanted to lose myself among the suits of New York City and feel cocaine residue on toilet seats. I wanted to hang off the edge of a whale skeleton. I wanted proof of the chaos. I wanted it so badly I didn't want it at all. I wanted what every human wants. For someone to tell me what to choose.

Yes, Lenka was right. I would return as a changed man, she would return as a changed woman. Some parts switched out, our casings the same. Who said these two brand-new humans couldn't love each other?

TWO WEEKS BEFORE the landing, I decided. It was time to discover Vasily. I had avoided him to forget my grief for Hanuš, but I needed to hear about his visions while we were still trapped in the same quarters together. Vasily had abandoned his sleeping chamber, they told me, and had set himself up in one of the ship's three laboratories. Klara no longer visited him; Yuraj made a visit every two days, officially to deliver snacks and mission updates, and unofficially (he'd say in a smiling whisper) to ensure that the "cookie fawk" was still alive. For the past few days, I had been monitoring Klara's and Yuraj's movements, looking for the small but certain overlap in their sleeping habits.

Finally, I had found it. During their nap time I slipped out of my cabin and made my way past their chambers and into the lab corridor, where the Russians (I guessed) studied the cosmic effects on bacteria, and how these mutations could be used in biological warfare. (Whether this was exaggerated Cold War paranoia, understandable distrust of the occupier, or a simple acceptance of the real world, I couldn't be sure. After all, what would my country have done with the Chopra samples? Look for any way to get ahead in the race of nations, or at least sell them to the highest bidder, the most convenient ally, before the spies of the world descended upon Prague's streets to find out for themselves?) I arrived at the last laboratory door, delighted at the comforts of floating freely in Yuraj's sweatpants, which slid off my hips regularly but which I was grateful for nonetheless. Finding the observation window covered and the access panel to the lab smashed, I knocked.

"Ostavit' yego tam," the man inside hollered.

"What?" I said.

"You are not Yuraj," he said in English.

"No. But you are Vasily?"

"Are you him? The dead man?"

I did not respond.

Several anxious minutes passed. I looked toward the entry corridor. Silent, but soon I could be discovered.

At last the door slid open. Behind it was a greased blob of a man, stuffed inside a white tank top and a pair of briefs. His hair had been reduced to a sweat-soaked pierogi at the center of his skull. In his left hand, he held a rigged remote for the door. Bare wires extended from the small box of the control panel to his side. His right hand was wrapped from the tips of his fingers all the way to his shoulder with gauze. His teeth were gray.

He nodded, as if knowing that I could not speak to him until gandering at the sty he had made out of a state-of-the-art research facility. Filthy underwear, microscope lenses, empty ration packets, pencil caps, crumpled pieces of paper, and individual potato chips floated around the room in an odd hoarder ballet, like an art show one might see at the National Museum as yet another condemnation of materialism. An unidentifiable yellow substance stained the lab chair, and the lab computer had been split in two with a hard steel pipe. At first, I thought that the walls were covered in twisted wires, but a closer inspection revealed countless pieces of paper with draw-ings. Every single one of them offered the same subject. A mess of dark shadows connected in a semicircular shape. From these black clouds erupted words written in an insidiously red Cyrillic.

The man, Vasily, uncrossed his arms. "You don't understand," he said quietly.

"I do. You've heard him."

His eyes widened. He grabbed me by the neckline of my shirt, his breath sour upon my chin. "You are the prophet, then," he said, "you. It could have been me, but do you know what I did when the god visited me? I thought it was a demon. I closed my eyes and I prayed him away. I haven't been to the church since my grand-mother died, yet there I was, my eyes closed for hours, and I begged for the god to be gone. Finally, he listened."

Vasily's English was nearly impeccable, only a slight hint of an accent. His bottom lip trembled. He picked at the gauze on his arm, tearing off small pieces and rolling them into balls before putting them on his tongue.

"You saw," I said.

"I did not see. Only heard. Heard a voice from the corners."

"And the voice told you of me."

"He told me to wait for you. The prophet." Vasily caught a potato chip and offered it. I shook my head. With visible disappointment, he returned it to its orbit, then strapped himself into the stained chair. I noticed that the microscope lenses were shattered, and braced myself for the possible glass particles swirling around, waiting to be inhaled.

"One must be lower than the prophet when the prophet is addressed," Vasily said. "The god returned to me again, yes, a few hours before we found you. He said I would not hear him again, no, but he would send a son in his name, and that is you! And he said we must rescue the son. I told Klara we must wait a few more minutes before leaving. We plucked you up, hmm, right before you perished..."

In front of me, then, sat a man who may have truly also known Hanuš, however briefly, the final proof I sought since I met him so long ago. I became immediately impatient with Vasily's tics, his muddled speech.

"He must have told you things about me, then. My name, who I am."

"Hmm, *da*. He did. Did I do good, prophet? I could have been you, you know. But I proved myself not worthy. At least I believe. You believe that I believe, prophet? I will spill blood, if need be."

From the depths of his sweatpants pockets Vasily produced a screwdriver and set it upon his neck. I stroked forward, seizing his wrist just as the tip broke the skin. I took the screwdriver out of Vasily's hand as he observed the tiny spheres of his own blood with childish delight. He poked at them with his finger.

"I need you to tell me everything the god told you about me, Vasily. So I'll know you are truly an apostle."

"Oh, prophet," Vasily said, "you are testing me. I haven't been told of your origins, because I am too lowly to know. I only have my mission. I will deliver you to Earth. And I will tell you the last words the god asked me to pass on to you." Vasily grinned, and now his fingers fully unraveled the gauze on his other hand and wrist, displaying a multitude of deep, infected cuts, wounds that would surely cost Vasily his arm.

I decided. Vasily and others like him were the reason Hanuš could never come to Earth. They couldn't cope with a vastness that was so outside their established knowledge of existence, even if they had seen Space up close. They would project their desperations, fears, and looming insanities onto types of intelligence incomprehensible to them. I had done so too, after all, when I nearly plunged a blade into Hanuš to satisfy my cult of the scientific method, hoped that somewhere within rested an answer to my unrest. I was ashamed.

The thought of hearing Hanuš's words to Vasily exhausted me and thrilled me at the same time. I took a few breaths to avoid impatience with the ill man.

"The god's message," Vasily said. "The prophet must not submit his spirit. He will find happiness in silence, seeking freedom, prayer, and he will know, know more than any other human, or any other... oh, now I am confusing words... the answer is in heaven."

Vasily looked around with panic, stuck his hands in his pockets, and from the ugly, twisted grimace on his face, I deduced he was looking for another weapon to hurt himself with. I asked him to keep his arms down. Hanuš would never have spoken of prayers, of prophets, certainly not of heaven. The hint of kinship I had felt with Vasily left me. He was a madman. I was not. I couldn't be.

I felt anger toward this man. He had been given a mission the same as me, and he had failed to retain his sanity, despite the luxuries of his ship and the benefit of other human company.

Or had I once been close to becoming Vasily? Had Hanuš saved me from this exact madness? Suddenly, mercy seemed necessary.

"Apostle," I said to Vasily, "you've done perfectly. You passed the test."

Vasily sobbed like a small boy, his hand on mine. "Now I get to go home," he said. "Take me from here now. It is too quiet. I miss the hum of mosquitoes above the lake."

I was glad. He didn't know Hanuš, I was the only human who'd ever truly know this cosmic secret. I did not want to share it.

He unstrapped himself and pushed me aside, leaping toward his sketch collection, and ripped off the page closest to him. He opened his mouth wide, crumpled the paper, and stuffed it inside. He chewed, swallowed, and stuck out his tongue to show me there was nothing left. He picked up the next page and did the same, occasionally murmuring, "It should have been me, the prophet."

Klara appeared in the door, just as Vasily consumed his last sketch. "You are bleeding," she said.

"A nonbeliever may not enter the shrine!" Vasily yelled, shooing Klara away with his hands. She gestured for me to follow. As I floated toward her, Vasily grabbed at my hand and kissed my knuckles, my fingertips, and I was too sick to speak, to look at the beastly grimace on the apostle's face. We exited his lair, the door slamming behind us. Klara crossed her arms.

"I'm sorry," I said, "I know I shouldn't—"

"I told you the man was not well," she said sternly.

"I had to hear about the—"

"His monsters? No, Jakub. You will stay inside your room from now. You never exit, only to use bathroom with permission. And if I find you out again, I will strap you to the wall and I will let you starve until Earth. Yes?"

I returned to my holding room. Vasily's words crawled through my ears, spun around the cranium. No, he couldn't have known Hanuš. Or did Hanuš appear and speak to Vasily, the former church boy, in a language he knew would have a real effect on a God-fearing man? I didn't want to believe it. Hanuš was mine.

FOR THE FIRST TIME since I boarded *NashaSlava1*, I could not rest. Klara came to me ten days before our estimated arrival on Earth. She said she had some things to tell me. First, she had sent a message to *tsentr* after seeing on her own the horrific state of Vasily's body and living quarters. She received a message back that Vasily was to be left alone unless he posed immediate danger to the crew or the ship. He was part of a separate mission ordered by the interior to study the effects of spaceflight on certain mental health issues.

I asked Klara why she would tell me this.

"Because I am tired of despicable men who rule empires," she said, "and because as soon as I return to Earth, I will move West and never think of this again. And because of the last thing I have to tell you. A friend of mine from *tsentral* told me what they will do with you. She said you will go to Zal Ozhidaniya. It is a place for special political prisoner, people who used to be spies, those sorts. And I feel responsible for this. Jakub, I want you to know, I have to bring you, I have to give you to them, but we are friends, still. I trust you. I want you to know this before they take you away. I would do something if I could, I swear."

"Will you kiss me on the cheek?" I said.

"Jakub."

"It doesn't mean anything. I just have not felt it in so long. I want to remember it."

Klara kissed my cheek, right next to my lips, and for a moment the dread of her revelation didn't matter. I asked her to leave before the elation expired.

* * *

I SPENT THOSE last two weeks on the ship hiding from the Russians, staying in my cabin and asking Klara to leave me alone. She said she understood. I pondered what life in a luxury political prison was like, how I would bear never seeing my country or Lenka again. The things I might have to do to free myself. Before we initiated the approach protocols inside the landing chamber, Yuraj wanted to strap me down, but Klara convinced him not to. She repeated that I could be trusted.

The universe deceives us with its peace. This is not a poetic abstraction or an attempt at twopenny wisdom—it is a physical fact. The four layers of Earth's atmosphere rest in their respective places like a four-headed Cerberus, guarding our precious skins from the solar poison thrown in our direction every second of each day. They are stoic guardians, as invisible as they are unappreciated by everyday thought.

As we prepared for reentry, I sat next to Vasily, who filled out a crossword on his tablet and paid no mind to our shuttle burning swiftly toward Earth. Klara and Yuraj sat in the front and handled the controls while speaking cheerfully in Russian to their mission command. As the shuttle flipped onto its belly, I looked out the deck window to see for the last time what we officially classify as outer space: the final frontier until a new frontier beyond it is discovered. It stared back, as always, with its insistent flickering, emptiness, lack of understanding for me or the necessity of my being.

We burned at a temperature of 1649 degrees Celsius, pushed through the mesosphere, the graveyard of dead stars and Earth's shield against rogue meteors, with the nose of the shuttle angled up. The air was too slow to clear our path in time and thus eased our fall. With the engines disabled the ship was now more of a sophisticated hang glider, using Earth's physics to slice through the atmosphere faster than the speed of sound. Deep below us, somewhere in

Moscow, or perhaps in the surrounding towns, a handful of people were bound to hear the sonic boom, two claps less than a second apart, the drumroll announcing our return. They would dismiss it as construction noise and move on with their day, placated by the silence of their media stations, their government. The pronounced *S* momentarily disrupting their skyline view—the unavoidable signature of the phantom astronauts—would be simply another weather anomaly ignored during a workday.

For 130 kilometers, we fell. The mesosphere—the protector. The stratosphere—eerie, calm, stable, and dry, the place without climate. A purgatory, occupying the properties of Space and yet a part of Earth. A deceptive non-world, a no-man's-land between the trenches. Then the troposphere, the last line of defense, from the Greek *tropos*, signifying change. The keeper of the world's water vapors and aerosols, a place of chaos, rising pressures, weather patterns. Perfect as the layer closest to human contact. Humanity summarized in a single sphere.

The Earth rested. There was no sign of the billions of volatile souls thrumming on its surface. We were so close to its oceans, its continents that contained the country that contained the city that contained the hospital in which I had entered this world, nude and small. The hospital now torn down and replaced by the offices of a snack machine manufacturer. Would I ever get to visit the place again, see the patch of dirt on which I had come to be?

The vision of my future life entered around my spine and made its way through the lower intestine, abdomen, lungs, and throat. Like a shot of bourbon traveling backwards. A Russian hostage, a man reduced to a state secret. And if I were, eventually, to return to my own country, what kind of life would await me? Dissected, intruded upon, loud. No peace in sight, no peace at all to continue my serene life with Lenka. I made eye contact with Vasily. He knew.

I couldn't accept it. If I made it back to Earth, I had to be a free man. It had all been taken away. Personhood, physical health, perhaps my sanity. I didn't know what happened to my wife. No further infringements would happen, at least not with my permission. Vasily's god had advised me. I wouldn't be a subject to Russian whims.

I unstrapped myself and jumped at the controls, shoved away Klara's arms, and activated one of the ship's engines. *NashaSlava1* turned and leaped, like a gazelle with a thigh torn to pieces by predatory teeth. I fell backwards onto the ceiling. Klara shouted, Yuraj unstrapped himself and dropped onto me, then wrapped his forearm and elbow around my neck with staggering efficiency, bound not just to pacify me but to kill me, grunting with frustration pent up during these months of isolation. I flailed my arms; life had begun to leave me, when suddenly more weight landed upon us. All I could see was torn gauze and Vasily's fists beating at the back of Yuraj's head.

"...*avariya posadka, ya povtoryayu...*" Klara shouted into her microphone, and I wanted to shout in turn, *I'm sorry, but how did you expect me to sit and wait?*

Blood poured into my eye and I was no longer weighed down. Yuraj had released me, and off to my right he screamed and pawed at his neck as Vasily spit out a piece of skin and meat. He had struck a major artery, and Yuraj's blood was pouring out heavily.

"The prophet will live," Vasily said. "I am the apostle."

The body must not be violated! I wanted to shout at Vasily, but it was too late. I had done this. It had to be finished.

The ship flipped back onto its belly, and Vasily and I crashed into the seats. Something cracked within Vasily's body, but he made no verbal indication of pain. Yuraj, barely breathing, was bleeding to death.

Klara looked back while holding the yoke with both hands, veins cutting through her forearm muscles as she tried to steady it. "Jakub," she said, as though she didn't know to whom the name belonged. She had gotten to know and trust a fellow phantom but she couldn't have guessed how much I wanted to come back home. I longed for the moment we had first sat over a meal together, the way I'd studied the sweat drops on her body and the way she'd pretended to ignore it. When we had thought only the best of each other.

Again I leaped toward the controls, beat at the keys, the screen, the panels, with my fists and cheeks and elbows. Klara dug her fingernails into any exposed piece of flesh she could reach, but she refused to unstrap herself, this genetically determined phantom astronaut trained for mission in the womb, and so I had a free rein. Once again *NashaSlava1* spun around, and again, and through the glass whirled those green fields of Russia, towns separated by hundreds of square miles of agriculture and nothingness.

Klara's fingers found their way into my mouth and she grabbed my tongue, eager to rip it out.

Vasily slapped her hand away from behind, his bloody teeth ready to strike again, and I shouted, "No, apostle, enough!"

He retreated back to appraise Yuraj, who was pale and barely moving. Vasily caressed Yuraj's cheeks, whispering, "You too could have heard the god."

I screamed at Klara to slow us down, pouring forth apologies and pleas and epithets. Earth's surface was so close now that we would collide at high speed, surely killing us all. I recognized the shimmering blues of water, even as I felt Klara's knuckles upon my back and forehead and eyes. She had finally unstrapped herself and was now unleashing her fury, perhaps in an effort to kill me before the landing killed us all. We collided.

The ship crashed into the water and the window glass exploded, its particles biting into my exposed face before the onrush of water washed them away. My body was at the mercy of Earth's elements now, much more savage than the calculating hostility of Space. The stream threw me against the cabin door, and Vasily landed on me,

grasping at my arms as the entire cabin flooded and the water separated us. I swam toward the window, toward life, then gestured
at Vasily to follow. I gave Yuraj, pale and unconscious and possibly dead, a final acknowledging look, and grabbed Klara's arm to
haul her up. She clawed at me and bit my hand, bubbles escaping
her nostrils, and I noticed that her arm was trapped underneath
the seat, which had been slammed against the wall by the pressure of the water. Her elbow was oddly twisted, surely dislocated,
perhaps broken, but Klara gave no sign of pain. Her eyes—deadly,
determined—were focused on mine. She was doing her best to kill
me with her one free hand and her teeth. I could not last much longer. I let go of her and searched for Vasily, who floated above Yuraj's
corpse, grinning from ear to ear, his apostle mission fulfilled. No,
he was not coming, and perhaps it was better. A broken man had a
right to leave this world. I too had made that decision once.

Again I tugged at Klara's arm, and she sank her teeth so deeply
into my thumb I thought she would rip it off. I could feel her teeth
breaking. I pulled back, freed my bleeding flesh, and swam out of
the observation window, swam upwards along the capsizing body
of a ship that had saved me. *NashaSlava1*, the pride of the Russian
people, though the Russian people weren't aware of its existence—a
phantom looming above their heads, protecting them from enemies,
delivering scientific glory and advanced warfare. A cumbrous blend
of metals designed to enhance humanity with an inflated sense of
importance, wisdom, and progress, but now subject to Earth's judg-
ment, as we all were, and drowning like a bag of unwanted felines.

When I emerged, I threw my arms about, swam so quickly I
thought my veins were going to pop open and bleed dry. I reached
land, dragged myself onto the shore, spit and coughed, grabbed at
the cold moist dirt under me, and I remembered—Earth. I licked
the mud. I kissed it, cackled, emitted sounds that terrified me, sounds
of pleasure that went beyond my comprehension, the pleasure of

insanity. At last the pain of the winter around me overcame the initial adrenaline, and Russia's frost bit into the skin underneath my soaked clothes. I rubbed my body in the dirt, now fully understanding why Louda the pig considered mud digging the highest form of living. The friction warmed me and I bit at the chunks of mud as if it were cake. It tasted of roots, compost, vegetable skins. I spit it back out. Behind me the lake that had welcomed me home expanded across a wide plain until it met a brown forest covering the horizon.

The broken surface of the icy lake gargled as the ship was digested along with the bodies and the samples of cloud Chopra, which now seemed a banal prize of the mission. I wished to sit and wait for Klara, Vasily, and Yuraj to emerge, healthy and well, before running around the frozen grassland and making my way through the woods. But the response team would swarm the lake any minute now, and I could no longer be subject to larger schemes, concepts, countries. I ran and I spit out leftovers of mud and I wept, wept for Klara, my savior, for her thirst to claw the life out of me. I expected at any moment the sound of helicopters, German shepherds, sirens speeding along the plains, chasing me down to throw me into a Saint Petersburg catacomb for torture and starvation. But there were no rotors, no barks. I reached the forest to the sinister silence of nature.

By nightfall, I had reached a village. I could not understand anyone's words, but they took me in, bathed me with water heated over a fire, clothed me, and put me into a reasonably soft bed. *Spasibo*, I kept saying, *spasibo*, calmly and generously, hoping this would prevent the villagers from thinking I was insane.

Outside, the night sky glowed with purple. Chopra was still alive, still tantalizing, but I would never again reach it. I longed for the black skies of old.

I woke in the middle of the night, held down by strong hands, with the taste of rusty metal in my mouth. I could not close it, or bite down. A pair of pliers shimmered in the dark. The pincer clamped firmly on my tooth and out it came, the blood pouring into my throat as this kind, crude dentistry was completed. The brown, puss-filled bastard was set next to my face like a trophy. I screamed, choking on the mixture of blood and liquor applied to my wound.

The next morning, I found a couple of men who spoke English. They were traveling to Estonia with sensitive cargo, they said. They could take me along if I promised to help guard their livelihood. I agreed.

The journey was rigidly scheduled, allowing for no breaks. We pissed into a bucket nailed down in a corner of the truck's cargo space. When Russian soldiers stopped us looking for a "dangerous fugitive," I hid under blankets and behind a mountain of Spam and bean cans containing twenty kilos of heroin. The driver gave the Russian lieutenant half a kilo of heroin for his trouble and oversight. We continued on.

Across the border, in Estonia, I shook hands with my accomplices. We were brothers now.

"I owe you," I said.

"No need," they said, "no need."

In Estonia, I jumped a freight train and rode to the coastal city of Pärnu. When night watchmen discovered me, I ran from the dogs snapping at my heels. With a painful bite on my unscarred calf, I entered the port and roamed from ship to ship, asking the sailors for a job, any job, which would take me closer to home. On my sixth attempt, a gangly Pole laughed wheezily and advised me that the captain was looking for someone to clean the bathrooms. The captain was a very clean man, he said. He couldn't stand the crew's crimes upon the ship's facilities, and would accept anyone willing to keep them presentable.

For weeks, I spent my days running among the three bathrooms, scrubbing each seat, each bowl. I bleached them and scrubbed them with such dedication I sometimes wished to lick them to prove my diligence, my commitment to the cause. I replaced soap and I provided oversized rolls of rough toilet paper. Some nights, the sailors got too drunk during their card games and their liquids and solids missed the bowls by miles. These were my emergency calls, apologetic voices waking me from uneasy sleep. I welcomed them. I had a purpose here. A simple one.

When we arrived in Poland, the gangly Pole offered to pay for my train ticket if I would keep him company until we reached Kraków. He spoke of his mother, who would welcome him with homemade smoked pork and garlic potatoes. He in turn would greet her with a surprise belated birthday gift he had saved up for with his wages—a new mattress and a certificate for weekly massages for her bad back. That's all he'd ever wanted to do, he said. Make enough money to ease his mother's life.

When he asked about my family, I asked if we could play some cards. He understood.

That night in Kraków, I flagged down a man with a pox-scarred face. He smelled of smoke and cheese puffs, but he was fond of reading philosophy and had published some poetry.

"It inspires you, the road," he said. "In life, you should travel as far as you possibly can, get away from everything you were ever taught. What do you think?" And he coughed, the same smoker's roar as my grandfather.

"What if everything you love is right where you are?" I asked.

"Then you find new things to love. A happy person must be a nomad."

"You haven't loved, then," I countered. "If what you love gets away from you, in the end you are only walking in a labyrinth with no exits."

Within six hours, we had arrived in Prague. The man offered no parting words, but he gave me the gift of intoxication. I drank his

Staropramen. The sun rose. I tipped the bottle three times, splashing brew upon the ground. An offer for the dead.

I walked into a phone booth and searched for Petr's name in the book chained to a broken telephone. That Petr resided in Zličín was the one personal detail I knew about him. Thankfully he was the only Petr Koukal in the city. I walked.

A tall brunette with a Ukrainian accent and gauged ears opened the door of a small but beautiful house. She told me that her husband was at the pub, *of course*. So Petr had a wife. I smiled at the long-awaited pleasure of resolving one of his mysteries. He knew what Lenka meant to me, after all.

I found him playing Mariáš with a group of old-timers, all of them collecting empty shot glasses and pints around the mess of cards. His beard was overgrown and resembled a rusted wire brush. He'd gotten a few more tattoos, and there was a hole in his T-shirt around the armpit.

When he saw me, he dropped his cards and tilted his head sideways. I quietly counted and at around the twelfth second he pointed at me and said to his Mariáš foes, "That man. Is he there?"

The men looked at me, then at Petr. He extinguished his cigarette and stumbled backwards as he stood. The men reached out to support him, but he waved them away. They groaned and grabbed at him, asking him to keep playing, but Petr no longer saw them. He put his arm around my shoulders carefully, as if expecting his hand to pass through me.

"This guy?" a toothless man said as he nudged me with his elbow.

In the silence, the man sized me up, as if now in doubt himself. He wiped the beer foam from his whiskers.

"Yeah," he said at last. "I'll say he's there."

No Penelope

THE STORY I GAVE Petr took the length of four pints of pilsner.

"You know when you wake up," he said, "and the second before opening your eyes you think you're somewhere else? In an old childhood bedroom, or inside a camp tent. And then you look around, and for a moment you don't remember which life you're living."

"That's very poetic for an engineer."

"Jakub. That's your voice."

"You recognized me. No one else seems to. I don't recognize myself."

"I've been seeing you everywhere. You can't be here. I must be hallucinating. Dreaming, maybe. But it's nice. It's nice to be with you again."

I did not mention Hanuš, my encounter with the core, how I had landed and found my way home. I told him that I had stepped into the vacuum to die honorably on the frontier and that a crew of Russian phantoms had saved me as I choked. He intuited that I was omitting things but understood he had no right to ask. By the time we returned to his house, his wife had gone to work. Petr told me he had retired early and was now making a record with his heavy metal band while his severance from the SPCR and his wife's work paid the bills. In the bathroom I shaved my neck and trimmed my beard, careful not to touch the spot where the infected wound of my former tooth rested on the side of my cheek. When I emerged and walked into the living room, I saw no reason to wait any longer. I asked about Lenka.

"Another beer?" he asked.

"No, thanks. Where is she now?"

Petr sat down and pulled a joint from underneath the couch cushion. He lit it with a burning candle. "I'm not sure if you're ready."

I slapped the cannabis out of his hand. "What the fuck does that mean?"

"I have something you need to hear. Don't ask about Lenka until you do."

I nodded, and Petr walked away. The joint was burning a hole in the carpet. I considered letting it turn into a full flame. I extinguished it with my shoe.

When Petr came back, he was holding a silver USB drive and a stack of disconnected pages. He handed them over.

"Listen to this. Then read the manuscript. I found these when I was clearing out the offices. Kuřák held sessions with Lenka. She needed someone to talk to, and didn't want you to know. Maybe these will have what you need."

I held the drive between my fingertips. It was light, too light for what it held. The manuscript pages were supposedly an early draft of Dr. Kuřák's biography of Jakub Procházka. So the man would make his fame as planned. Petr gestured me into a den, where a laptop rested next to a guitar and a piano.

"Have you listened to this?" I asked.

"Yes," Petr said. "I couldn't resist. I'm sorry. Take your time."

Four hours' worth of sound files. As I listened through earphones, Petr brought me a glass of water and a bowl of ramen soup. He touched my shoulder as if I might disappear, then lingered in the doorway. I heard him strum an acoustic in the next room. Outside, the sun was setting.

After these four hours, I ejected the USB drive. I walked into the bathroom and washed my face, ran my fingers through the wiry, curled hairs of my beard, the dry skin underneath. My eye sockets seemed hollow, detached from their mooring, as if my eyes were eager to retract and hide inside my skull. My lips were the color of vegetable oil, chapping in the middle. I had come too close to death ever to look young again. But there was something about the way my cheekbones protruded, creating lines I hadn't seen before. There was something about their color, how the faded sunburn from my spacewalk had left behind a healthy hint of brown, which seemed somehow fitting on my otherwise pale skin. Whatever form I now occupied, I could grow to like it. I threw the flash drive in the toilet and I flushed.

"I'm so sorry," Petr said. "I deserve the punishment, we failed you, we failed the mission, but I still have to ask that maybe you don't bring the whole story to the media."

"Petr," I said, "don't you understand? I don't care. I just want my old life back."

Excerpt from interview of subject Lenka P., Session One:

Kuřák: So these concerns, they came to you only after the mission started? Or did you feel this contempt before Jakub left?

Lenka P: I tried not to think about it too much. He was getting sick all the time, you know? I could tell how happy and how horrified he was. I could tell how badly he wanted to leave a piece of himself with me. There was no room for me to feel contempt. But once he was gone...people become abstractions. And the things weighing on you become clear. That's why people are so afraid to be away from each other, I think. The truth begins to creep in. And the truth is, I have been unhappy for a while now. Because of his expectation that we have a family, because of the guilt he carries around, because his life was always in focus more than mine. My struggles, my insecurities, they had always been mostly on the back burner. The project of our marriage has predominantly been to figure out Jakub. But I digress.

Kuřák: Tell me more.

Lenka P: Aren't your questions supposed to guide me better than that?

Kuřák: Is this session irritating you?

Lenka P: I'm irritated about feeling these things. And I hate that I've agreed to these meetings. He would consider it a betrayal.

Kuřák: His contract bars both of you from seeking unapproved psychological help. He would understand that this is your only option…

Lenka P: Can I tell you something? Maybe it will make sense to your analytical mind, somehow. Jakub and I, we used to have this hiding place. A small attic in a building where I lived as a kid. It looks so different now than it did the last time Jakub and I came there. It used to be an old, dusty, mice-infested dump, you know? It was our dump, covered in fake stars and condom wrappers. Now, it's a room where the residents hang their laundry. The walls are painted mint green, there's a plastic window. To see if there was anything left behind, something I could collect and hold on to, I tore through the wet towels and sheets of the room, tore my way to our corner, and then I saw them. The first girl, in a bomber cap and shorts and a leopard-print shirt, holding a Polaroid camera. Haven't seen one of those in forever. A few feet away from her, leaning against the wall, was another girl, completely nude, her back against the wall, hips sticking out. At their feet were hundreds, maybe thousands of pictures, all of them of this nude girl in different positions. I had so many questions, but I asked none. What I knew right away was that the girls were lovers, and this was their contract. They had a hiding place, a place of their own, where they explored their rituals. Tell me, can't you recognize these contracts as soon as you see them? A man pours more wine for his wife than for himself. A contract. Lovers watch Friday night movies in the nude with containers of Chinese food on their laps, General Tso's sauce dripping on their pubic hair, they cool each other's bodies with bottles of beer. A ritual, a contract. Jakub and I spoke of these contracts often, the importance of their preservation.

Kuřák: You feel that there has been a violation.

Lenka P: It took me ten minutes after I left those girls to realize that the nude girl was Petra, the girl I used to play with in the attic as a child. And there she was, probably didn't even recognize me, and yet she made me realize. Jakub and I, our contract declared that we were meant to knock around this world together, explore it, make it better or ruin it, live young for as long as we could. But then he left, and now every minute of my day I expect the call to let me know he is gone. Even if he returns, what kind of man will he be? The things he's seeing, the loneliness, the sickness...you see, Jakub chose to become forever someone else. That is his right as a person, but it does not bode well for contracts. He's the one flying away from me, but sometimes? Sometimes it feels like I'm in a spaceship too, and I'm soaring in the opposite direction. And there's no chance we will ever collide again, not unless the universe is a loop, and that, Dr. Kuřák, is why I wake up standing next to my bed, arms limp by my sides. Like some sleepwalker of grief.

Kuřák: What would Jakub say of these contracts?

Lenka P: I don't think Jakub has any idea. He thinks he's going to come home to the same Lenka, the old Lenka, and he will be the same Jakub, and we'll pick up where we left off, like those eight months aren't very long. But it isn't the time, it's the distance, the likelihood of failure, the danger he's put himself in. I'm no Penelope. I don't want to wait around for a hero's return. I don't want the life of a woman in epic poetry, looking pretty as I stand on shore and scan the horizon for his ship once he's finished conquering. Perhaps I sound awful. But what about my life, my hopes for myself? They can't all be tied to Jakub. They just can't.

Kuřák: I don't think you're selfish.

Lenka P: I appreciate that.

Kuřák: Do you consider Jakub an idealist?

Lenka P: Jesus Christ, what a question. He's flying a spaceship to nowhere. What else would you call a man who does such a thing?

[END]

THAT EVENING, after I had listened to Lenka tell her truths to Dr. Kuřák, I determined that I must stay dead, hidden from the shocked, warm embrace of a nation that had built me statues and would surely smother me with cries of miracles. I had died for the country. They had no right to ask me for a resurrection. I discussed this with Petr until I unwittingly slipped out of consciousness. The next morning, I woke up with a pillow underneath my head. Petr and his wife, Linda, stood over me with mugs of coffee and a plan. It was clear that Linda now understood the identity of her guest, and that the plan was a team effort born of their sleepless night.

Petr insisted that my body was devastated by zero gravity and in need of healing. He noted my swollen cheek, the result of my crudely extracted tooth. He noted my blocked sinuses and my slight limp. He explained that approximately 12 percent of my bone mass had vanished due to spaceflight osteopenia and that without therapy, I was looking at a lifetime of excruciating knee pain. Stomachaches, gas, gums swollen with gingivitis. I imagined those emaciated bones carrying my pounds of organs, flesh, and skin like an overloaded mule climbing a mountain.

And so they convinced me. I would spend three weeks in Carlsbad, Bohemia's famous town of healing, dip myself into the hot springs, and drink mineral water. I would lift weights to rebuild bone density, wearing Petr's borrowed gray sweat clothes, whose elastic band had worn thin from an indeterminable amount of time holding in his girth. I would also submit to the dentist's tools to rid me of infection, and I would let Petr drive over once a week and provide me with physical examinations. Petr assured me that no one was going to recognize me. It was because people don't think of dead men as physical bodies, he said, but glorified concepts. Aside from that, I knew that no man, woman, or child could confuse my transformed cheekbones and sagging eyes with the fresh-faced hero of posters and television screens. After these three weeks, Petr promised, he would take me to Lenka himself, if that was what I wanted.

When he dropped me off, Petr handed me a bag with eighty thousand crowns in it. Part of his severance package from the SPCR. I did not think about rejecting it for a single second. I was owed.

DURING HIS RULE in the fourteenth century, Holy Roman Emperor Charles IV blew off steam after a day's work by hunting on horseback around the Ore Mountains. One day, his pack discovered a hot spring flowing from the earth, a miracle sent by God to heal the emperor's injured leg. Charles IV experienced instant relief after dipping his majestic limb into the spring, and declared that it possessed divine healing powers. He granted city privileges to the settlements surrounding the springs and this new town was named

Carlsbad, after its beloved founder. As the town grew, renowned physicians from around the world published papers about the effects of the spring, and by the nineteenth century, Carlsbad had seen the likes of Mozart, Gogol, and Freud. To build a proper social playground for these celebrities, architectural behemoths in the style of art nouveau were constructed around Carlsbad's trees and fountains, turning the town into a man-made Eden if ever there was one. Colonnades, hot springs, parks named after rulers and composers, buildings with curves and edges so delicate only the devil himself could have carved them. And silence. The silence of serenity, the silence of human beings too content to speak.

My room in Carlsbad wasn't much bigger than the lounge area of *JanHus1*. By all standards, it was sufficient for a dead man. Its rough gray carpet itched my feet and there was a chair that smelled of chlorine and a table that creaked constantly for no apparent reason. The bed was magnificent just as fresh food was magnificent, just as humans walking around without a care were magnificent, their sheer existence a wonder for my starved senses. I ate all of my meals in this bed and shook the crumbs from the sheet out of the window before smoking a cigarette. Yes, since the pox-scarred driver had given me one of his menthols, I had taken up smoking. I hated the smell of cigarettes, the taste, even the smoke I found aesthetically overrated, but I chain-smoked regardless in an effort to form a habit, to build a structure for my lonely days. I woke at nine in the morning sharp with a prebreakfast nicotine craving and I smoked my last stick around midnight, right after ingesting sleeping pills. Tobacco was a timekeeper, the tuner of my biological clock. A friend.

Every morning at ten, I had my physical therapy. A kind-eyed woman named Valerie helped me submerge in a blue tub filled with hot mineral water. During our first session, she asked me where I came from, whether I was married. Prague, I said. I didn't answer the second question. She got the implication of my brief answers and began talking about herself instead. Her father used to work in a factory that manufactured weapons for the Nazis. Near the end of the war, he and a few other workers decided to sabotage the guns — to damage magazine springs so the ammo wouldn't feed, or to pack the ammo with too much powder in order to cause explosions and the loss of fingers. The inspector, a German, was a drunk, always loaded on slivovitz during his shifts, and it was easy to distract him enough for the weapons to pass through undetected. By the time these weapons were put into circulation, the Germans were retreating, and Valerie's father never found out whether his rebellion had much of an effect. But he would walk around town for the rest of his life, chest puffed out, receiving free beer in exchange for his story of great sabotage, cutting those magazine springs with pliers, slicing his hands, bleeding with pride over those fascist tools of murder.

"My father never did anything else after that," Valerie said. "Mostly, he became a drunk. But a man only needs one thing to be proud of. It will carry him through the rest of his life."

Once, she ran her hand over the burn scar on my calf. She asked how it had happened.

"My father is responsible," I said.

"Hmm," she answered.

DURING THE SECOND WEEK of my stay in Carlsbad, Petr took me to a dentist's office. A woman wearing a white mask set a tube over my mouth. The gas was dense and sweet, like kettle corn in Wenceslas Square during a hot summer. I didn't feel the tools scraping the rot away. I woke up expecting pain, but all I could feel was a gap, another piece of my body gone. "It's done," the woman reassured me. I consumed a pill the size of a locust.

Back in my room, I woke to a strange scratching coming from the air-conditioning vent. It began with hesitance, a creature feeling its way around a new environment. After a few minutes, the scratching gained a rhythm—*shka shka shkashka shka shkashka*—the rhythm of work that some small rodent figured would bring it to freedom. Consistency. Work without interruption, work with intensity. Surely, working at a steady peace, without breaks, the creature could reach its goal. I listened to my companion, refusing to take away its dignity by opening the vent. It took twenty minutes for the rhythm to reach its climax—*shkakakakashkakakakashkakakaka*, now with true desperation, as the rodent beat at the world to convince it of its worth, not a plea but a demand: *Hear me! Let me out! I am here!* I decided it was time for relief for the both of us, and when I stood up I saw a small brown nose peeking through the bars, two black eyes fixed on mine. I unscrewed the cover with a coin. When I opened it, a small tail was peeking from a dark corner deep in the shaft. It was hiding from me. It would not be rescued. I tried to reach the tail without any luck. I sat on my bed with the vent uncovered for an hour, waiting for my new friend to come out. It didn't. I put the cover back on, and while I was fastening the last screw, the nose appeared again, followed by the laborious scratching. *Work will save me. Diligent, patient, never-ending. It must.*

I put a coat on and walked outside.

A yellow hue spilling from the windows of a hotel facing the Smetana Park spread across the last bits of dried, frozen oak leaves paving the road. The fountain ahead glowed red, which made the statue of a nude woman pouring water from a vase seem mischievous, in cahoots with the devil. I removed my shoes and stepped into the grass, then leaned on the fountain and massaged my right knee, observing the lightless sky, which an upcoming storm appeared to have coated in tar, masking even the effect of Chopra. I was grateful for the darkness. Stars didn't seem the same anymore—to me they did not invite fantasies, did not symbolize aspiration, did not arouse curiosity. They were dead images of things for which I had no use.

Inside the fountain, a black, sleek thing splashed around. It seemed too large to be a snake or a cat. The red lights dimmed. I looked closer, reached toward the swimmer, and then he rose, lifted himself on eight bamboo legs and extended a pair of human lips toward the naked woman's vase, lapping up the cascading water without giving me a single glance with his many eyes.

"Hanuš," I said.

He did not respond. He drank, coughed, spit, and drank some more with suckling greed. I stepped into the fountain, and the cold water soaked through my jeans. I reached for Hanuš, but before I could touch him, the statue came to life. Above us stood Lenka, her firm calves attached to the fountain. Her hair was tied into thick braids. My Lenka, she looked like a Bohemian queen. I touched the soft flesh of her calf, no longer interested in Hanuš, and a sharp pain stiffened my knees and knocked me backwards. I was submerged, and for a moment I wasn't sure which way was up, the surface, the light, and which way was down, the depths, the darkness. The water stung my nose and eyes and at last I found my bearings and lifted myself up. I was alone in the fountain, alone with the statue. The stream of water from her vase landed on my chest and I lowered myself to have a drink. It tasted of copper, or maybe zinc. It tasted of things that weren't alive. I wanted her so badly.

When I returned to my room, the mouse was on my bed. The air-conditioning vent was undamaged. The creature studied me, ready to leap. I went to the minifridge to get a Kolonada wafer for it, but when I returned, the mouse was gone. Had it stayed around to thank me for helping, or to emphasize it didn't need help—*see? I can take care of myself.* There had been an escape route for the mouse the whole time. The vent was simply another obstacle to be over-come for the sake of overcoming. I ate the wafer, its hazelnut flavor melting on my tongue. We could make such great things. Smooth liquors, wafers melting on touch, statues so close to life.

The idea of Lenka's calf, the feel of its skin, guided my hand below my waist. My body did not respond. I massaged, caressed, but the sensation was mechanical, devoid of pleasure. Desires used to come to me so easily.

Failing to achieve a climax, I stopped. My ear itched, something moved around my eardrum. I stuck my index finger inside and fished at the speck of dust bothering me. When I took my finger out, a small black creature hopped off onto the carpet. This was no dust. I leaped, upending the television set as the Goromped escaped my thumb, then I grabbed the carpet and hurled it into the air, my eyes locked on the small black dot bouncing up and falling back down. I caught it as it struck my cheek, held it between thumb and middle finger. My first instinct was to squeeze, to squash the beast and wash it off my hand with soap, but its outer shell was as hard and sleek as a stone. It gnawed at my friction ridges with its miniature teeth, and wriggled its legs to free itself. I seized an empty preserves jar and dropped the Goromped inside, then secured the lid as the creature jolted up and down, up and down at a frantic speed, its force almost tipping the jar over. I put a heavy book on top. Now there was nothing but tapping.

"I got you, you maleficent fuck. I got you."

I gathered the pieces of the old television. Inside the jar, the Goromped spun like a helicopter rotor, emitting a mild whistle reminiscent of wind blowing through a small alley.

"Clever. Momentum theory won't help," I said. "You are mine."

On and on through the room's darkness and cold, the Goromped spun without pause.

EXCERPT FROM INTERVIEW *of subject Lenka P., Session Four:*

Kuřák: You sounded very urgent on the phone. Would you like to tell me about the incident?

Lenka P: It's not much of an incident. A freak-out, rather. It was
when the *Lifestyle* magazine people came over. They took pictures of me sitting on the couch all by myself. They asked me
how I was coping with the waiting. Whether I still slept only
on one side of the bed. There was something about their questions that suggested I wasn't whole, like they were interview-
ing a person who had half of their body removed. They want
to sniff out my rituals of loneliness and parade them out for
the world. I just don't want to do it anymore. I want to...this
is awful to say, but I just want to be separate, from the mission,
from Jakub's fame. I want to live how I choose. And I don't
want to entertain the world with my sadness.

Kuřák: Do you blame Jakub for this unwanted attention?

Lenka P: I guess so. Friends, family, they all ask me about him,
treating me like a temporary widow. Like he's my world and
my world chose to depart. And you know, there is some truth
to that. I am the spaceman's wife. I can make my pancakes in
the morning, go to work, come back home, go to the gym,
run my five K, and do my squats, but at the end of the night,
in bed, I'm the half of the marriage that's been split apart by
this mission to nowhere. I do ache for his touch—understand,
I don't need men, I never have, but I want Jakub, because I love
Jakub, I love him and I have chosen him to share my Earthly
life with. I ache for that serene sleep of his, the way he can
wake me when I'm tossing too much and bring me a glass of
pineapple juice, which somehow calms me. I ache for our magnificent fucking, and I ache for the days when I didn't have to
anticipate a call about his death, when his living was obvious,
without interruption. But then, I don't know if that Jakub can
ever exist anymore. The Jakub existing now is the one who
chose to leave.

Kuřák: This is the most you have opened up in here.

Lenka P: Is that all you have to say?

Kuřák: Lenka, I can't tell you what you want. You have to arrive there yourself.

Lenka P: That's not at all helpful.

Kuřák: Therapists are mirrors.

Lenka P: Whenever you say that, I want to hit you.

Kuřák: I apologize for upsetting you. But my verdict remains the same.

Lenka P: Fine. What I want is to get away from all of this. The reporters bugging me for interviews, my family looking at me like I should be getting ready to wear black and grieve. I want to get away from the fashion companies asking if they can pay me millions to be on their billboards. And I'm tired of looking at the face of the man I love, Dr. Kuřák, puffy from zero gravity, his voice raspy and sad, telling me those same terrible jokes he told on Earth but without the energy and flair that come with Jakub Procházka. I am tired of the doubt in his voice, betraying his thoughts—*Does she still love me? When I am so far away? Does she expect the call announcing my demise so she can at last move on?* I am whining, am I not? He is the one up there, and the cause is great and noble, don't think I don't realize that. It's just that... Dr. Kuřák, the problem is, he never asked me. When he got the offer, he called me, and I dropped my phone into the fountain. He thinks it was out of excitement, but it was out of fear. I was paralyzed. He came home and we drank champagne. He made steak and played music for me. But the question never arose—Lenka, what do you think? Should I do this? What will it do to me, to you, to us, to the world we've built? Perhaps I would have said no. Perhaps he would have listened, stayed with me on this Earth, and I would have hated myself for it, but I would still have my husband. He turned me into Penelope. He made it about himself.

Kuřák: So you would have chosen to stifle his dream in order to keep him in your — what did you call it before — your contract?

Lenka P: Well, when you put it that way, I sound monstrous. *Stifle.*

Kuřák: There are no monsters in this room.

Lenka P: It goes back to the other things we've spoken about in here. He doesn't ask. He never asked me if I wanted children — he just assumed I did because he does. It's how he operates. He has this guilt from his childhood. He carries his father's transgressions in a big bundle around his shoulders. He had to become an astronaut, of all things. It is noble, it's lovely, but I don't know if I'm willing to keep up with him while he chases redemption, like there's some magic out there that will set him free. The resentment, it builds. And so I have to ask — I still have a good chunk of life ahead of me, and what do I want? Need. While Jakub chases his purpose and thinks *She'll just wait, always wait*...what do I do?

Kuřák: I think we have arrived at the root of this, Lenka. You said you wanted to get away.

Lenka P: Yes. For a while.

Kuřák: Why can't you?

Lenka P: Because I can't leave him when he's all alone, stranded, with me his strongest link to Earth.

Kuřák: But what if you just...go.

Lenka P: I can't do that.

Kuřák: But you are no Penelope.

Lenka P: No.

Kuřák: And yet you wait. In spite of yourself. Jakub freed himself. He said good-bye to Earth. Someone theatrical would say he went off to fulfill his destiny. Yet you aren't allowed to do the same for yourself.

Lenka P: It would kill him.

Kuřák: With all due respect, that is nonsense. You are making
   yourself into a hostage.

Lenka P: So, in your imagination, I just go. I go away.

Kuřák: You go and you determine what it is you want for yourself.

Lenka P: I can tell you've never loved anyone.

Kuřák: I have. And I have always allowed them to do whatever it
   is they need. It is the very basis. Not trapping one another.

Lenka P: I need to go. I need to buy things for dinner.

Kuřák: Go. Have dinner. Think.

                              [END]

THE GOROMPED HAD BECOME an important part of my daily routine in Carlsbad. I smoked my morning cigarettes inside, and found
that if I let a bit of smoke inside the jar, the creature would become
momentarily paralyzed. While it lay on the bottom of the jar, I
stuck the burning cigarette against its hard belly and heard a faint,
high-pitched whistle that came along with a headache. I lifted the
cigarette. The Goromped's shell had turned red. It took about five
minutes for its natural hue to return, and a few more for the creature to buzz around the jar in rabid circles once again.

   After my afternoon excursions around Carlsbad's streets and
attractions, I attempted other methods. Filling the jar with water
did nothing. In fact, the Goromped simply kept moving in circles
as the liquid engulfed its body, as if it didn't even notice the change.
When I sprayed it with insecticide, it plunged itself into the puddle
and somehow absorbed all of it, lapped it up like a dog until the
glass was dry. What truly seemed to bother it was laundry detergent. After I poured it inside the jar, the Goromped shot directly
upwards and smashed into the lid until it bent. And again, and
again. Quickly, I transferred the creature to a clean jar.

   As I observed the creature, I tried to decide whether I was angry with Dr. Kuřák. There was eagerness in his support for Lenka's leaving, but he did seem to treat her with understanding and kindness. I could not be furious with a man who was good to her when she needed it. What truly haunted me were my alleged crimes of ignorance, outlined within the session recordings as clearly as the opening arguments of prosecution. How could I so deeply misunderstand something I cared about? Those small moments in which I had wronged Lenka were now cruelly apparent. When I was in Space, I manufactured moments in my head during which I had asked whether she would allow me to go on the mission, but really these questions never came up. All was decided by me from the start. I wondered whether I had behaved like this all my life, whether such disregard for a loved one was yet another genetic legacy I carried, representing my father's traits in full denial.

The Goromped experiments began to keep me shut inside the room for most of my days, which made the recovery seem slower, more painful. Suddenly I was aware of the soreness in my cheeks, my inability to walk without a slight limp. Outside, the sunshine touched upon the shoulders of women and men who seemed so without worries, a city of strollers without a destination. I too craved motion, but not that of a casual stroller—I wanted the thrilling speed of the Goromped.

I shrouded the jar with a black handkerchief and went outside. For the first time I made my way to the residential parts of town, the ones that belonged to neither patients nor tourists, and there I noticed a blue Ducati motorcycle leaning against a shabby house. A reasonable price tag hung around its neck. I hurried home to withdraw some money from the bag Petr had given me and I purchased the Ducati in cash, along with a helmet, from a man exposing his rotten teeth as he counted the cash. I rode out of Carlsbad and into the hills, past the forest filled with men reinforcing their winter wood supply, past teenagers sitting around a van without wheels, sniffing either paint or glue. The road was rough, filled with pot-holes, and I liked the vibrations it gave off. It felt as though I was working against something, making an effort. I rode through vil-lages, caught the disapproving glares of old women sitting in front of their houses, the lustful envy of village boys working in the fields after school to afford a Ducati of their own. I escaped bewildered dogs snapping at my ankles, zoomed along miles and miles of bare potato fields, wheat fields, cornfields, the postseason desolation of the countryside. The landscape elicited a raw sense of survival: wood prepared, food hoarded, and now it was time to stay inside and drink liquor to warm the belly until the winter passed. After a full day's ride I returned to Carlsbad, feeling hungry and already missing the smell of burning petrol.

The next day, I rode an hour outside Carlsbad, to Chomutov County. I stopped in front of the church in the village of my grand-mother's birth, Bukovec. In the cemetery out back, my grandmoth-er's gravestone rested underneath a willow tree. She'd always told me stories about this tree—she had been afraid of it when she was a little girl but grew to love it as she matured and its sagging shape transformed from monstrous to soothing, like the blur of moving water. When her appetite for cabbage soup—another comfort of her girlish years—at the hospital had lessened, and it came time for us to say our last words, she told me how much she hated leaving me. I asked what I could do, how I could repay the lifelong adoration she had given me, how I could show my love, and she said if there was a space anywhere near that damn tree, I should put her there.

I knelt at the grave and brushed the dried catkins from the sleek stone. I was sorrowful that I hadn't been able to release her ashes in Space along with my grandfather's. But this had been her wish. At the end of his life, my grandfather wanted to become dust, to have all trace of the body destroyed so the soul could be free. My grandmother had an agreement with nature. She wanted her body to be buried whole, to become one with the soil, with the tree, with air and rain. With a heavy heart, I had separated them, but I knew that if any remnant of cosmic justice existed, they were already together again in another life, another reality. I stayed at the grave into the night, told my grandmother of Hanuš, as I knew she would've asked him many questions. I returned to Carlsbad as the sun began to rise.

PETR SAID THAT my recovery was coming along as well as it could. I had regained some muscle, my limp was not as severe, I even slept for a full evening here and there. My healing weeks were coming to their conclusion and I started asking the question forbidden to me until now: *Where is she?* "In time, Jakub," Petr would say, "in time."

During my last therapy session, Valerie ran her fingers along my leg scar. She was an older woman with deep wrinkles alongside her eyes, and a voice so deep she must have spent her life smoking tobacco and drinking vodka to numb (or enhance?) her desires. Her stories were almost erotic in their precision and in her desperation to narrate the truth without a word one could deem unnecessary. She was the only woman who had touched me since my return. She was Earth's presence upon my body, made me feel as though she could be simultaneously a lover and a mother. Her fingernails teased my scar.

"I've come to love your silence," she said. "You're a blank canvas. I can imagine upon you any kind of life. Like a man from old folk stories."

I kissed Valerie on the cheek. She allowed it. I put on my underwear, pants, and shirt and walked out of the spa whistling. I realized too late it was the tune of an Elvis song.

On that last Sunday in Carlsbad, I purchased a gallon of liquid detergent with added bleach and quickly tipped the Goromped's holding jar into the plastic container. A frenzied sibilance brought me to my knees, but I held the cap on the bottle firmly to withstand the Goromped's attempts at freedom. The bottle cracked along the edges, the liquid inside it warming. I clamped my fingers along the sides, desperate to hold it together and smother the cosmic vermin cunt in the one substance it couldn't withstand, until finally the bottle exploded all over the room, spewing plastic shrapnel that carved a shallow cut into my cheek. Mountain-scented goo covered everything—the bed and carpet and ceiling and my clothes. I touched the walls, searching without success for a sign of a corpse, until at last I thought to pick over my shirt and face, and there in my beard I found the smallest remnants of dead legs and a particle of shell. The Goromped had split in half in the eruption. I spit on the remains, threw them in the toilet, and flushed. Yes, I took pleasure in its killing, science be damned. For a brief moment, my scientific convictions were loose enough to let me believe that Hanuš was watching from some kind of afterlife, grinning with satisfaction at this last act of revenge.

I left a seven-thousand-crown tip for the cleaning service. Removal of the havoc caused by the Goromped's detergent grenade would take considerable work. At the downstairs shop, I purchased a box of chocolates and wrote, *For Valerie*. Her kindness had been unconditional. Her life consisted of welcoming men, women, and children in pain, some temporary, some chronic; she attended to people waiting for death, to humans praying that their despair and bodily imprisonment could be eased somehow, lifted, and Valerie effectuated this with her hands, her voice, stories, with a determination to find good in every word and every movement of a weakened limb. Valerie was an unknowing force. Leaving her chocolates seemed banal and almost insulting, but she didn't need to be the victim of my glorification of her, idolatry in itself a certain kind of death.

* * *

WE LEFT BEFORE DAWN, the world still dark. Petr offered to carry the bag of clothes he had lent me downstairs, but I refused. When he opened the passenger door to his Citroën, I pointed at my Ducati and strapped on my helmet.

"Back to Earth in style," he said.

I asked Petr to put the bag of clothes in his trunk. We started our engines, destination Plzeň, where Petr would take me to Lenka's apartment. I was not feeling the expected joy over our drive. Certainly I craved to see Lenka, so much that I could not bring myself to keep still. But our reunion would be tainted by the truths that her conversations with Kuřák had made me aware of. The various ways in which I had hurt her, ending with the suffering of my death, which would now be nullified. Everything about my return, the good parts and the bad, was extreme, painful, unprecedented. I couldn't possibly know what she would say to me, what I would say back, or even how to begin to speak across the ever-widening gap of the universe between us. She was right. I had changed too much to feel like an Earthman. The intricacies of human emotion seemed incomprehensible, a foreign language. I could explain nothing of my journey, and I could not explain who I was now. What to make of such a homecoming?

Out on the road, the Ducati's recoil shook my bones and filled my blood with chemistry. I was subject to velocity, a violator of the speeds at which the human body was allowed to travel. In Space, the speed of my ascent was masked by my vessel, but here physics was felt without mercy. This was my habitat, a planet I ruled with an iron will, a planet on which I could build a combustion engine and a set of wheels to carry me at the speed of two hundred kilometers per hour as I felt every jolt and every disturbance of the air particles struggling to get out of my path. Why go anywhere else? We've already done so much to the place.

I snapped at Petr's heels, my wheel millimeters away from his bumper. We needed to go faster. To Lenka. Back to home. Back to life.

Excerpt from interview of subject Lenka P., Session Five:

Lenka P: It keeps piling up.

Kuřák: Go on.

Lenka P: I keep thinking about the miscarriage, years ago. I didn't even want to be pregnant, not yet. And one day I'm just on the treadmill and suddenly there's blood everywhere, on my legs, on the running belt. For weeks after, Jakub just stayed at his office. He snuck in to change his clothes every so often and he gave me this look, like he was doing me a favor by staying away, like it was all his fault. Things were never really the same after that. We did have good days still—there was this one time we went to the astronomical clock tower together, and it almost felt like we were those kids in love again. But really, we weren't. Jakub thought everything was fine, but we had lost parts of ourselves.

Kuřák: Do you think he chooses to be oblivious?

Lenka P: Jakub is smart. Brilliant. But he never understood the work it takes. He always thought, we fell in love, we had this story of us, and that would sustain us for the rest of our lives. It's not that he didn't put the work in. But he thought that just showing up, just being there, would be enough. He put his research first, poured himself into everything else. When it came to us, he thought the marriage could be fueled by nostalgia and physical presence. Sealed by having a child.

Kuřák: You sound like you've made up your mind about some things.

Lenka P: Well, I've been asking the right questions. What would things have been like had Jakub not agreed to go? Would we be together for much longer? How do I welcome him when he returns home? I'd want to feel his body on mine, of course, because I love him, but I'd also want to beat him over the head, shout at him.

Kuřák: Perhaps, if he hadn't gone, you wouldn't have the catalyst for these thoughts. You would have gone on, just living one day at a time, without tackling the things causing your unhappiness.

Lenka P: Well, the catalyst is here. Now I have to decide what to do with it.

Kuřák: And?

Lenka P: I want to take long walks without anyone expecting anything from me. I want to be blank. Ithaca no longer expects Penelope to sit and wait. She gets on a boat and sails toward her own wars. Is it so terrible for her to want her own life?

Kuřák: Not at all.

Lenka P: I love him. But I just don't see the way ahead anymore. I've lost it.

Kuřák: It's okay for human beings to change their minds. You can love someone and leave them regardless.

Lenka P: I keep thinking about his sweet face. His voice. How it will sound if I tell him any of this.

Kuřák: Waiting until he returns is an option.

Lenka P: I need to be away now. I need to leave Prague, leave these people who won't stop calling, emailing, taking pictures of me without asking. Like I've done something special by getting left behind.

Kuřák: What will you do?

Lenka P: I have a phone session with him this afternoon. I'm going to try to explain. Oh God, his voice, what this will do to it.

Kuřák: It will distress him. But it seems that leaving all of this behind is what is necessary for you now.

Lenka P: I'm surprised you're not talking me out of it. For the sake of the mission and all.

Kuřák: The timing, admittedly, is not great. But such things cannot be avoided.

Lenka P: Such things?

Kuřák: Unhappiness. Wanting to do something about it. And you are now my patient, just as Jakub is. The context doesn't matter—my work is to bring you to realizations that are the best for your well-being.

Lenka P: And Jakub's well-being?

Kuřák: Our unique situation presents some conflicts of interest, of course. I'm doing my best to take care of Jakub, considering he will barely speak with me. To be honest, effects of your marriage worry me less than the memories he has buried. The old life he tries to outrun. I would like for him to liberate himself.

Lenka P: You are not a bad man. It is harder and harder for me to see why Jakub dislikes you so much.

Kuřák: I have a theory. Perhaps I remind him of someone he does not like to be reminded of. Or perhaps it is because I made him speak of things he'd rather not have spoken about.

Lenka P: He keeps his secrets.

Kuřák: Clutches them to his chest.

Lenka P: I tried. I am trying.

Kuřák: I know that. So does he.

[END]

PLZEŇ. The town that served as a frontier to many Bohemian wars and produced a beer that soon became a worldwide sensation, featuring ads with half-naked women holding the ale above their heads like an ancient artifact, as if the green glass bottles contained the Fountain of Youth. Plzeň is colorful, with magnificent architecture of the Old World, but modest about the culture and history pulsing within the veins of its streets. A challenger to Prague in many ways, and no Bohemian says such things lightly.

This was Lenka's new home. We arrived as the town woke up with the sun. Petr parked his car in front of a cake shop in Plzeň's downtown. As I slid off the Ducati, I felt as though gravity might once again give up on me. Even the heavy cube bricks lining the street could not force the numbness from my calves.

"Her building is around the corner. Number sixty-five. Apartment two. It has a black roof—"

"Petr, I have to do this alone now."

Hesitant, he handed over the bag of clothes. I turned to go but he grabbed at my sleeve, then pulled out a cigarette and lit it with a single hand. "You're saying I won't see you again," he said.

"Don't think about it anymore," I said. "You did everything you could. I made my own decisions. I wanted to go."

"What do you think will happen with her?"

"You know, on the bad days, I thought I made her up. This great love of mine. And you, frankly, and Central, and many other things. When you wake up in a room you don't recognize, you feel lost, right? What about walking to an outhouse in perfect darkness, using only muscle memory. Chickens pluck at your feet. You walk until the senses catch on to familiar clues. Until you feel the spiderwebs upon the wooden door and the rabbits stirring as you interrupt their sleep. You walk into the darkness until something becomes familiar. I don't know what should happen, Petr. Please keep me in your thoughts."

Petr put his arms around my shoulders, then returned to his car and drove off.

* * *

I STOOD IN front of Lenka's apartment door, lacquered in a brown similar to the color of my grandparents' gate in Středa. There was no doormat, that usual square pancake serving to cleanse one of the dirt of cities before entering a sacred space. I knocked, listened, knocked again, waited with my cheeks hot and sweat soaking through my shirt. I leaned on the door, rested my forehead, knocked once more. What would Lenka say when she opened the door? Surely I looked appalling, perhaps unrecognizable even to her, in comparison to the man she'd married. I pushed myself off the door, straightened my spine. Maybe I wouldn't need to say a word. Maybe she would be so ecstatic to see me alive that she wouldn't expect a thing. No answer.

I reached above the doorframe, where Lenka had always left a key during our years together, terrified she would lose hers and lock herself out as she had done when she was a little girl, with her parents out of town and the streets full of unknowns. Under my fingers I felt the coldness of brass, took the key down, and slid it into the lock. I entered Lenka's world.

It was a railroad apartment, four rooms locked together in a single line without doors. I walked into an office in which bookshelves held books that were only hers, novels from all over the world, while my nonfiction tomes of theories were gone. Even our literature proved that I'd wanted to conquer everything outside Earth, while she wanted to know every inch of the planet I desired to leave. I put my hands upon these books, remembering those nights of silence when our forearms had touched and we had read until sleep took us, the pages mixed between limbs and sheets.

The next room, her bedroom. The bed was not ours. It was hers, smaller, and a crater in the middle suggested that Lenka had slept comfortably without having to choose a side. The sheets were folded neatly, another morning ritual of hers. Above the bed was a painting

I had never seen—cormorants rising over a river, a sunset with hues so orange the beams looked like napalm. Lenka's signature in the corner.

What would happen if Lenka were to come back home, capture the poltergeist lurking in her space? How to explain that I had passed through the core that had seen the beginning of the world? That I had fallen through the atmosphere and crashed into a Russian lake. That I had come for her.

The third room was an undecided space. A yoga mat and weights lay in one corner, while the center was dominated by an easel supporting an unfinished painting on a large canvas. This new project was a night sky above Plzeň's horizon. One star was particularly thick, glowing, with a tail behind it that suggested movement. This was how Lenka had seen me when I left, guessing at which of the moving reflections in the vast darkness could be her Jakub.

There was also a closet. I opened the doors and leaped into her clothing, sniffing at the familiar detergent, the armpits of blouses still holding traces of sweat mixed with deodorant, notes of her apricot perfume. As I put my face in the clothes, they began to fall, and soon I too fell to the ground, burying myself under the pile until I couldn't breathe.

The final room was the kitchen, in which I could still smell all of Lenka's favorites—fried eggs, bacon, the goddamn bacon, mushroom stew. There was a high bar table littered with a week's worth of newspapers (was she still searching for articles about me, or embracing the new world without me in it?). Above the table stretched a framed photo of the sunset on a Croatian beach.

I walked back to the office at the front of the apartment. There weren't any photos of me, no photos of our wedding. I considered rummaging through the closets to see if these items still existed, or whether Lenka had scrubbed her life clean of the reminders. Their absence wouldn't upset me. It would bring clarity.

I exited the apartment and walked outside. If I kneeled down and put my ear to the sidewalk, would Plzeň speak to me, tell me where to search? I turned in all directions with my eyes closed and chose one at random, then embarked, knowing I would scour these streets day and night until I found Lenka.

As I stepped forward, faint music drifted from the direction of the River Radbuza. It came into sight and I realized that Lenka's cormorant painting had been conceived at its shore. The music grew louder as I walked into the city's historic center, where the Cathedral of Saint Bartholomew dominated the skyline. A mass of tents, stages, and food stands opened before me, organized into neat rows for the winter festival. A group of Roma musicians unleashed their soothing folk, accentuated by the smacks of steaming grog spilled upon the ground, the sizzle of onion, and above all the cheers of voices unified in the pagan ecstasy of human celebration. I entered the masses, searching above their heads. Lenka had to be here, with her love for ritual and for life. I bought a cup of grog, proof that I too belonged here, that I could still run with my kin, my species. Hours passed, the afternoon sun began to retreat, and the air grew cooler as I circled the square. Then, at a table ahead, a hand picked up a slice of bread smeared with goat cheese. The body belonging to the hand was concealed by the crowd. I tore through the mass, now seeing that those hands which had memorized my own body so thoroughly were not a mirage.

Lenka. Her sweet hands.

She paid the vendor and turned her back, the green tunic over her shoulders flowing in the wind like a queen's robe. For a moment, the tunic slid off her right shoulder, and the few inches of bare skin inspired a lust that made me dizzy. I stumbled, but kept following nonetheless. What was the best way to approach her? I couldn't put my hand on her shoulder before she saw me. She needed to see me first, recognize me, recognize the man who had so selfishly gone away from her to chase his own ambitions, the man who had returned now that she had made this new life to ask that she drop her solitude and, once again, change everything for him.

Lenka. Her sweet hands, the skin of her shoulders. Was I worthy of her still? I quickened my pace, pushed through the herd to get ahead of Lenka, and turned back into the lane in which she strolled. She was now walking toward me, thirty meters, twenty-five. But there were too many bodies obstructing us. My eyes sought hers, ten meters. For the first time since I had left Earth, I saw Lenka's face clearly. Peaceful. Adoring every sight and every breath. As if the world had been her creation and she a carefree supervisor walking the floor on the seventh day of rest.

She was changed, happier than I'd ever seen her. Happier even than in our best days, our orgasmic slumber in the Orloj tower, the peak of our love. Five meters.

I froze in my steps. Lenka looked directly at me. No. She looked past me, with no sign of recognition, no acknowledgment of my material form. She walked past me. As though I were just another stranger in too large a crowd.

Could I be anything else, in the new world she had built for herself? She had to see me. There was no other way to begin anew. I cursed the enveloping masses.

I shadowed her, searching for a better opportunity as she ate boiled peanuts, purchased a few canvases, and made her way home with the setting sun. I was drunk by then, mostly on samples of liquors flowing across the border from the rest of Europe, belching menthol, caraway, and coffee from the earthy shots I had picked up as I stalked. My mind a warren of confusion, uncertain whether I belonged to Earth anymore at all. But my body ran on autopilot— where Lenka went, I went.

She retreated into her apartment and I sat on the pavement outside, down the block. The ground was cool to the touch, and the distant voices of people coming home from the festival, drunk on simple pleasures, encouraged me. The street lamps came on with their low buzz of static. A beautiful night. I imagined walking up to Lenka's door and ringing the bell. She would have to see me then. The possibilities of her reaction terrified me, each of them bringing their own special sense of horror. If she touched me, put her arms around me, would my bones hold together? Or perhaps she would run, thinking me a corpse come to haunt her. This endless loop of thought kept me confined to the sidewalk. Her words to Kuřák replayed over and over. She wanted a life of her own, one that wasn't overshadowed by my obsessions, my needs. And then I had seen her face in the crowd, serene and impassioned, and the lightness in her step.

Was she her happiest like this? I needed to leave Earth, pick at the particles of Space. What did Lenka need?

She walked back out of her building holding a large canvas bag, and I took cover behind a building at the end of the street. Lenka stepped toward the river. I followed her down the path, but still I kept my distance, still I could not bring myself to reenter her world. It was so easy, I had only to shout out her name, to run the short distance separating us and touch her. But with each passing moment I felt more and more like an intruder.

She set up an easel and began work on the unfinished painting of the night sky.

Her voice from Kuřák's recording, counting up all the things I had done. Yes, the winter of 1989 was the Big Bang of my life. The guilt of my father's servitude had followed me everywhere, leading us here.

She took a sip of something from a thermos. Coffee? Wine? All I had to do was ask.

The paint upon the easel, grains of powder and oil staining the cotton fibers, the solvent evaporating to leave a pigmented, dry oil to oxidize. This resinous film was now the new dimension of reality, confined within a rectangular cloth. A new world. A perspective. Lenka had painted the edges purple to allow for Chopra's influence. She raised her hand to her head, and though I couldn't see I was sure the purple on her fingers colored a streak of her hair. What if this reminder of a phenomenon so distant, yet one that uprooted our lives, remained there forever? Within the painting existed the sum of our lives. My decision to leave. My decision to put something else above Lenka. I chose the dust, I chose Space, I chose the trip to nowhere, I chose to live above humanity, I chose higher missions, I chose symbols, I chose to claw at redemption.

I didn't choose Lenka. I failed our contract. Now she had made a life for herself. Of course, I could merge into this life. Rid myself of any ambition left, drop any designs for my future and simply live alongside Lenka in any way she wanted me to, do as she would tell me, cause no further disruptions. But such life didn't seem worth consideration, not only because I would never be able to truly embrace it, but because Lenka would reject it as an insult to what life is supposed to stand for.

She rested the brush upon the ground and sat by the edge of the river. She rolled up her pant legs and dipped her feet into the water. Frogs dispersed with protesting croaks. The air grew chalky with smoke from a nearby bonfire. Lenka hummed and leaned back into the grass. Peaceful, alone. Looking out over the calm surface.

There was no space for me here. I took a step back. And another.

Lenka returned to her easel and began to disassemble it. The cup used to rinse the brush tipped over, the water marked by all colors of the palette spilling on the grass. Lenka leaned over and began to draw something into the stain with her finger. I had never been as curious about anything as I was at this moment about what Lenka was creating out of view. She was an unmatched engineer of these small moments. Embracing accidents and curiosities. She judged the work below and laughed to herself.

I couldn't exist here. In the world that had come into being due to my absence.

Within me now lay the mystery of Hanuš, the violent rejection of Chopra, the bodies of the three humans whose deaths I was responsible for. Klara's eyes wild with betrayal, her effort to murder me with a single arm, her teeth sinking into the meat of my thumb like fangs.

I had nothing to give anyone else. Not here.

I turned and ran back up the pathway. I jumped onto the Ducati and started it, throwing my helmet to the ground.

She had loved me so well. I could never have asked for a better life as an Earthman.

Now I was a specter. Fragments of pasts, futures, gates through time and space. I was the series of particles released by Chopra's core. My only destiny: motion. I rode at the highest speed. Away from Plzeň. Lenka had freed herself of the things haunting me. She was to remain free.

Thus we never see the true State of our Condition, till it is illustrated to us by its Contraries; nor know how to value what we enjoy, but by the want of it.

EXCERPT FROM FINAL PHONE CALL *with Lenka P., approximately one day after Jakub P.'s projected death:*

Lenka P: He didn't suffer? You're telling me the truth?

Kuřák: Yes. It's reported that he took the cyanide pill. His passing was without pain.

Lenka P: And you gave my message to him?

Kuřák: I was assured he was told.

Lenka P: I let him die thinking he'd lost me. I should've pretended it was all right until he returned.

Kuřák: Again, a certain role imposed upon you.

Lenka P: That's what loving someone is.

Kuřák: I'm not sure I agree.

Lenka P: Jakub did what he needed to. He was fulfilling his destiny.

Kuřák: His, not yours.

Lenka P: Why are you so adamant about making me feel better?

Kuřák: Nature of the job.

Lenka P: I'm terrified by my reaction. I can't feel anything. It's like it didn't happen. It's like I'm going to come home and the Jakub I first met, so cleanly shaven, will be there waiting. What if time really works that way—we can manipulate it like that, we just haven't wanted it hard enough.

Kuřák: This is how you grieve. Don't be afraid of it.

Lenka P: I married a sweet boy who walked around the city like he was lost. And then, he goes to Space. What a life. Amazing. Wonderful. Terrible. All at the same time.

Kuřák: Do you feel free?

Lenka P: I feel like I've lost too much.

Kuřák: Freedom can feel that way.

Lenka P: You promise me?

Kuřák: What?

Lenka P: You swear he was told? That I loved him. That our life together was not a forgery—that everything we did in those years came from the best parts of ourselves? That we'd have that, at least.

Kuřák: He was told. I swear it.

Lenka P: I keep having this image of Jakub, like a thick star highlighted in the darkness, with a line of movement behind it. I see it every night, as if he's leaving all over again. How can things get so far away from us? What use are the physics of Earth, these layers of atmosphere? They keep things from reaching us. But I wish they could've also trapped him here.

A Child of the Revolution

WITHOUT THE PURPOSE of finding Lenka, my time became an endless orbit on Earth's concrete. Days ceased to have beginnings or endings as I rode my Ducati in circles on the highways surrounding Prague, teasing out ever higher speeds, much like the Goromped that had lived in my Carlsbad room. The singular purpose of motion. No schemes to it. No plans.

At a gas station, I purchased a clearance hooded sweatshirt sporting the colors of the national football team. I pulled it over my head, still nervous whenever a person stared at me for too long, afraid that in the correct light I might be recognized, despite the forever-altered facial structure, despite the sunken eyes, despite being severely underweight. I did not look strangers in the eyes, I turned my head so no one could ever see me fully in daylight. Now the hood made me feel slightly more invincible.

When I grew too tired to hold myself up on the motorcycle, I stopped at a trucker motel and ate vending machine chips on a rough bedspread. The TV set in my room would not turn on. I had almost convinced myself that it didn't matter, that I didn't need it, but I knew it'd be hours before I could sleep, and complete silence worsened my headaches. I asked the attendant downstairs for help, and with an abundance of loud sighs, he gave me a television set from another room. Victorious, I opened a beer and switched to a news station.

Milk prices rising. (I snickered, recalling my conversation with

Tůma.) France, another country to leave the crumbling European Union. Then, suddenly, the faces of men I knew. Their hands cuffed.

Prime Minister Tůma himself, clothed in sweatpants, his hair unkempt, was being led out of his Barrandov villa by policemen. These images were from two days ago—history happening as I had been riding in circles.

Then, different footage from a different place appeared. This was downtown Prague, an office building modeled after a New York skyscraper. From within its depths the police led a man whose face I would have recognized in a lineup of millions. It was Him.

I felt my foot dampen and glanced down at the beer bottle I had dropped without knowing it.

According to the newscaster, the two men had been arrested, along with two other politicians and another businessman, for siphoning cash from phony government contracts. The media called them ringleaders of the scheme who, in the span of three years, had managed to steal seven hundred million crowns of tax-payer cash. Prime Minister Tůma, the self-professed savior of his nation, and the other man, supposedly a close childhood friend of Tůma's and his phantom adviser throughout the years. The man, Shoe Man, whose Christian name was introduced to me for the first time through this cracked, dirty television screen—Radislav Zajíc.

I set the television on my knees as if I could reason with it to give me more detail. After their arrest two days earlier, the men had immediately posted bail and retreated to an undisclosed location. The image of their arrest flashed by again, and although there were signs of gray in the sleeked hair I had last seen as a child, it was him, inescapably. With all the cruelty of the modern news cycle, the story melted away and into a report on a new red panda born in Prague Zoo.

I ran downstairs and tossed the room key and cash for the spilled beer stain at the clerk. I rode back into the center of Prague, to the streets near my former university, a village of pubs and Internet cafés filled with intellectuals blowing off steam. How I used to fit in here—but now, as I entered one of their Wi-Fi lairs, the young minds of the future looked upon me with distrust, perhaps even with wrinkled noses. Did I smell? No time. Something was afoot, pieces of my life suddenly did not form a whole, or perhaps they fit together too tightly. I paid for two hours of computer time and sat down with a cup of coffee that cooled as I ignored it and stretched my fingers over the keys. A few taps, the humming of a processor, an instant name, social networking profiles, emails. Radislav Zajíc, his life laid out before me. A light breeze traveled through the café, scented with car exhaust and blooming trees.

Finally, I drank down half of the cold coffee. I wasn't sure what to do with the name now. Perhaps I wanted to spend the rest of my life as an avenger, haunting Him, displacing Him. What else was there to do? Perhaps he was the only person who knew me anymore, who knew my life before the headlines, before my ascent and before death. Maybe I wanted to do nothing at all.

Business tycoon Radislav Zajíc and Prime Minister Jaromír Tůma: childhood friends, victims of communist persecution, post-revolution opportunists. Their focus had gone in different directions but they had remained close, Zajíc being Tůma's number-one adviser and largest fund-raiser. Within one search, again I had a purpose on this Earth, a purpose contained inside a small white rectangle and its blinking cursor. The two men had built a lifelong coalition, with Zajíc working in his preferred shadow, raising capital through his investments in energy, real estate, and the importation of Western brands, while Tůma became the political apostle of the boundless market, his haircuts, silk ties, and influence paid for by Zajíc and his brethren. Now the shadows had been lifted by the ministry of interior, and the Internet was once again proving a court of the people, the Arena of Rome in which the crowds declared *Thumbs down*. The entire affair had already been summarized on

Wikipedia, the apparatus of justice rushing ahead to imprison the men as people of the republic protested these high-level crooks in the streets of Old Town. I glanced outside. No protests at the moment, not currently revolutionary.

I finished the terrible coffee. Shoe Man and Prime Minister Tůma, boyhood friends. Where did I fit between the two? I slammed down the cup and logged into my old student email account, knowing the university allowed these accounts to exist indefinitely without oversight. I pasted Radislav Zajíc's email—his private information leaked by a vigilante hacker group—into the recipient field. Sure, it wasn't likely he'd be checking it much, with the venom citizens were bound to send his way. But I had to find him. Before the day I died, I would look Shoe Man in the face and ask my questions. *What had he done?* This was the first step.

I considered soliciting one of the students around me for a cigarette or a swig from their flask to calm me. Given the ban on caffeine during training and the mission itself, the single cup of coffee was already affecting me with a vengeance—making my hands shake and causing a variety of typos that prolonged the writing of only a few simple sentences:

You offered me gum and I said no.

You took our house. Stalin's pigs, oink oink.

My grandfather died in a twin bed from IKEA. My grandmother died in a hospital bed after eating cheap cabbage soup.

What else have you done?

I'm here.

I sent the email.

Beside me, a young woman with a thick book in her lap looked around conspicuously and poured from a silver flask into her coffee cup, and I leaned over to ask if I could impose in exchange for my silence on the contraband. She answered that I could have a little, and that blackmail is impolite, and I thanked her and drank down my own spiked cup as I stared at my email inbox. Refreshed, stared some more, massaged my stiff knees. Students began to depart, and as the young woman next to me left, the barista began to wipe the counters and I noted the café was to close in a few minutes. Refreshed, refreshed—once a known astronaut, now reduced to a customer overstaying his welcome to check email. The barista tapped me on the shoulder. My two hours had passed—I was welcome to return tomorrow morning.

I hovered my cursor over the browser window's red X. It seemed more red than usual. The color of a stop sign. I hesitated. Behind me, the barista's deep exhale.

A new subject line appeared. The preposition "Re," bold, thick with life. I opened the email. The barista tapped on my shoulder again.

Little spaceman. If it is really you, call me.

I took a two-hundred-crown bill from my wallet and offered it to the barista for some paper, a pen, and whatever coins he had on him. He hesitantly accepted the bill and brought me a pencil and a napkin. I scribbled down the number Shoe Man had sent. The coffee and alcohol in my bloodstream made my heart knock against my rib cage. I shut off the computer and thanked the barista thrice as he locked the doors. He shrugged, and I ran to the end of the street.

I slammed twenty crowns into a pay phone around the corner. Where do the coins go? I wondered. The concept seemed like pure science fiction. Tossing a piece of metal into another contraption of metal, and voilà, hearing a voice.

I dialed the number as the sun outside descended, creating an array of shadows within the booth. Around me the city wound down, humans with their business concluded going about the pre-leisure rituals of getting dinner ingredients or hiding out in a bar. My headache and bloated stomach reminded me that I had been living on junk food and beer. But what was a body, after all? Why keep it pretty for the dirt?

On the other end of the line, a click, followed by hesitation. Then a voice I knew, as if I were still hearing it through the keyhole in the closed door to my grandparents' kitchen.

"Let me hear your voice," he said.

"Where are you?"

"It is you."

"What have you done?" I said.

"You're not dead. This is your voice. Unless—"

"Answer me."

"I want to see you."

"What if I kill you?" I said.

"Something your grandfather would say. The number you're calling from, it's Prague."

"I'll be by the statue they built. Tomorrow. Noon."

"You used to study in that park. That's why I asked them to build it there. But maybe I'm just talking to myself here," Zajíc said. "Going mad. Is it you?"

"It might be better for you if it weren't," I said, and hung up.

I found shelter in a shuttered bakery shop offered for sale and ate a slice of cold pizza for dinner. Soon an entrepreneur would take the place over and give it a new mission. The floors were prewar, when stonemasonry was still an art. They were cool to the touch and I spread a tablecloth underneath myself, looking upon the withered and sagging signs advertising the former menu. Millennia ago, the earliest people found that they could pulverize grains of wheat to form a putty which, upon baking, would redefine the species. Even now, with culinary pleasures having gone global and the world offering complex delicacies, what comforted me as I rested in the bakery was the image of a simple roll, golden on the outside with pure white dough on the inside. The crack you make with your thumb as you rip into it.

The purpose of my newfound mission thrilled me. I couldn't go back to Lenka, I didn't belong in her world anymore. With the universe ever expanding, we could never circle back around to each other. But Shoe Man...

Radislav Zajíc. He defied these laws of physics. He had returned, somehow. He knew me. He knew Tůma. I'd always figured he knew *of* me, if only from the newspapers. I had counted on him watching my triumph. But his friendship with Tůma opened its own separate cosmos, one that did not begin with a random incident of energy exploding into being, but was carefully designed. As I fell asleep in the bakery, with mice bumping into my shoes, I was certain that everything that had happened was somehow his doing.

In the morning, I woke early. I rode to Vyšehrad, a fort overlooking the River Vltava. There the ghosts of the old kings kept guard over alleys and fountains, towers and shops, the souls of children dragging themselves to school and tired adults jumping onto the tram. Perhaps the ghosts watched over me too. More than a thousand years ago, Princess Libuše had stood on the hill of Vyšehrad and looked across the River Vltava, where she declared, "I see a great city whose glory will touch the stars." She instructed her men to travel to the settlement and find a peasant constructing the threshold of a house. Atop this threshold, Libuše claimed, was where the Prague Castle should be built. "And because even the great noblemen must bow low before a threshold, you shall give it the name Praha." *Threshold. Práh.* The founding of Prague depended on such staggering duality. Across the river, Libuše had seen a vision of a thousand towers extending up to the skies, towers so high they could be seen from Istanbul, from Britannia, perhaps from God's own divine throne. And yet the name of this city of glory was based on the humblest part of any structure: a threshold, a line marking entry and exit, a symbol no person considers twice. Was this duality—the humble name and the contrasting vision of grandeur borne out when Přemysl the plowman, a simple villager, married Princess Libuše and became the first ruler of the Bohemian lands— the reason Prague had survived civil wars, the Austro-Hungarian cultural purging, and occupations by fascists and Bolsheviks? Perhaps the world is enslaved to its own dualities, a humble beginning with an impossible dream attached. Libuše's vision across the river was the beginning. I am the end. With me, Prague had touched the skies at last, and fulfilled the prophecy that Libuše bestowed upon its cradle. Never mind that the Holy Roman Emperor once resided in the Prague Castle, or that the first council of Bohemia had congregated within its walls. It was with me that the history of the city had finally come full circle.

I rode to New Town and parked my motorcycle a few blocks from Charles Square, which had been a home to me during my first university years. It had changed quite a bit. No longer did students loiter around with their heavy bags. They had been replaced by headlong tourists consulting their maps and agendas. I roamed the streets around the square and took part in the city that had given me life. I handed money to a group of three actors performing Shakespeare on top of a parked van. I ate hot dogs and paid bathroom attendants to hand me carefully folded toilet paper. Church bells tolled in the distance, and a small boy dropped ice cream at my feet, his parents lamenting in Italian. I walked into an alleyway that turned into a pop-up bookshop, with young people rummaging through boxes of literature and paintings. The street ended in a homeless commune of tents and piles of clothes, the outpost secured by a vigilant street dog. I fed the dog the remnant of my frankfurter wrapped in a napkin—in Prague, the likelihood of running into a dog, feral or domesticated, was high, and I liked to be prepared—and the guardian of the commune's treasures licked my fingers.

At eleven o'clock, I returned to the square, its grass dark and littered with wandering birds. The square was surrounded by walls of trees that sheltered its inhabitants from the city life around it. There, in the middle of the plaza, stood the spaceman's statue, dead eyes of carved stone, a nose much smaller than mine, helmet in his right hand, left hand over his heart, a gesture to the people. The base, towering above me as if it held the weight of an emperor, was decorated with a sign of pure gold, whose letters had been carved by the same stonemason who had curated the main stairwell of the National Museum. Part of the etched name was concealed by growing vines.

Beyond the statue I encountered a group of middle school children on a field trip. They frolicked under the supervision of a frowning teacher, and their youthful twittering carried an eerie song to my ears. Impossible, I thought, but no, I had heard them correctly. They were singing of the dead spaceman, of being just like him someday.

No other sound would ever force the tune out of my head. It would return without invitation for a lifetime to come, like the flu or the scent of lovers. I stood there in the flesh and observed the children, my attention unreturned, while the stoic, bloodless version of me placed a few meters away earned the praise of their song.

I sat on a bench across from the statue. Noon was a few minutes away. My nausea, the tightness in my knuckles, the violence of the moment, the fear forced me to lean forward. The man who'd banished my family was on his way over. In this earthly life once again resumed, he was now all that mattered.

One minute late. Was he coming?

A figure emerged between the trees. He made his way toward the children and put his hand on the teacher's shoulder. The two spoke and the newcomer pointed toward me. The teacher nodded.

Radislav Zajíc walked briskly toward me. He stopped some fifteen meters away, his arms awkwardly limp at his sides, like a boy told not to pick his nose. He seemed shorter than I remembered, but it was his face, marked by those same pox scars and gray scruff. His suit, the body armor, was smooth and perfect at every crevice, as if it were another layer of fresh skin.

"I asked that teacher if he saw you sitting here," Zajíc said, "and he said yes."

I rose and walked up to Shoe Man. I was taller than he was. "You see me," I said.

"I do. Jakub. You are here. And you look like your father."

He knew me. He had recognized me instantly. This man was the last living remnant of my early history. A proof that those childhood days weren't a mirage. Against my will, the anger and nausea dissipated. Shoe Man soothed me.

Probability theory examines mathematical abstractions of nondeterministic events. It also studies measured quantities that may either be single occurrences or evolve over time in an apparently random fashion. If a sequence of random events is repeated many times, patterns can be detected and studied, thus creating the illusion that human observers can truly know and understand chaos. But what if our existence itself is a field of study in probability conducted by the universe? Each of us a character, a mathematical abstraction set up with attributes copied from previous subjects, with a slight variation (switch Oedipal complex for Electra complex, exchange crippling social anxiety for narcissism), sent out with similar instincts—the fear of death, the fear of loneliness, the fear of failure. Our outcomes—poverty, starvation, disease, suicide, peaceful death on a bed plagued by shame and regret—being collected by a researcher above, a cosmic tally gathering the likelihood of happiness, likelihood of wholeness, likelihood of self-destruction. Likelihood of luck. Can a subject born impoverished and diseased finish in the upper luck bracket at the end of her life? Can a subject born into privilege and health crash and die in utter misery? We've seen it all. We've seen it all and yet where are these patterns, when will the universe publish its findings in a respected peer-reviewed journal? What is the ratio of probability for one cosmic event to occur over all others? How unlikely. Yet here we are.

Radislav Zajíc saw me. I raised my fist and slugged him across the jaw. He fell to the ground too easily, and I studied the spot on my wrist where something had cracked. My third knuckle collapsed, creating a darkened crater. Blood burst out. The schoolteacher hurriedly gathered the children and led them away from the square.

Zajíc stared up at me. Gone was the defiance he'd shown to my grandfather—he was not daring me; he was not baiting. He simply waited, looked on with gentle curiosity. *If you decide to beat me to death, that is your business.*

I extended my hand and pulled him to his feet. He walked to the statue, and I followed.

"You know, it's been many years since someone's hit me," he said. "It has a sort of relief to it."

"I've been saving it for a few decades."

He put his hand on the base of the statue, brushed the vines from my name. "You should've seen it," he said. "I've never witnessed something pass through the Parliament so quickly. People were outbidding themselves on how much we should spend on building this statue. They wanted to make it as tall as a tower. But I argued that you'd prefer something smaller, in a place that matters. I know you spent most of your time here as a student. Looking up at the sky and studying all night."

"You and Tůma. You did this."

"Yes and no. How did you do it, Jakub? How'd you make it back."

"I flew, you son of a bitch. I flapped my goddamn wings and here I stand."

Zajíc leaned against the statue, massaging his jaw.

"You sent me to Chopra. You put Tůma up to it. Say it."

"I gave him your name, Jakub. There was nothing diabolical—"

"For what? To take the last Procházka off the Earth? I almost died. I lost her. For what."

"It's not the reason, Jakub. If I may."

My hands trembled, and I put them inside my pockets. I could not show weakness. Not to him. "Yes," I said.

"After you left Středa, I couldn't let go of you. I've been married a couple of times, and each of my wives had caught me whispering your name in the dark, thinking you were a lover of mine. I watched you grow up, saw your grade reports, statements of purpose for university. I wanted to ensure they would admit you, but you didn't need the help. I watched your grandfather's funeral from a distance. I asked the vineyard where you and Lenka married to quote you a small rate and I paid for the difference. You've been a charm from the old life, and I wanted to see, always wanted to see—were you going to turn into a bastard? Was it in the blood? And you kept being good. Determined."

"You've lost your mind. So what? You chose me for the suicide mission as some kind of restitution?"

"One night, when we were drunk, Tůma told me about his space program dream. I laughed at him at first, but he was serious, he grabbed me by the collar and swore it would happen. I used to think he was the man the country needed, you know? Before we became cynical together. He used to believe in feeding both the citizens' stomachs and their souls. He believed in science and curiosity and books. He made me think of you. And so I gave him your name, Jakub. It seemed inevitable, the two of us in that moment. It was not to punish you or to reward you. It was a reaction to what seemed a cosmic calling. Tůma gave you the choice, and you decided to do something great, just as I expected."

"I've done nothing. I should've stayed with the things I knew. Certainties. You've never been anything but a sad, hateful man. You let my father win and you let him ruin us both."

"Hmm," he said, "yes, some of that is true. But you have done everything, Jakub. The mission was a failure but the country believes we can be great. You should have seen the funeral. The whole city was alive like I've never seen it. Dignitaries came from all over the world to pay their respects. And now you're back—I don't know how, I don't know what you've had to do, but you are here, and we can bring you back to the nation. A hero's return. They will go apeshit for it, Jakub. You will be a king. Whatever you think you have lost, you will get it back a thousandfold."

I thought of it. The news headlines, the interviews, everything I had expected upon my return but intensified to a point of frenzy, endless questions, how is this possible, what brought me back? Would this resurrection mean the return of Lenka? The end to her peace.

No. I could not. I had given them everything. They had no right to ask for more.

"That won't happen," I said. "I stay dead. I've earned it."

"You're certain?"

"I am. I want the quiet life."

"Well, I suppose it makes no difference to me. My trial is in a month. Unless I decide to flee the country, which I'm still considering. My own quiet life in the Caribbean. Either way, Jakub, it seems that the big missions of our lives are over."

"What was yours?"

"Helping democracy with heaps of cash."

"You're a thief."

"I became one, yes."

"What do you think of my father now? You can't think you are better than him, not anymore. This pain you've caused to get revenge on a dead man, the people you've ruined in the process. The point of it all."

"May I show you something? It requires a short trip."

"I'm not going anywhere with you."

"Don't be stupid, Jakub. I've watched you grow up. I wish you no harm."

What else was there to do? I did not want for this meeting to end, for this man who knew me, the last remnant of my life before the mission, to leave. I followed him through the grass field and between the trees, where we reentered the city and a suited driver opened a door to a black BMW. We sat on the leather seats and Zajíc offered a glass of Scotch. I drank it down without pause. Was it a betrayal to my grandfather that I sat next to this man, spoke to him? He couldn't blame me for wanting to understand. To know every bit of influence that had gotten me here. The seat cooled my back, I poured another drink, wondering what it was like to be a man who lived such luxuries every day, molding them into a barrier shielding him from the terror of being ordinary. Zajíc studied me and all these decades later I still worried he could read me easily, the gestures of a frightened boy.

We arrived at a building in New Town. The chauffeur opened the door and I stood before a delicatessen storefront. The building was eight stories tall, made in the old republic, before the war and before the communist housing projects. Shoe Man gestured for me to come through the front door to the top of the stairwell. There he removed a set of keys from his pocket and opened a door made of metal. It creaked, and I noticed deep scratches upon it.

As I hesitated, Zajíc entered the room. The windows were covered in black paper, leaving the room concealed in shadow. Something clicked. Lamplight illuminated the room, and Shoe Man stood by a desk stained with blood, its drawers having been removed. The lamp—small, with a rusty neck and harsh, invasive light—and a green folder were the only items on the desk. The only other piece of furniture in the room was a wooden chair covered in thick deep cuts, pieces of duct tape sticking to its legs and back. The chair faced the blacked-out windows. On the dusty stone floor in front of it rested the artifact of my life's history. The iron shoe.

"Is this real?" I said.

"When I met your father, the basement where the usual torture rooms were located was being fumigated for rats. The secret police kicked a few of the less important bureaucrats out of their offices, and made these provisional chambers. Can't let vermin get in the way of interrogation."

"This is it? This one?"

"This room. Your father's feet walked upon this floor. Of course, by the time I bought the building, the space had been changed back into a nice office. I had them re-create the room as I knew it from memory. Don't worry, the blood is fake. But the shoe I think you recognize."

I pictured myself at nineteen years old, with baby fat still on my cheeks. Men I've never seen, never spoken to, coming into my university classroom and taking me away. Taking me here, blacking out the world beyond these windows, a separation like dirt tossed upon a coffin. Causing me pain, hurting me with the full conviction that they were on the right side of history, the moral side, the side of humanity. My father had done this for a living. He had done this and it had kept us in a nice apartment and in nice clothes and with secret Elvis records stashed away.

"Why did you bring me here?"

"I wanted you to see it, the place where I was born. The man I was before I knew this room—he was probably going to become a chemist. A scientist, like you. But once they kicked me out of university, took everything from my family, the only focus of my life became not ending up in this room again."

"Why are you telling me this?"

"Don't you want to know me?"

I turned to the wooden chair and sat down. My knee pain was returning, reminding me I hadn't taken my medication all day. I removed the bottle from my pocket and swallowed a pill dry.

I slid my foot inside the iron shoe. "Tie it," I said.

Zajíc bent over and pushed down on the safety, then pulled the heavy leather belt inside a loop.

I tried to lift my foot. I could not.

"That's the most terrifying thing," Zajíc said. "It grounds you. It makes you feel like, perhaps, you might never walk again."

"It's a comfort now. To be still. Bound."

"How did you do it, Jakub? How did you come back?"

"We're not going to talk about that now."

He nodded and walked toward the window. He opened it, and the black paper ripped at the edges. Sun came into the room for the first time in many years. Without the darkness to lend it isolation, it seemed like a regular sad office keeping human beings away from living wildly, not unlike the office of Dr. Bivoj.

"You made me think I was a curse," I said. "Like my whole existence was some kind of spiritual stain. The last remnant of Cain's sperm. Those aren't good thoughts for a child. For a man. I've wished you dead in so many different ways. Before I started shaving I fantasized about what I could do to you with a blade. Your voice has resonated through my head all these years, uninvited. I should throw you out that window, but I no longer see the point in it. I don't know what to do after we leave this room. I don't know. When I couldn't bring myself to speak to Lenka, I thought that finding you would be another mission, the last possible way of living. But I look at you and I know that retribution is not life."

He turned to face me. He bent low before me and unstrapped my foot. The brief suspension, the release from weight and pressure, felt again as though I was floating in Space, with Hanuš by my side, about to encounter a core that would take us to the beginnings of the universe.

"I've built a life around a couple of hours in a room with an unkind stranger," Shoe Man said. "Jakub, it took me too long to realize it. Your father did what he did to me, but the decision to live as I have—it was still mine. For me, the catalyst was this room. For your father, the catalyst was the day he decided the world was full of his enemies. For you, the catalyst doesn't need to be anger or fear or some feeling of loss. The significance of your life doesn't rest with Lenka, or your father, or me. I've done heinous things, yes. I've watched you, asserted myself into your affairs, but the choices— those were all yours. You're so much better than your father and I. You won't let this cripple you. It doesn't have to end for you like it ended for us."

Shoe Man remained kneeling at my feet, and I saw that the man who'd walked into my grandparents' house with a backpack had been gone for some time. The eyes looking at me from beneath these gray brows were dead, like windows leading into a deep, starless night; his limbs and features sagged—victims to both gravity and his lifetime of money.

"Now that you've been caught," I said, "you feel sorry for yourself."

"I wish it was as simple as that. Being in a room with you now, I've ceased even to wonder about my punishment. It seems clear. You are freed of imprisonment and I will face mine."

"Now you're a philosopher."

"We understand each other, Jakub. You know it too."

"A flash of the old life."

"A flash of the old life."

"I miss it. The flow of the river through Středa. It would carry me to the village limits and I would swim against the current to shore. I never wanted to leave there, not for a second."

"I had a home like that too," he said. "They took it."

"I don't know what I'll do now," I said. "She's gone. I returned for her but I couldn't bring myself to face her. I know I should chase after her, but I can't. There's a life for her outside all of this. Without me."

"And for you too. There is something you could do, Jakub."

"You're advising me."

"I won't, if you don't want me to."

"No. Advise me, Shoe Man."

"Shoe Man? Is that what you call me?"

"All my life."

"The house is still there, you know," he said. "And it belongs to you. I always kind of knew that you'd come back for it."

Still kneeling, Zajíc pulled a pair of keys out of his pocket. The originals, the same ones that had once rested inside my grandmother's purse. The same ones she had used to lock the house after she ensured that my grandfather and I were safely in our beds.

He rested them on my palm. Much lighter now than when I was a child.

"I've gone so far, and back," I said.

"I have too. Why live otherwise."

"I hope you'll take the punishment. Go to jail. Do what ought to be done."

"I can't promise it, Jakub. The one thing you and I have in common—we love being alive too much to get in line for what's coming."

Both of us noticed at the same time that my laces had come untied inside the iron shoe. Zajíc held them, one in each hand. He stopped and stared out the window, his cheeks ruddy, thought finally catching up with instinct, but he was already committed, and so he tied my shoelaces into a neat bow. The cloth of my trousers had ridden up a few inches, revealing a small part of the scar on my calf. Zajíc froze, rolled the cloth up just a bit more.

"Mine has faded," he said. "You can no longer see the numbers. Just a single white line cutting across."

When he stood up, he seemed old—ancient and small—subject to the crushing weight of conscience. The finely fitting suit, the reflective surface of his leather shoes, the diminishing gray hair—none of it could fool me any longer about the true state of his being. Zajíc was not a menace. He was a man displaced and looking for a new purpose.

Radislav Zajíc checked his watch and walked toward the door. He turned halfway, without looking at me.

"You haven't asked what is in the green folder," he said.

"Well?"

"It's my poetry against the regime. I did write it, you know. Only as a joke, a dare of sorts, to impress someone I don't remember anymore. But then my fellow pupils took it seriously, and spread it around. Suddenly I was a published revolutionary. You see. The slightest gesture makes up our history. And so I met your father. And so I met you."

He left. The sound of his steps, larger than life, lingered for minutes, until at last the front door, eight stories down, thundered shut and I was alone with the afternoon sun. The rusting shoe defiantly eyed me with its mouth agape, as if in shock at being so suddenly abandoned by its loyal keeper. I picked it up and, once again, like so many years before, I considered whether any part of it still held genetic leftovers of my father, physical evidence of the encounter that had defined my family's fate.

I cast the thing out the open window facing the courtyard, and it screeched hideously along the stone walls until it too faced the inevitability of being forgotten, its pieces split apart, guts disemboweled along the grass and dirt, the shoe finally drained of evil and rid of purpose. A fat pigeon hopped around with its brothers, searching for parts to satiate their instinctual greed. Finding nothing, the birds arose, bound to scavenge in greener pastures, but the fat one, which I imagined to be the flock leader, performed an elegant pirouette against the iron shoe's corpse, and, as it soared away, dropped thick, cream-white phlegm, the liquid forming a petite dumpling that splattered with crude efficiency all along the metal scraps.

For a moment, the leap looked soothing. I could jump after the iron shoe and my aches would split apart like the shoe. No more thoughts of Lenka, no more knee pain, but *the body must not be violated.* The body was the most important thing, carrying within it the code to the universe, a part of a larger secret that was significant even if it was never to be revealed. If the body mattered to Hanuš, it mattered to me, and I would worship it as he had. I would never cause the body harm.

Pleased in some vulgar fashion over the shoe's undignified demise, I walked back to Charles Square. Around me, Prague crooned: bike messengers darting along important routes; troopers of business big and small marching with those shining loafers and heels, *one two, one two;* children with colorful backpacks skipping their way home from the wisdom and enlightenment of institutions (and what disappointment awaited them!) to the safety of their homes. It was exhilarating, all of it—was existence alone not revolution? Our efforts to establish routines in the nature that forbade them, to understand depths we could never reach, to declare truths even as we collectively snicker at the word's virginal piousness. What a mess of contradictions the gods created when they graced us with self-awareness. Without it, we could run around the woods like wild boars, dig in the dirt with our snouts to find worms, bugs, seeds, nuts. During breeding season, we could howl like wolves in December, alpha females pawing at the backs and ears of alpha males. We could mate for weeks and then toss aside the burdens of sex for the rest of the year. After this, we could hoard food in underground foxholes and sleep, sleep through *Leden, Únor, Březen, Duben,* no *have to go to the office grocery shopping oh God is that person looking at me do I have something on my face my shoes are falling apart is North Korea threatening us again my back pains have returned do any massage parlors actually provide handjobs and are they open to servicing women otherwise that is sexism and I've had a stomachache for three years now, should I get it checked out but it is fear and stress and what will the doctor prescribe?* There, in our underground paradise, shying away from God's sun and his fucked-up curse of Eden, the cocktease heaven that never comes, we could be like Hanuš and his race, the floating connoisseurs who do not know fear despite the looming threat of Gorompeds.

Alas, we are what we are, and we need the stories, we need the public transportation, the anxiety meds, the television shows by the dozens, the music in bars and restaurants saving us from the terror of silence, the everlasting promise of brown liquor, the bathrooms in national parks, and the political catchphrases we can all shout and stick to our bumpers. We need revolutions. We need anger. How many times will the Old Town of Prague host the people who've been slighted bellowing for a change? And are the people truly speaking to the charlatans of Politik, calling to the bone and flesh of their leaders, or is this a disguised plea to the heavens? *For fuck's sake, either give us a hint or let us perish altogether.*

I was not a part of the revolution. I was a slogan left on the side of an abandoned building, a mum witness to changes in weather patterns, moods. I was the statue of Jan Hus, with his sharply sculpted cheeks covered in a finely trimmed beard, his spine straight like a king's and not like a scholar hunched over his books, quietly observing Prague with turmoil in his heart and peace in his soul, both of which conspired to get him killed. I was the work of Hanuš, the ticking timekeeper of the universe, a jester performing his trick dance again and again to fresh hordes of eager visitors. I was the lion of Bohemia drawn within the crest, the dark eagle of Moravia, the crown jewels resting in a display case inside the castle. I was organic matter transformed into a symbol. My existence would forever be a silent statement.

As I passed Old Town, the protesters gathered by the hundreds, loitering around the statue of Saint Wenceslas upon his horse, holding signs condemning Tůma and Zajíc, condemning all men of power sitting in rooms and designing the future of the world, chanting against systems, chanting for change, chanting for hope, and it was still early in the day and I wished that by nighttime the crowd would grow into the thousands, like in the days of the Velvet Revolution, when our nation was so alive that its outcry thundered across the globe, breaking free of the greed and exploitation of men who'd lost themselves. Every single one of these bodies who'd decided to cast aside the ceaseless distractions, who'd decided to put on shoes and take a sign and march around the cobblestones of the nation instead of watching a bit of television, was a single act of revolution, a single particle within the explosion of the Big Bang. I felt confident in leaving the fate of this world in their hands.

I left the revolution behind me. The way horse hooves echo on the cube bricks of the main square. The way languages sing together over beer and coffee with whipped cream. The shivering visitors of the winter markets, their gloves soaked with grog spilling over the edge of a flimsy cup. The excited shouts of boys about to try absinthe ice cream. The bringers of change, actors in their own destinies. Those who love Prague, have always loved Prague, those who stroll every weekend around the same street and project holograms of history onto its physical reality. Those who dream. Those who lean on the statue of Christ crucified and kiss and grope each other with the hunger of dying beasts. Those who hope to die by jumping into the River Vltava, and fail. Those who use the free subway newspaper to wipe the sweat off their brows inside the sweltering train. The massive history, this metropolis of kings, of dictators, of book burning, of bloodstained tanks standing still in indecision. Through it all the city is here, its pleasures small and large cast upon the daily walkers rushing to offices and shops to participate in their habitual existence. They will not quit. God, they'll never quit, and though I had to leave them, I loved them all the way to hell and back, through peace and through turmoil.

Even the Sun Burns

I RETURNED TO STŘEDA, the village of my ancestors.

The houses that used to thrive had been scarred by winters, their walls cracking open and rooftops sagging. The old distillery was boarded up, gagged, sprayed over with the bawdy truths of graffiti. As the motorcycle engine sliced through the disturbing serenity of the main road, curtains behind windows opened, eyes on the intruder—a man coming home, perhaps, but they had no idea where he'd been. The old convenience store was shuttered and a few houses away a brand-new Hodovna supermarket stood out like an empty plastic bottle in a field of daisies. Ahead, the sky was morose and sable, and the sour smell of an impending rain shower crawled underneath my helmet. The scar on my leg itched, and I could not scratch it.

Half the gate of my home had collapsed and rotted through, a spongy mess of black bugs and dirt. The other half stood tall, faded brown, a welcome memory of my grandfather coughing and cursing as he painted over the judgments cast upon us by our countrymen. I let the Ducati fall into the dirt and stepped over the ruins, into a field of tall grass covering every inch of the front yard, including the sandbox and a tub of green still water. The walls of the house were cloaked in vines and the front doormat was topped with a generous pile of dried cat shit.

The backyard. Feathers and brittle, dull bones of chickens were scattered in the mud. No flesh, no skin, all eaten away by the elements and by felines. Inside the rabbit cages, bits of fur stuck to the ceiling. The coney skeletons recalled Sunday afternoon feasts, haunches and loins slowly roasted with bacon and paprika, with Grandma presiding over the crockpot and muttering to herself, *Almost, almost there.* Everywhere lay engorged worms, dead gluttons that had reached nirvana, having stuffed themselves with game until they burst and dried out. Mixed with the mud, the remains of the farm had become mush, a porridge that pulled on my shoes like quicksand. The strings on which my grandfather had suspended the rabbits after execution swung in the breeze. I looked closely, marveled at the resilience of the simple material through storms and scorching summers. It had wanted to remain as much as the vestiges of things that used to be alive. The outhouse smelled of nothing at all—the pounds of excrement underneath it had long ago become soil, and perhaps the outhouse could be taken down and the few square meters it occupied turned into a strawberry field. I wished for a cigarette. The piercing smell of my grandfather's tobacco smoke hit me, as if he were right there puttering around, working and cutting, presiding over his own piece of the world.

The garden. A mess of groundhog piles and dirt bike tracks— the local youth had found a good place to blow off some steam. The apple tree had been ripped out of the earth and was covering the potato patch, just as my grandmother had always predicted during storms—*Someday that damned tree will ruin our entire harvest*—the claw of its root menacingly curled toward the skies. Names and hearts were carved into the bark. I was not angry. The space was here. It existed without a claimant. It belonged to these vandals as much as to me.

I stomped in this graveyard, crunched it underneath my boots. *I'll rent it to some nice Prague folks,* Shoe Man had promised once. And then he'd left it all to die.

I inserted the house key into the lock before realizing that the front door was open. Scratches around the handle suggested many attempts at picking the lock before the intruders had succeeded. I entered to a smell of mildew. Thick layers of mold had colonized sections of the carpet like hair on an old man's back. It had seeped through the walls too—stains of it had metastasized wherever the rain had managed to circumvent the decrepit structure, wherever the drunken vandals had chosen to piss.

I left the hall and stepped into the living room. With blood thumping into my fingertips, I stumbled toward the kitchen counter, my eyes open wide and searching for ghosts. The faint haze of leftover cigarette smoke thickened the room's ozone; the smell of tobacco overpowered even the musk of fungi. Where was he, the shape of my grandfather, smoking cigarettes and reading the newspapers well into his death? Was his passing a lie too? But this doubt dissolved as soon as I spotted the Monument of the Vandals. Where the living room table had once rested now stood a pyramid, nearly as tall as I was, composed of beer bottles at the base, on top of which rested pounds upon pounds of cigarette butts, all burned to their very nubs, all Camels, the brand my grandfather despised. The squatters had left the monument as a reeking flag of their presence, much like the first men on the moon, a statement of ownership of this forgotten land, this house of no one.

What did my arrival mean to their conquest? Did it erase their authority, or was I the squatter, my presence nothing but a haunting in need of exorcism?

I kicked the pyramid. It fell apart, spilling forth like the gushing blood of a pig. The stink of stale tobacco and saliva put me on the verge of retching, and I retreated into the hall to embrace the much more pleasant aroma of withering. I chose to ignore the bathroom and pantry for now—no good things could await there.

Then there were the bedrooms. In the room that had been mine was a single bed littered with rags stained with semen and blood, and spent condoms dry and shriveled. I pulled the rags off. And there, on the mattress beneath, were the two small stains from my boyhood nosebleeds, along with a bigger, darker blotch from the feverish, salty sweat of my back. This was my bed. The small form of my child self was imprinted on the fabric like a postnuclear shadow. The bed had been gnawed on by mice and burned with lighters, but it was unmistakably mine, surrounded still by collapsed shelves holding my grandmother's history books, also marked by rodents. I sat down on the mattress, not at all concerned whether the juices of teen carnage had seeped onto it through the rags.

Above me, a giant hole in the ceiling and roof provided a direct view of the clouded heavens. The cave-in must have happened a long time ago, as there was no sign of rubble.

From underneath the pile of half-eaten books emerged a daddy longlegs, its torso fat and dragging on the floor—so rich was the house with insects for it to feast on. It made its way toward me without any hesitance, then stopped a few feet away from the bed. I felt its eyes upon me. I felt at home.

"Is it you?" I asked the spider.

It didn't move.

"Lift a leg if it's you."

Nothing. But it was there, its gaze upon me consistent. Interested.

"Stick around," I pleaded. "I'll be back. You stay."

I walked outside, leaned the Ducati against the cracked wall of the house. I had no knowledge of what time it was—it seemed that it was still early in the day, a good time for the errands ahead, but with the village streets so empty, I couldn't be sure. I followed the main road, no longer comforted by the hallucinogenic speed of an engine. Gravity reached from beneath the concrete and clawed at my ankles, keeping me slow but steady.

An old woman whose face I didn't recognize waved at me from a bench in front of her house. She puffed on a pipe, pulled her skirt up to expose legs colored with black-and-blue veins. How soothing the winds flowing from the east must be to the pain of aging. I waved back, asked after the time.

"Haven't owned a watch in thirteen years," she responded, toothless.

I made my way to the new market. In my basket, I collected potato chips, bacon, eggs, milk, brownie ice cream, deodorant, a loaf of fresh sourdough, smoked mackerel, two jelly doughnuts, lard, a cooking pan, and a jar of Nutella. The stuff of Earth. I held a newspaper in my hand before putting it back on the shelf. Too much.

With my filled plastic bags, I circled around the market and down the gravel path next to the closed distillery. I reached what we the children of the village used to call the Riviera, a beach of rough sand and grass patches flanking the river. The currents ran wild and deep as they reached past the distillery, and there we used to hold on to the thick wooden poles hammered into the river's mud that emerged above the surface. The water would wash over our shoulders, and we'd play to see who could hold on the longest before the current loosened their grip and took them away around the bend. I'd almost always won.

It was obvious the Riviera hadn't seen swimmers in a while. Half-buried newspapers and plastic bottles peeked from the sand. A black snake slithered from the bushes and vanished underneath the water's surface. I considered taking my clothes off and following its example, but the water would be too cold for at least another couple of months. Setting the bags down, I rolled up my pants just below my knees and entered, shivering momentarily as my skin touched the ice-cold river. I stood there until the feeling of cold dissipated and the mud beneath my toes became warm. Everything had changed except for the water. Whenever I got in its way, it simply poured around me and continued on. It welcomed me for a swim and cared not when I left again. Even its attempt on my childhood life had been without evil intent. So close I'd been to my life ending early, to perishing here and never knowing Lenka, or Hanuš, to never seeing the golden continents of Earth from above. But again and again I had come to the shore, clawed myself onto it, and lived.

I left the Riviera's desolation behind and walked to Boud'a's house on the main road. The door was shuttered, the windows broken, the front garden that had formerly been so meticulously kept by Boud'a's mother now filled in by concrete. Leaning against the side of the house were four planks of wood covered by plastic. I looked around the empty main road, then threw the planks over my shoulder. I studied the door a bit longer, hoping an old friend might still emerge, another human who might recognize my face.

On my way back, I asked the old woman without a watch about the fate of Boud'a's family. They had fled to the city, she said, as most people had, fled to the city for jobs and for supermarkets the size of circus tents, where you could choose between tomatoes from Italy and tomatoes from Spain. I stopped myself from asking if she knew what Boud'a was now doing with his life, fearing the answer could be something like banking. I imagined instead that Boud'a had stuck to his desire to own a restaurant that served mussel pizza. He'd eaten mussel pizza in Greece once, and after that, all he wanted was to grow up and make the best mussel pizza on Earth. The old woman asked if I needed anything else, and I waved good-bye.

I returned to the house and carried the planks inside, in case of rain, then went to the bedroom to check on the spider. It was gone. In the kitchen, I chopped up one of the planks and filled the stove. As the fire grew, I spread lard along the new pan and laid out eight slices of bacon. Within ten minutes, the odor of cigarette butts had been dominated by pure animal. Saliva dripped from the corners of my mouth—I could not contain it. The plan was to cook up some eggs too, but I couldn't wait to eat as I cleaned the small pan for another round. I ripped a hunk of bread from the loaf and separated the soft middle from the crust. Over the middle, I cracked a raw egg. I stuffed the bacon inside the crust. I fell upon the improvised sandwich like a beast, tasting blood from my gums as it seeped into the food, but I chewed with greed, without a concern for dignity, with the carnal pleasure of an unsupervised animal. I lost track of time. As I finished, the sun, concealed by clouds to begin with, crept somewhere behind the horizon.

The shed still held all of its tools—rusty, sure, with some of the wooden handles having rotted, but in the fading light I found a hammer and nails, some of which still seemed factory fresh. I dragged the ladder from the shed, checked each step for damage. So much of my grandfather's kingdom had been preserved here—with some additional tools, I could again convert the shed into a powerhouse factory. Make a new table, new bookshelves, encase the single bed with a fresh wooden frame. I could rip out the molding carpets and bathroom tile, smash the piss-soaked walls, replace electrical cables, install indoor plumbing. I did not lack time. I did not lack patience. I would remove every organ, haul it to the garbage dump by the ton. I would be an artist restoring his own painting—rejuvenating colors I had once known to be radiant. I would be the plastic surgeon of history. Retain the ghosts and refresh their facade.

Yes, I could do it. It could be my life. Jan Hus had died for country and lived for himself. If only he could live in our age, become my phantom brother. We would attend Dr. Bivoj's village festivals of small pleasures, drink the tainted hooch. We would visit Petr and learn to play the guitar. Hus would tell me of his widow and I would tell him of my Lenka, what used to be.

I walked out of the shed, tools in hand, and looked over the reclaimed backyard. Here again, animals would roam. I could raise a Louda, scout the Internet for a flintlock pistol to employ in executions. I could scythe the fields of grass behind the village every morning, carry piles of it on my back, allow it to dry beneath noon sunshine, and feed it to rabbits. I could obtain chickens for the harvest of yolk and the carnal sincerity of their nature. Small dinosaurs. I could keep a few guinea pigs, perhaps a ferret. Creatures of routine to look after.

And the garden beyond? I would resow every crop. I would grow my grandfather's carrots, potatoes, peas. My grandmother's strawberries, tomatoes, celery. After caring for the animals, I would pull on my galoshes and get ahold of the shovel. Whistle songs of the past as I tended my earth.

Yes. This life awaited. I saw children's feet marking the fall mud in the backyard. My daughters and sons picking their first tomatoes off the vine. The children of my children digging for potatoes when my knees were too old for bending. And there was Lenka, silver-haired, watching the bursting life grow around us. Somehow I'd gotten her back. Somehow we'd found each other again.

For a moment, Lenka's face transformed into the face of Klara. Her hair so thick I couldn't stop running my hands through it. She had never died, she'd run away with me and we'd become phantom lovers.

In this future, we were free of systems. Other humans went on to become symbols, sacrificed their lives to serve. Other humans handled the torture, the coups, the healing. We simply sowed, harvested, and drank a bit before dinner. No one tried to take what was ours. We had too little. We were invisible, and in this slower life we were our own gods.

Yes, there were things left in this world. I had traveled through Space, I had seen truths unparalleled, but still, in this Earthly life,

I had barely seen anything at all. Something rests in the mortal soul, hungry to feel anything and everything in its own boundless depths. As boundless and ever-expanding as the universe itself.

Back inside the house, I pushed the bed to the wall, where it used to rest when I was a child, and leaned the ladder against the interior wooden frame of the roof. I climbed, and I set each plank against the frame, nailing them in until I had finished the first layer. As I worked, the night map of the universe above was startlingly clear, as if once again trying to lure me. It looked exactly the same as it had on the day my grandfather and I sat by a fire and spoke of revolutions. The purple glow of Chopra still remained, though it was weakening, collapsing in on itself and saying its last good-bye to the Earthlings dying to know its secrets. I appreciated this gesture, yet I could not bring myself to leave even the smallest gap between the planks to stargaze. I needed the intimacy of an enclosed house. A structure to trap me.

The patch created a nearly perfect darkness. I slowly made my way down the ladder, lit a match, and held it over a candlewick. The silence infiltrated my muscles and spread their fibers apart, inducing soreness and serene warmth. The only force present was a small flame. I had built a dam to deter the murmur of the cosmos.

From the kitchen pantry, I retrieved the jar of Nutella. I lay on the bed, opened it, and scooped some out with my fingers. Spread it along my tongue.

The darkness overtook me. I woke up sometime later to the faintest tapping on my skin. On my forearm rested the daddy longlegs.

"Is it you?" I asked.

I smeared some Nutella on my wrist, right next to the arachnid. *Taste. You loved it.*

No movement. Its fat belly remained lodged on my forearm hairs.

"Are you still afraid?" I said.

The weight is nice. What would the world be without it. Nothing but fear and air. Yes, the weight is nice.

Is it you?

Because it is me. I can promise you, I am here.

It is me. The spaceman.

Acknowledgments

I'd like to thank:

My country and my people. For their resilience, wisdom, art, food — and their humor in the face of great adversity.

The magnificent women of my family — my mamka, Marie, and my babička, Marie, my teta Jitka and sestřenka Andrejka. My little synovec Kryštůfek.

Ben George, an incredible editor and friend, who's given this book more than I could ever ask for. Everyone at Little, Brown for giving *Spaceman* such a welcoming home, especially Sabrina Callahan, Reagan Arthur, Sarah Haugen, Nicole Dewey, Alyssa Persons, Ben Allen, and Tracy Williams.

Drummond Moir, for his brilliant editorial insight and for bringing *Spaceman* to the UK. Everyone at Sceptre, especially Carolyn Mays, Francine Toon, and Caitriona Horne.

Marya Spence, agent superhero with endless powers, remarkable human and friend, fellow appreciator of strange foods. Everyone at Janklow & Nesbit, superhero central.

All of the brilliant writers and mentors I have had the pleasure of encountering through the years, especially Darin Strauss, JSF, Rick Moody, and Dr. Darlin' Neal.

Everyone at the NYU Lillian Vernon Writers House — what you do to foster future literary voices is imperative. We owe you so much. The Goldwater Writing Project for making the writing of this book possible and for enabling me to meet the talented, extraordinary residents of the Goldwater Hospital. I think of them and their writing every day.

The friends and colleagues who have kept me sane, provided wise notes, shared in alcohol and food and anxiety—especially Christy and Scott, Adam, Emily, Bryn, Peng, Tess. All of my friends in the Czech Republic, the United States, and in between who make this. Earth a magnificent place.

Most importantly, I'd like to thank all readers of books, for keeping the conversation alive across centuries.